Praise for

THE BOOK OF IVY

'Well-developed characters and intricate world-building, combined with complex relationships, political corruption, and betrayal, leave readers begging for the second book in this series.'
SLJ

'An intriguing start with a brave heroine.'

Kirkus Reviews

'The novel is less about the devastation of the world and intriguingly more about the people left behind. The promise of a second book will excite potential readers.'

Booklist

'There were points in which I found myself clutching the covers, shaking the pages in a little disbelief and a little rage. Overall, if you're looking for a suspenseful book with a great, and at times almost heart-wrenching romance, don't miss *The Book of Ivy*.'

Teenreads.com

'Thought-provoking, poignant, and sexy! Readers will burn the midnight oil to finish *The Book of Ivy* and fall asleep with the name Bishop Lattimer on their lips.'

Mel, Erin, and Regina Read-A-Lot

'*The Book of Ivy* has every ingredient you look for in an epic novel: from the spine-tingling plot and exhilarating characters, to every entrancing word penned by Amy Engel.'

Insightful Minds Reviews

'With her debut, Amy Engel has pulled off one of the best dystopian romances that I have ever read. It was impossible to put down.'

Bibliophilia, Please

'This is an intense story of love, family, romance, and betrayal, that kept me on the edge of my seat (with my heart in my throat) until the very end!'

Jenuine Cupcakes

'I enjoyed this novel so much that I polished it off in two sittings. There is no insta-love! There is no love triangle! Best of all, the protagonist actually has common sense, and she uses it!'

Julie at Magna Maniac Café

'What a finale! I was trembling with grief the second Ivy's plan took shape (and shed more than a few tears in its wake). I inhaled this book and desperately miss the characters already.'

The Reading Café

THE
REVOLUTION
OF

Amy Engel was born in Kansas and after a childhood spent bouncing between countries (Iran, Taiwan) and states (Kansas; California; Missouri; Washington, D.C.), she settled in Kansas City, Missouri, where she lives with her husband and two kids. Before devoting herself full-time to motherhood and writing, she was a criminal defense attorney, which is not quite as exciting as it looks on TV. When she has a free moment, she can usually be found reading, running, or shoe shopping. *The Book of Ivy* was her debut YA novel and *The Revolution of Ivy* is its sequel. Find her online at amyengel.net/ or @aengelwrites.

Also by Amy Engel and available from Hodder:

The Book of Ivy

THE REVOLUTION OF

AMY ENGEL

HODDER

First published in the United States of America in 2015
by Entangled Publishing LLC

First published in Great Britain in 2015 by Hodder & Stoughton
An Hachette UK company

2

A CIP catalogue record for this title is
available from the British Library

Paperback ISBN 978 1 473 62934 9
eBook ISBN 978 1 473 62933 2

Printed and bound by Clays Ltd, St Ives plc

Hodder & Stoughton policy is to use papers that are natural, renewable
and recyclable products and made from wood grown in sustainable
for ests. The logging and manufacturing processes are expected to
conform to the environmental regulations of the country of origin.

Hodder & Stoughton Ltd
Carmelite House
50 Victoria Embankment
London EC4Y 0DZ

www.hodder.co.uk

For Holly,
my sister in all the ways that matter.

TEARS SLIP DOWN MY CHEEKS, THEIR SALT STINGING MY lips. I give in, allow myself to weep for everything I've lost, for the fear of what's to come. I grieve the daughter I was, the wife I never wanted to be, the killer I refused to become, the traitor I pretended to be.

I am none of those things now. I raise my head and wipe my eyes. Daughter. Wife. Killer. Traitor. They are all old versions of me. Now I will become a survivor.

I take a deep breath and let go of the fence.

1

 o one survives beyond the fence. At least that's what my father always told me when I was a child. But I'm not a little girl anymore, and I no longer believe in the words of my father. He told me the Lattimers were cruel and deserved to die. He told me my only choice was to kill the boy I loved. He has been wrong about so many things. And I'm determined that he's going to be wrong about my survival as well.

If I want to live, I have to move away from the fence and head toward the river. But even after I start that direction, my fingers still clench and release, clench and release, as if they are searching the air for the comforting familiarity of chain link. I know that last night I was lucky, considering what could have happened while I was passed out and injured on the wrong side of the fence. An animal could have found me. Or a person. I can't count on that type of luck again. I need to reach the river, quench my thirst before the sun sets, and find some shelter from the coming night.

The river can't be far, but it still takes what feels like hours for me to get there. I lose count of how many times I have to stop and rest, my breathing ragged and my body aching. My thoughts move sluggishly inside my head, and dizziness is an ever-present companion, hovering over me, waiting for a moment of weakness. I probably have a concussion from the blow to my head, but I'm not sure I remember what you're supposed to do for one. And it's not like I can put my feet up anyway, grab a cold compress, ask someone else's opinion. A laugh bubbles in my throat, but when it breaks free all it sounds is wild, just this side of insane, and I press my lips together tight.

Keeping my thoughts from returning to Westfall takes almost as much effort as walking. But I push the memories aside. Out here, longing for things that are no longer mine will only lead to weakness that will be my downfall. Instead, I concentrate on the simple act of putting one foot in front of the other and continue moving forward even as part of me is left behind, beyond a fence I cannot breach.

When I finally reach the river, it's not a placid pool like Bishop showed me inside Westfall's borders. Here it's wide, and although not raging, the current is running strong. The water looks brownish in the afternoon sun, silt stirred up by the rush of water. But when I kneel on the riverbank and cup it in my hands, it is mostly clear, and I gulp it down. I reach with both hands and shovel it toward my open mouth as fast as I can. I hadn't realized how thirsty I was until the first drops hit my tongue.

Once I've slackened my immediate thirst, I splash water onto my face. I take off my sweater and set it on the bank beside me, then cup handfuls of water and scrub gingerly at my face and neck, cataloging injuries as I go. The guards who threw me out were definitely not careful with me. My lower lip feels puffy and raw, and the back of my head is so tender I can't even run my fingers over it without sucking air in through gritted teeth. My arms are crisscrossed with dozens of deep scratches. I plunge my hands into the cold water and rub the blood away, try to work the dirt out from underneath my nails.

The sun is beginning to sink lower in the sky, and a thin strip of light cuts through the trees and glances off my wedding ring. I straighten my left hand out underneath the water, watch the gold glimmer and shift. I remember the day Bishop put it on my finger, the way my hand shook. The way I wanted to rip the ring off, how foreign and confining it felt against my skin. Now it takes me a long minute to work the ring off my finger. It leaves behind a dent in my flesh, a smooth band of skin that feels naked without it. But I can't bear to wear it anymore, this reminder of all the things I have lost. I hold the ring loosely in my palm, and then open my hand, let the river carry it away.

I scoot back on the riverbank, content for the moment to listen to the play of water over rocks, feel the warmth of the fading sun on my back. I try not to think about the coming night. I try not to think about anything beyond my basic needs, afraid that if I do I will simply collapse under the weight of my fear and grief. There's no room for second-guessing the decisions I made back in West-fall. No room for wondering what might have been. I don't consider myself a victim—it was my choice to sac-rifice myself, after all—but out here, turning into one will be easy if I don't stay focused.

Behind me there is a small stand of trees, as good a place as any to take refuge once darkness falls. My more immediate worry, now that thirst isn't at the top of the list, is finding something to eat. My father, in all his end-less lessons, never spared a single second talking to me about how to survive beyond the fence. He never taught me how to start a fire or catch a small animal. I suppose he never considered the possibility that all his planning might come to nothing, that we might be caught, that he might need to give me some kind of alternative training. It is just one more time he has failed me.

A slight movement to my right catches my attention and I watch as a small lizard scampers across the rocks, stopping to sun himself. I hold my breath, willing him closer, although I'm not entirely sure what I'll do with him if I'm able to catch him. But the gnawing hunger in my stomach forces me to try. I lean my weight onto my left arm and inch my right hand closer. At the last second the lizard must sense my intent because he tries to scuttle away, but I'm faster, or more desperate, and my fingers close around his scaly back.

I hold him in my fist, and he stares at me with dull black eyes. I pick up a small rock and use it to crush him, ignoring the bile that fights its way into my throat. I eat methodically, not allowing myself to think, trying not to taste the bitter tang that coats my mouth. It takes all my concentration to swallow, my eyes focused on a spot across the river. My stomach wants to heave the lizard back up, but when I'm done I set my jaw, take deep breaths through my nose. My days of eating Bishop's hamburgers and turkey sandwiches are over. Now I will eat whatever it takes to stay alive.

When I'm sure the lizard is going to stay down, I crawl forward and rinse my mouth with water. I swish and spit until all I taste is river. The sun has almost set now, bands of orange and pink threading like gauze through the trees. The air is still warm, but there's the promise of fall's chill underneath. The weather will not cooperate with me for long.

I pull my sweater back on and drag myself over to the stand of trees. I curl myself into a ball, trying to make myself invisible. I haven't seen another person since the children at the fence, and I don't have the sense that anyone's watching me. But I still feel exposed, with no way to defend myself if someone were to come along. I anticipate it taking hours for me to find sleep, but my battered body has other plans, and almost as soon as I close my eyes, I'm sucked down into darkness.

When I wake, it's difficult to tell what time of day it is, whether it's morning or afternoon, whether I've slept twelve hours or twenty. The sky is overcast, dark clouds rolling in from the west, the rumble of thunder promising storms. I have a feeling that my sleep was closer to unconsciousness. I don't feel rested. My body is sore and stiff, my vision fuzzy, like I'm looking at the world through a pane of dirty glass. I push myself to sitting, hissing in air at the sharp spike in my head.

I need to find better shelter from the coming storm. The day is warm, but I worry what will happen if my clothes get soaked and the temperature drops. I hate to leave the river, but promise myself I won't go far, just to the nearest available shelter. My stomach is cramping with hunger, so before I head out I kneel by the river and gulp down handfuls of water to ease the ache a little.

I walk due east from the river, looking for anything that would offer good protection from the rain. At first there is nothing, only the empty expanse of land. I know that before the war overpopulation was a real concern, the idea that the earth might simply run out of space and resources for all its inhabitants. Such fears are hard to imagine now, when I am the only human as far as the eye can see, the sole evidence of life.

The sharp crack of thunder moves closer, a stiff wind blowing my hair into my face. I top a small rise, and in the near distance I see the rusted hulk of a car. I approach it cautiously, but there's no indication anyone's touched it in decades. The tires are shredded to nothing, both doors on the driver's side ripped away. The front windshield is smashed in and there's a faint rotten smell from the interior, but the car is still the best option I've seen in terms of shelter. I climb into the backseat, easing myself over the cracked and torn leather.

The storm hits only a few minutes later, rain lashing down against the car, driving in sideways so that I'm forced to curl against the far side in order to stay dry. I'm grateful for the protection from the rain, but staying still, without the benefit of any sort of distraction, allows my brain to circle back around to Westfall. To my family. To Bishop. The longing I feel for him is a physical ache, pinched and throbbing inside my chest. I bite down on the inside of my cheek to keep myself from crying, press my hands against my closed eyes. It shouldn't be so hard to forget someone I barely knew. Bishop was in my life for only a few months, but somehow he left an imprint that has absolutely no relationship to the length of time we were together.

I lower my hands and open my eyes, watch the rain beating down against the long grass outside the car. I work to clear my head of thought. Perhaps this is how I will survive now, by keeping myself an empty white blank, pretending my life began only yesterday and nothing came before. My eyelids grow heavy, my breathing deepening with the sound of the rain. I let myself sink down, my head resting against the dirt-streaked window. I have a fleeting thought that maybe it's not a good thing to be sleeping so much, but I give in to the oblivion. If nothing else, it's a welcome respite from the pain.

At first I think I'm dreaming about the dog that bit me. The one my sister Callie strangled with his own chain. I hear the snarling, smell the scent of wet fur and rancid breath. I shift, batting against nothing, and my hand slams against something hard and slick. My eyes fly open, take in the interior of the car, my hand resting against the leather seat. My body is already scrambling backward, registering the threat before my mind can process it. There's a coyote in the open doorway of the car. Saliva drips from its mouth, its light brown fur matted and mud-clogged. It bares yellowed fangs at me, growls ripping from its throat. I've never seen a coyote in real life, but my father talked about packs of them roaming outside the fence. So far, there is only evidence of one, but his pack might not be far.

"Go away!" I yell, kicking out with my foot. Panic is flooding my veins and part of me knows I need to calm down, *think,* but the rest of me is simply frantic to get away. My foot catches the coyote in the head and it retreats. But only for a second before it returns, this time putting its front paws up on the backseat, watching me with predatory eyes. I don't know if it is strong enough to kill me, but it can definitely inflict serious damage.

I draw my foot back to kick again and the coyote lunges forward, its jaws snapping the air only millimeters from my canvas-covered toes. I scream and flail backward, eyes searching the car for some kind of weapon. For a split second, I consider trying to launch myself over the coyote and out of the car, but I know on the open ground it will outpace me easily. My frantic eyes land on the broken front windshield. A portion of the metal frame yawns inward, the end sharp where it's broken in two. I keep one eye on the coyote as I shift forward. I'm scared to try kicking it again. If it gets a hold of my foot, it will mangle me in seconds. I take a deep breath and vault over the front seat, screaming as the coyote shoots into the car, its hot breath brushing against my neck.

I can hear the coyote growling frantically, scrambling on the backseat behind me, but I don't look back. I reach out and wrench the loose piece of metal from the frame, only distantly aware that I've sliced through my own fingers as I pull it free. I turn, heaving out air, lunging at the coyote just as it springs toward me. I bury the jagged metal in the coyote's eye and we scream at the same time, both of us spouting blood.

The coyote falls onto the floor of the backseat, shaking its head wildly, trying to dislodge the metal. Warm drops of blood spatter onto my arms as it writhes. I shove myself out of the car and run, not looking back. I can feel my own blood gushing out of my fingers and I clutch my hand against my chest. After only a minute of hard running, I have to stop. My head is spinning and my stomach heaves. I lean over, vomiting up water and bile, acid stinging my throat. Even before I've finished wiping my mouth with my good hand, I'm looking behind me, eyes searching the long grass. But nothing moves. If the coyote is still alive, it is not following me. At least not yet.

By the time I make it back to the river, blood is running down my forearm, dripping off the bend of my elbow. I sink to my knees on the bank and look at my hand closely for the first time. All four of my fingers on my right hand are cut across the bottom joint, the deepest gash on my ring finger where a thick flap of skin hangs loose, revealing a flash of white bone. I tip my head up, take deep breaths until my stomach settles.

I pull off my sweater, the front of it soaked with blood, and toss it beside me. Using my teeth and hands, I manage to tear off a strip of cotton from the bottom of my tank top. I press the cloth hard against my fingers, willing the flow of blood to stop.

Only one day outside the fence and already I'm losing the battle. Part of me is surprised I'm not crying, not shaking with fear. But the rest of me knows this is probably only the first of many injuries, many tests, I'll face. I can't afford to fall apart every time.

The cloth is soaked through with blood by the time the flow begins to slow down. Using my teeth again, I manage to knot the sodden piece of tank top around my fingers. I don't know how much good it will do, but maybe it will keep some pressure on the wounds. I'm so tired I can barely move, my whole body screaming for sleep although I haven't been awake for all that long.

I lean over the water, splash some on my face with my good hand, bring a handful to my mouth. Now that the rain has stopped, the sun has come out from behind the clouds, just in time to set. I can barely see my own reflection in the water, which is probably a blessing. Only the outline of my head and neck. The lines of the trees behind me.

And a man's shadow over my shoulder.

I whirl around, my legs skidding out from under me where I was crouched on the grassy bank. I throw out an arm to stop myself from tumbling into the river. My injured fingers dig into the ground and instantly begin to bleed again, but it hardly matters. My breath is a harsh rasp in the early evening gloom.

At first I can't tell who it is, just a man, his face masked in twilight. But he steps forward and I see his blue eyes, eyes I would know anywhere.

"Hey there, pretty girl," Mark Laird says. And then he smiles.

2

For an endless moment there is only silence as we stare at each other. Instinct tells me not to let him know how scared I am, how even now my stomach has twisted itself into a hard knot of fear, the hair on the back of my neck quivering in anticipation. I haven't seen him since the day I followed Bishop to the fence after Mark was put out, but I realize now that some part of me has been anticipating this moment all along.

"Hi, Mark," I hear myself say, my voice surprisingly normal.

He cocks his head at me, the smile fading from his cherub cheeks. Even now, after all I know about him, he still looks deceptively innocent with his round face and sparkling blue eyes. He takes a step closer and I start to push myself up. I have at least a few inches on him; I'd rather be towering over him instead of prone below him. But before I can stand, he lifts his foot and brings it down on my ankle. Not hard enough to break bone, but hard enough that the threat of damage hangs between us like an ugly promise.

"You shouldn't get up," he tells me. "You look like you've been through a lot." Slowly, as if he has all the time in the world, he squats down beside me, replacing his foot with one hand chained loosely around my ankle.

"I'm fine," I say. And now my voice has a slight quiver. I don't miss the way Mark's eyes go dark and hungry at the sound. My gut feeling was right; he likes gorging himself on other people's fear. I tell myself not to think of the nine-year-old girl he hurt, how her cries were probably music to his sick, perverted ears. "Please let go." I give my leg an experimental twist and his hand clamps down, fingers gouging into my Achilles tendon.

"What happened to you?" he asks, as if I haven't spoken. "They put you out?"

I nod. He stares at me and belts out a laugh, making me flinch. "What for?"

I hesitate, weighing my options, trying to decide what to tell him. "Because I tried to kill the president's son," I say finally.

Mark shakes his head. "You're lying. I saw the way you looked at him." He grins at my shocked eyes. "You thought I didn't see you that day? When he came to give me his pathetic charity?" His index finger sneaks under the cuff of my jeans, slithering against my skin, and my leg jerks like I've been shocked. But there's nowhere for me to go. He's got me trapped. "I know who you are," he says. "And I know who he is."

"I'm not anyone anymore," I tell him, a painful truth that hurts me to speak aloud. "I'm out here alone, just like you." Comparing myself to him on any level makes me want to scream, but I want to keep him talking. If he's talking, he's not trying to do anything else. "Have you met other people?" I ask. "Is there somewhere safe for people who've been put out?" Maybe if he sees us as allies, part of a pack, he won't be able to hurt me.

But Mark doesn't care about what I have to say. He reaches forward with his free hand and caresses my cheek. I twist my head away from him, my breath coming so fast it burns on the inhale. "Don't touch me," I tell him.

"You've got blood on your cheek," he says and the gentle tone of his voice makes my fists clench, nails biting into my palms. It's so much worse than a yell. He acts as if I'm okay with his hands on my body. As if I've given him permission. "Your poor face." His fingers slide over my lips and I slap his hand away.

"I said, *don't touch me.*"

He grabs the back of my neck and squeezes, his thumb pushing against the tender spot where the guards hit me. I cry out, pulling at his arm with both hands, as a bright, electric bolt of pain shoots through my head, leaving a trail of white stars in its wake.

"Don't you ever, *ever* tell me what to do," he says, lips pulled back from his teeth in a snarl. "You stupid bitch."

He's done pretending, done with even the slightest pretense that this a friendly encounter. Terror surges through me, so fast and vicious I think my heart might burst. My earlier exhaustion vanishes in an instant, every single cell in my body suddenly wide awake and poised for battle.

Mark shoves me backward, catching both my wrists in his hands, and launches himself on top of me. I kick my legs upward and buck wildly, desperate to throw him off. Standing, I might have had an advantage with my height, but on the ground his heavier weight puts the balance in his corner. If he gets me pinned, it's all over.

He grunts when my knee connects with his side, his breath hot and fetid in my face. I don't bother screaming. I can't spare the air, and there's no one to help me anyway. The only sound is our ragged breathing, harsh exhales as hard bone meets soft flesh. He punches me in the face and sparks explode in my head; my eye feels like it's bursting from the socket. I wrench one hand free and my nails make contact with the side of his face, leaving behind three bloody furrows in his skin. His scream of pain gives me a burst of strength and I manage to flip onto my side, belly-crawl away from him, using my elbows like pistons to pull myself forward.

But I only get a few feet before he's back on me, his hands gripping my hips. He straddles me, grinds my face into the ground. Dirt fills my mouth and nose, making me gag, snot and saliva smearing across my face as I fight to breathe. Mark slams my face into the ground and I feel my lip split. He lets go of my head and grabs my right arm, wrenching it up behind my back, my hand pushed almost to my neck.

"That was fun," he pants from above me. "I don't mind a good fight. But now we're going to do things my way." He twists my injured fingers with his free hand and I scream. "What happened here?" he asks, voice conversational, as if we're discussing the weather.

I don't bother answering and he lets go of my fingers, but increases the pressure on my arm. My shoulder throbs in time with my heart; I can't move without making the pain unbearable. "Let go," I wheeze. "Let go and I'll stop fighting."

"Yeah?" he says, and I can hear the laughter in his voice. "You're a shitty liar. But I tell you what, I'm such a nice guy, I will let go."

"What—" Before I can ask what he means, he wrenches my arm up in one quick jerk, my shoulder slipping from its socket in a white-hot flash of agony. I shriek, a long, high-pitched wail that reaches up into the evening sky and brings darkness rushing toward me like the wings of a raven.

My breath is whistling out of me, and Mark gives a satisfied hum of approval. Proud of his work. I am still terrified, and seriously injured now, too. But underneath the fear and pain there is an unexpected, but not unwelcome, pit of boiling, surging anger. Anger at Mark, my father,

Callie, President Lattimer, my mother. Even Bishop. It stirs inside me, a seething red mass of pure willfulness. And that determined part of me knows that if I give in to the darkness, I will never wake up again. Mark Laird will do what he wants with me. Leave me dead and violated along this riverbank. After everything I've gone through, I refuse to let him be the one to end my life.

I bite down hard on my tongue just as the blackness descends, flying in along the edges of my vision. Bite so hard I taste blood, salty and slick against my teeth. The blackness recedes, but not enough. I bite again, in the same spot, and the sharp pain forces me to focus, sweeps the darkness away.

Mark is moving off me, confident he has me at his mercy. My left hand is outstretched, resting in the grass, and I move it carefully sideways, close my fingers over a rock and grip it tight.

"That's better," Mark says, talking almost to himself. "Let's turn you over. I want to see your face."

He flips me onto my back, heedless of my dislocated shoulder, and I have to bite down again to keep from screaming. I force myself to lie still and compliant, eyes half closed, as he pushes my hair away from my face. I don't move as his hands skim down my chest, even though it takes everything I have not to fight him. I remind myself that now, maybe more than ever before in my life, I need to think, not just act. He leans over me, but still I wait. I will only have one chance.

"Hey," he says, "are you in shock or something? Wake up." He slaps my face and I let my head loll on my neck. "Hey," he repeats, leaning closer, his blue eyes only inches from mine. I bring my arm up fast, slam the rock into the side of his head as hard as I can. It doesn't knock him out, like I'd hoped, but he's stunned, head hanging down as he sways on all fours. I use my good arm, rock still clutched in my hand, to push myself up to sitting and hit him again, this time on the back of the head. His hands go out from under him and he falls across my legs. I kick him off, making a high-pitched keening sound in the back of my throat. He's still conscious, and he tries to grab my foot as I stand, but his fingers slide away. I hit him a third time, on the temple, and his eyes roll back in his head.

I stand over him, panting, somewhere beyond tears. My fingers ache from their tight grip on the rock. I know I should hit him again. Hit him until his head is a bloody, pulpy mess like the lizard I killed yesterday. I bring my arm up, but I can't make myself bring it down. I can hear Callie inside my head, telling me to *Kill him, damn it, what are you waiting for?* Even Bishop is whispering in my ear, urging me to end it, make sure that in a future with no guarantees I can at least rest easy that Mark Laird won't hurt me, or anyone else, ever again. I know that Bishop would not want me to hesitate.

But I can't do it. Just as I wouldn't allow Mark Laird to kill me, I don't want him to be the person who turns me into a killer. I let the rock slide from my numb fingers. Instead, I bend down and rip off his shoes. It takes me twice as long as it should, with only one working arm, and I'm practically sobbing with frustration when I finally pull the second shoe free. I turn and throw them into the river, watch as they drift away on the black current.

It's almost full dark now, the sun long since disappeared, but we're blessed with a full moon, and I notice a bag on the ground that I didn't see earlier. Mark must have dropped it when he spotted me. I pick it up without bothering to look inside and sling it across my body, crying out a little as I work the strap underneath my injured arm. Beside the bag is a round object, glinting in the moonlight. A canteen. I crouch at the edge of the river, one eye on Mark's still form, and fill it with water.

I need to leave the river, at least for now. It doesn't offer enough cover. I doubt Mark is the only person out here who will hurt me if he can. And having water will make staying hidden easier. I will have to find somewhere else to get fresh water, but the canteen buys me a little time, at least.

I grab my sweater off the ground and head south without looking back, following the line of the river. I'm searching for someplace to cross where I won't be swept away. Every step jars my shoulder, but the pain, while ever-present, feels distant, as if I'm watching someone else suffer instead of actually experiencing it myself. Soon enough it's going to hit me, though, once the shock or

adrenaline wears off, and I want to be far away from Mark
Laird before that happens.

I've been walking for at least fifteen minutes when the
river narrows, a series of rocks spread across its width.
There's probably no way to avoid getting wet, but hope-
fully I can cross without falling in or being swept away.
It seems as good a place to try crossing as any. The rocks
are slippery and jagged, and my equilibrium is upset by
not being able to use my right arm for balance. I lose
my footing about halfway across and come inches from
somersaulting into the water. Kneeling on a rock, hair
hanging in my face, shoulder screaming in protest, ruined
fingers still dripping blood, I draw a deep, unsteady
breath. My earlier anger, the anger that helped me beat
Mark, has dissipated like smoke in the wind. All that's
left is exhaustion. I have never been so bone-weary, so
tired all the way to my soul. Do I want to give up or keep
going? Live or die? Fight another day or wave the white
flag and let the water wash me away? I tell myself this is
the last time I will ask this question. Whatever the answer,
it will be final.

Come on, Ivy, you can do this. It's not my own voice
urging me on, but Bishop's. I imagine him next to me,
how he would look straight into my eyes and expect me
to keep going. How he always believed in me, up until
the bitter, ugly end when I forced him to lose his faith. If
he were here, he'd help me get to my feet and we'd finish
crossing the river together, leaning on each other when

slippery rocks threatened. Because with each other, we were always our better, stronger selves.

I know that thinking about Bishop is an indulgence I can ill afford. And in the harsh light of morning I may regret my weakness. But now, with only the indifferent silver moon as witness, I allow myself the comfort of pretending he is beside me, offering his warm hand for me to hold.

I stand up and finish crossing the river.

3

The screech of morning birds wakes me, the sun shining into my face. I jerk, disoriented, and my shoulder is suddenly replaced with glass shards and fire. My fingers ache, pulsing underneath their filthy bandage. After crossing the river last night, I walked east until my exhaustion and injuries caught up to me, forcing me to find shelter in a small grove of trees when I couldn't stop shaking, could barely take another step without falling. But a night spent on the hard ground, my back wedged against a tree trunk, has done nothing to improve my condition. My right arm hangs limp at my side, and the skin of my shoulder feels hot and swollen when I run my fingers over it light as butterfly wings. I don't bother unwrapping my fingers; I already know what I'll find.

I sit quietly for a minute, listening for any unnatural sounds around me, but I hear nothing other than the shift of leaves overhead. Mark's bag is still slung across my body, and I open it, something I never bothered to do last night in the dark. The mere fact that he had a bag and a canteen means that, at the very least, there must be houses around here somewhere. Maybe a whole abandoned town where I can find some type of supplies.

The bag is worn brown canvas, not too big and relatively light. I send up a quick prayer that there's something to eat inside its depths. The first thing I pull out is a second canteen, empty, and I curse myself for not checking the contents last night. Two full canteens of water would make me feel a lot more confident, but there's nothing to be done about it now. My fingers close around something wrapped in cloth and I pull it out, unwrap it carefully. I doubt it's severed fingers, but with Mark Laird you never know. Underneath the cloth there are half a dozen strips of what look like beef jerky. I lift it and sniff. It's not as well-made as the kind we had in Westfall, but the long, lean winters left all of us familiar with jerky. My mouth fills with saliva at the scent and I tear off a ragged chunk with my teeth. It's tough and gamy, and still one of the best things I've ever tasted. In just a few minutes I've already eaten an entire strip, barely taking the time to chew. It hardly touches the gnawing hunger in my belly. But I'm not sure when I'll find food again, so I force myself to rewrap the rest and set it aside.

The remainder of the bag holds a battered paperback book, one I've never read before, some type of mystery with half the pages torn out, probably used for starting fires, and two bruised apples. And at the very bottom of the bag is a broken knife, the blade snapped just above the wooden handle, which is lucky for me. If the knife had been a factor in our fight by the river, the result would've been very different.

Mark travels light, which tells me his camp or the place he got his supplies can't be too far away. I polish one of the apples against my denim-clad thigh and bite into the slightly too-tender flesh. I lean my head back against the tree and allow myself to enjoy the moment, knowing it might be a long time before I have this much to eat again. Have a peaceful morning where I'm not fleeing or fighting for my life.

I need to decide where to go next, and the only thing I'm sure of is that Mark Laird is not alone. He hasn't been out here long enough to have dried and cured the beef for jerky, if he even knows how. I have no way of knowing if he stole the jerky or befriended the people who made it. But there are others in close enough proximity that Mark has crossed their paths. I'm not sure whether to be cheered by this thought or terrified.

I have to keep moving. I can't walk forever; eventually the seasons will change, and by the time the harsh winter snows arrive I want to make sure I have someplace to hole up. To make it through, I'll need food and a water supply, not to mention warmer clothes. I'm not going to find any of those things by sitting here, waiting for rescue that's never going to come.

I roll to the side and push myself up with my good arm. The heat from my injured shoulder radiates up into my jaw and down to my fingertips. I need to get my shoulder back into the socket, but I don't know how to do it by myself. Instead, I fashion a crude sling by tying and looping the arms of my sweater around my neck, slide my arm into the cradle it makes, and sigh with relief when some of the pressure on my shoulder joint eases.

Once I'm up, I continue heading east. Not for any particular reason, just because that's the opposite direction of where I last saw Mark Laird. I'm hoping to come across a road or path, something I can follow that might lead me to an old town where I can look for supplies. It feels good to have a goal in mind, even a small one, rather than just blundering about aimlessly in this empty landscape.

Bishop would love it out here, I think, as I cross a field of tall grass, brambles catching against my legs every few steps. The quiet, except for insects and the sound of my own breathing. The sun, warm but not yet hot. The clouds, puffs of cotton in a crystal-blue sky. I try to convince myself that this is peaceful, but I'm all too aware of how alone I am. Growing up, I used to wish for a day to myself, one where my father and Callie would leave me to my own thoughts instead of trying to stuff me full of theirs.

But now the isolation is smothering. If I discovered I was the last person alive in the world, I would not doubt it.

By the time I come across a road, more weeds than asphalt, I'm limping from blisters on both feet, and my entire right side sparks with pain at each step. I sink down to the ground on the edge of the road. I can't afford to stop for more than a few minutes. I won't want to continue if I don't keep moving forward.

My canteen is only half full, but I take a swallow anyway. I meant to make the water last longer, but the unforgiving sun is making a joke of all my good intentions. I debate whether to eat the last apple or another strip of jerky and finally decide on the apple. It will spoil before the jerky. I make it last as long as I can, sucking on the core until every last bit of moisture is gone, then toss it away.

It's a risk to go out on the road. I'll be more easily spotted there than if I keep to the tall grass or trees. But the uneven landscape is quickly proving too difficult for me to navigate with my useless arm and shoulder. Better to take the road, where at least I can keep my footing and avoid a fall. Decisions are easier, I'm finding, when there are no good options to begin with.

Turns out it's not easy going on the road, either. I have to watch for cracks in the asphalt, ragged chunks that hide behind clumps of creeping green plants. But it's still less challenging than navigating the tall grass. The sun shimmers off the broken asphalt for as far as I can see, the gray snake of road disappearing into the far horizon, and I follow it into a future I cannot yet fathom.

Four days. More than a hundred hours I've been on the road, and I haven't passed a single abandoned town. The only signs that anyone's ever inhabited this land in the entire history of the world are the skeletons of rusted cars I navigate around. But there's never anything more, just this endless stretch of road and the broad, blank sky. If not for the position of the rising and setting sun, I would think I'd gotten turned around at some point and was simply retracing my steps over and over.

My water is gone, my thirst slackened only by a brief rainstorm that partially refilled my canteen and a small puddle of stagnant water at the side of the road. Water I knew I probably shouldn't drink, its surface dark with dirt and the smell of rotten things rising from its shallow depths. But in the end, my thirst beat out my good sense. My brain's dim warning bells were no match for the desperate need to drink.

Earlier today I could have sworn I heard someone calling my name in the distance. And in that moment, I didn't even care if it was Mark Laird, I was so relieved to hear another human voice. But it was only the harsh cries of a few crows circling overhead, their wings turned a glossy blue-black by the unrelenting sunlight. As I watched them wheel above me, I understood how easy it would be to slip into madness out here. How quickly it could happen.

I expected it to be difficult outside the fence. And dangerous. But I never anticipated how relentlessly empty it would be. How vast the land and how small I am in comparison, almost like I'm steadily shrinking into nothing under the endless expanse of late-summer sky. I might have done better out here before I met Bishop. Before I got used to having someone listen to me, walk next to me. Before someone loved me.

I used to be better at loneliness.

I haven't dared to take off my shoes; I don't want to see the wreck of my feet. But I won't be able to walk much longer. A few more miles is what I tell myself. I make it a challenge. Take one hundred steps. If I'm still alive, take one hundred more. It's a sick little game, but it keeps me going. I passed a sign a few hours ago, knocked over into the weeds. Barely legible words across its rusted tin surface: Birch Tree—8 miles. After all the distance I've covered, eight miles is nothing. But I have an irrational fear that I'm never going to reach Birch Tree, that the town will just keep moving farther away from me, somehow always creeping beyond the far horizon.

But at the top of a small hill it took me much too long to climb, I finally see something in the distance besides grass and trees. Houses. The road I'm on passes right between the cluster of buildings. A harsh, choking sound escapes me, part laugh, part sob. I walk faster downhill, a kind of shuffling run as I try to protect my shoulder and favor my feet at the same time.

I have no idea what I'm going to find in Birch Tree. Maybe nothing. Maybe something worse than Mark Laird. But right now I don't care. The town may be empty, but it once harbored life and some remnant of that time will remain, some proof that people once populated this barren land. A reminder that although I'm alone now, maybe I won't always be.

I slow down the closer I get to the town, the back of my neck prickling with awareness. I don't see any movement, no sounds of human inhabitants, but my body is sending out warnings anyway. I feel watched, eyes crawling over me as I limp along the road. I'd be easy pickings for someone, my arm useless in its makeshift sling, my body weak from hunger and dehydration. And while nothing moves in the shadows between the houses, the uneasy feeling in my gut doesn't leave.

The first house on the left has been partially burned, the roof collapsing inward, fire-blackened boards pointing their jagged remains toward the sky. The second house is in better shape, a squat little bungalow, its front windows smashed. A bit of tattered curtain, faded to colorlessness, blows inward on the hot breeze. I pick it for no other reason than because it reminds me of the house I shared with Bishop.

I climb the front steps, my back still tingling with the knowledge I'm being watched. It could be my imagination, my mind playing cruel tricks, but I don't think so. I push open the cracked front door anyway. If there is someone out there, they can catch me on the road as easily as they can inside the house. It's not like I'm going to be able to outrun them.

People have been inside this house since the war, although how long ago I can't tell. There's a coating of dust on every surface, but not thick enough to have been undisturbed for fifty years. And everything that once made this house a home is gone. No pictures on the walls, no knickknacks on the mantel. The only things that remain are those too large to be easily moved. A weather-beaten dining room table, missing part of one leg so that it slouches lopsided, partially blocking the doorway. A couch in the living room spews stuffing onto the floor, holes in the mildewed fabric probably providing nests for all manner of small animals over the years. There is a dark stain that runs almost the whole length of the entryway, practically black against the wood. Blood, years old. Probably spilled sometime after the war ended. So many people weren't killed by the bombs. They were done in by fear and mindless panic, their own neighbors as lethal as weapons. Survival of the fittest taken to its most deadly conclusion.

I walk into the kitchen, wincing at the screech of the floorboards under my feet. It sounds like I'm announcing my presence, my exact location, to the entire town. The kitchen is bare, all the cabinet doors hanging open to reveal empty shelves. Not a single crumb left to scavenge.

I didn't expect anything different, but I'm still hit with a sharp pang of something close to panic. For the first time I accept that I may die, that this long-abandoned town may be my final resting place. I don't know where to go from here. There doesn't seem to be any point in climbing the stairs. It would take too much energy, and the thought of being trapped up there if someone followed me inside keeps my feet firmly planted on the first floor.

The sun is blinding when I reemerge onto the sagging front porch. I put up a hand to shield my eyes from the harsh light. Nothing moves in the midday heat. In the distance, I can hear what sounds like a door swinging in the breeze. Beyond that, there is nothing. Even the crows have fled.

I was wrong. Being here, in the skeleton of this ruined town, is worse than the open road. I've never believed in ghosts. The things that frighten me have always been right in front of me, easy to see and categorize. But if there are ghosts, this town is full of them, haunting all the cobwebbed corners and dusty yards. Whatever I was hoping to find here has long fled. All that's left behind are the husks of lives that ended decades ago, tainting the air with sorrow and waste.

I stumble down the porch steps, back out onto the parched pavement. And again it hits me, a steady thump right between my shoulder blades. The knowledge that something is watching me, even now tracking my unsteady steps.

I turn in a slow circle. Only the lifeless houses stare back at me, dark windows capable of hiding anything within their shadows. The smart thing to do would be get off this road. Find some cover among the trees and hope I can outsmart whatever is tracking me. Maybe become the hunter instead of the hunted.

But I'm too tired for that. Too weak and too angry. I hold my good arm out from my side, beckoning into the hot, still air. "Come on," I yell. "You want me? Come and get me." Nothing. I nearly stamp my foot in frustration. *"Come on!"* My voice, furious and fragile in equal measure, spirals off into the silence, as though swallowed up along with everything else that used to be alive.

4

Bishop is pressed against me, his bare chest heating the skin of my back and shoulder. I can't see him, but I can feel him, smell him, and the relief is so immense it threatens to engulf me, rolling over me like a wave I'm happy to drown in. I try to speak but all that comes out is a sobbing breath. "Shhh," he says, barely a whisper. I want to roll over and look at him, but when I start to turn, his hand on my shoulder tightens, hurting me. The pain confuses me. Bishop would never hurt me. But when I cry out, he only squeezes harder. My hand scrabbles upward, desperate to loosen his grip, but I don't find his fingers. Instead, something slithery-soft and faintly greasy slides through my hand, making me recoil. A long black feather. I wrench my head backward and Bishop is gone. In his place is a huge crow, its talons digging into my shoulder, slicing through the swollen flesh. Blood that burns like fire runs down my arm. I scream, try to bat the bird away, but it only stares at me, my own pain-twisted face reflected back in the vacant pools of its eyes.

"Here," a voice says. "Drink this."

My eyes feel glued shut, and I don't try very hard to open them. I don't have the energy. Something clanks against my teeth. "You have to open your mouth." The same voice. My lips are pried apart, and a trickle of liquid hits my tongue. Now I open my mouth without hesitation, my hand coming up blindly to grab.

"Hold on, you're going to spill it. Slow down."

Water wets my lips, my tongue, the back of my sandpaper throat. I give a cry of anger when the flow of water stops, force my eyelids apart in order to chase the source. There's a girl leaning over me, dark hair, brown eyes, wrinkled brow.

"Callie?" I say, and don't recognize my own voice. I sound a thousand years old, more dead than alive.

The girl's eyebrows shoot up. "Not last time I checked," she says. Even before she's done speaking, I realize my mistake. This girl's hair isn't as long, just skimming her collarbone, and her eyes are the muddy blue-brown of river water, not dark and inky like my sister's.

Too late I notice the man slouched in the doorway, watching me, and realize I'm inside a house. Lying on a bed. Panic slaps me hard and fast, and I lurch backward, succeeding only in smacking my head against the headboard and waking the pain in my shoulder.

"Relax," the girl says. She holds out a hand but doesn't touch me. "We're not going to hurt you."

"Yet," the man in the doorway says with a smirk. He has a crossbow slung across his back, the tip of it just visible over his left shoulder. His eyes glow pale brown against his dark skin.

"Shut up, Caleb," the girl says, her eyes still on me.

"Who are you?" I ask. "Where am I?" I look around, my eyes bouncing from doorway to wall to bed, not able to land on anything for more than a second. Not sure where the biggest threat lies. "Where's my bag?" That bag is the only thing I own in the whole world; I can't lose it.

There's a beat of silence. Caleb shifts into the room, takes a step closer to the bed. "You mean Mark's bag?" he asks.

My heart leaps sideways in my chest, and I'm instantly alert. Anyone who knows Mark, who speaks of him with such familiarity, is a potential threat to me. I have to be careful. "I found that bag," I say. "It's mine now." I try to hold Caleb's gaze, but my eyes slide away before his do.

"We can worry about Mark and the stupid bag later," the girl says. "Right now we need to get your shoulder fixed."

Ever since Mark dislocated my shoulder, getting it back in the socket has been all I can think about. But now, faced with the prospect of these strangers touching me, I shrink back, bring my knees up protectively. I notice for the first time that my cut fingers are freshly bandaged.

"We cleaned those up," the girl tells me, following my gaze. "You should have had stitches, but it's too late now. You may have some scars, but they should heal up fine."

"Thank you," I say.

"No problem. But now we have to take care of your shoulder. It's going to hurt," she says. "But we have to do it. The longer it stays like that, the less likely it's ever going to be right." She looks at Caleb. "Come on."

Caleb has to be close to a decade older than the girl, but he listens to her like she's the boss. He crosses the room, stopping next to the bed so that he's on my injured side. He has a length of faded cloth stretched between his hands like a cradle. Or a noose. I look up at him. His face is impassive, waiting for the girl.

"Lie down," she tells me. "On your back."

I uncurl my legs slowly. I feel like prey, exposing my delicate underbelly as I flatten out on the bed, the two of them looming above me.

"Are you good with pain?" the girl asks.

That surprises a hoarse little laugh out of me. "Getting better all the time," I say.

The girl smiles, revealing a slight gap between her front teeth. She tucks her hair behind both ears and nods to

Caleb, who bends down and loops the cloth under my armpit, pulling it taut. I clench my teeth to keep from crying out. I try to keep my breathing even, tell myself if they were going to hurt me there'd be no point in healing me first. *Unless they're sadists*, a little voice in my head whispers, but I tell it to shut up.

The girl nods at Caleb again, and then reaches forward and takes hold of my injured arm, pulling steadily downward, while he keeps tension in the cloth. My shoulder, already filled with broken glass, explodes, pain rippling up into my jaw and shooting sparks from my fingertips. The girl pulls harder and I can't keep quiet any longer, screaming into the humid air as she gives a final yank and my shoulder shifts back into place with a *pop* that sends me pinwheeling down into darkness.

I jerk awake, gasping out the last of another horrible dream. No talons this time, but something equally as horrifying, involving Bishop and blood and my own guilty hands. I can hear my shuddering breath and I count backward from one hundred until it evens out, slow and steady. My head aches, a dull, insistent throb. It takes me a few seconds to realize I'm in the same room as earlier, still in the narrow bed, although the daylight is fading fast, purple-tinged light edging in around the cracked and dusty shutters. I lift my injured shoulder off the bed, just an inch, testing.

"Better not," a man's voice says from the gloomy corner to my right. "Likely to pop it back out. Gonna be a while before it's ready for normal movement."

My eyes swing wildly, landing on Caleb, who is sitting on the far side of the room, his body slouched on a wooden chair. His relaxed stance is deceptive; he has the lean, hungry look of a predator. One false move from me and he'd be up and out of that chair before I could blink.

"You scared me," I say, fingers twisting in the worn quilt someone has thrown on top of me.

Caleb shrugs, doesn't apologize. His eyes pulse with a quick, clever intelligence that warns me to be careful. "Ash is always looking for someone to save," he says after a tense beat of silence.

I have no idea what he's talking about. The smoky early-evening light shades the whole room with the foggy, underwater quality of a dream, making me wonder if I'm still asleep and my nightmare has simply taken an unexpected detour. I blink fast, pinch the back of my hand. "What . . . I don't know what you mean?" I say eventually. "Who's Ash?"

"Ashley, the girl who was here earlier."

He sounds impatient, but only half of me is really listening. Now that I'm sure I'm awake, I'm wondering if we're alone in this house, whether he's dangerous, calculating whether I can beat him to the doorway. And where to go from there if I do.

"Hey," he says, loud and sharp. "Pay attention to what I'm saying."

I try to focus on him. I don't want to make him angry, or any angrier than he already seems. But I can feel my own irritation rising, too. "I am paying attention," I snap back.

"She's looking for someone to save," he repeats. As he speaks he points in my direction. It has the ease of a gesture he's done a thousand times, probably so much a part of him he doesn't notice it anymore. "Even if they're not worth saving."

I shift upward in the bed, scooting up to sitting. Caleb doesn't try to help me, just watches. "So what are you saying?" I ask, once I'm upright. "I'm not worth it?"

Caleb shrugs again, apparently his default reaction. "Too early to know." He kicks at something on the floor, and for the first time I notice my bag lying there. Well, Mark's bag, if we're being truthful. "I'd be interested to hear how you got this bag."

"I already told you. I found it."

"Where?"

"By the river. I slipped on some rocks and dislocated my shoulder crossing the river. When I finally got to the other side, I found this bag on the bank. So I took it." I'm not even sure why I'm lying to him. All I know is that he knows Mark, knows him well enough to wonder why I have his bag. If he finds out I hurt Mark, regardless of the circumstances, I'm not sure what he'll do to me. Until

I have a better idea of who, and what, I'm dealing with, lying seems like my best option.

"How'd you get beat up?" Caleb asks. "If you never saw Mark?"

"That happened before I found the bag." I keep my voice even, my gaze steady.

Caleb watches me as the shadows grow longer in the fading light. He probably thinks his silence will force me to speak, that I'll be so desperate to fill the void I'll tell him things I've promised to keep to myself. But he doesn't know me. I may not be a very good liar, but I'm an old pro at silence, forever listening for my cues and keeping what I really want to say buried deep. I can match silence with silence any day of the week. It's when I let my temper get ahead of me, when I open my mouth, that things usually start getting tricky.

"And when you took the bag, you didn't see anyone around?" Caleb asks when it becomes clear I'm not going to talk first.

I shake my head. "What's the story with this Mark guy, anyway?" I ask, fighting to keep my voice casual. "Is he a friend of yours?"

"I know him," Caleb says, and although his face doesn't give anything away, I can hear him measuring his words the way I'm measuring mine. It reminds me of those first days with Bishop, when I tasted each word before it left my tongue. "He went out hunting a few days ago," Caleb continues. "He never came back."

"Well, I can't help you," I say, trying not to think about Mark, the look on his face when he was hunting *me*. "I never saw him."

Caleb knows I'm lying. I can see it in the flare at the back of his eyes, the way his body is still slouched in the chair but his fingers tighten on the arms. But he can't prove it, not without Mark here, and so I hold his gaze as the sun slips behind the house and bathes us both in dusky shadow.

Sometime in the night Caleb leaves, and Ashley takes his place. She brings water with her and rations it to me in tiny sips so I don't get sick trying to gulp it all down in one huge swallow. She brings a small piece of rabbit, too, greasy and tough.

When I wake in the morning, she smiles at me, unlike Caleb, and sits on the edge of the bed, her legs curled up beside her. More like a companion than a warden, but it doesn't make me any less nervous. She has a wicked-looking knife dangling from her belt, and although her face is friendly, I don't doubt that she could gut me in a second if she felt threatened.

"We found you passed out in the road," she tells me. She hands me a small bowl of blueberries and another glass of water. I think I could drink for a month and still be thirsty. "You didn't even make it ten steps after you left this house." She lets out a little laugh. Her voice is deep for a girl's, her laugh scratchy to match. "Which is probably a good thing, since Caleb had to carry you back here."

Caleb carting me around when I was unconscious is not an image I want to dwell on. "You were the ones watching me?" I ask. It's comforting to know I wasn't imagining it, that my survival instincts are in proper working order. "Caleb and you?"

Ash nods. "We didn't mean to scare you. But we had to see if anyone was with you, what you were doing, before we showed ourselves."

"Are you two alone out here?"

"No, we're part of a larger group. But Caleb gets restless," she says with a grin. "He likes to get away sometimes, so I tag along."

"So you don't live here? In Birch Tree?"

"Nope. In the warmer months we actually have an outdoor camp. When it gets colder, we settle into a town. But not this one. Ours is closer to the river." She smooths out the blanket on my legs. "You can come with us, if you want," she says. "Back to our camp. It's hard to make it out here alone."

I still don't know if I can trust them, but she's right. I'm not going to survive alone. There is strength in numbers, even if you're unsure of the people making up those numbers. "Okay," I say.

"Good." Ash smiles, tucks her hair behind her ears. "I don't even know your name," she says. "Caleb said he told you I'm Ashley. But I go by Ash."

"I'm Ivy."

"Nice to meet you, Ivy." Ash holds out her hand for a brief shake, her fingers gentle around my injured hand. "Where are you from?" She must see something in my face, because she's quick to add, "You don't have to talk about it, if you don't want to."

"Yes, she does," Caleb says, back to lurking in the doorway. I take the opportunity to glare at him. He glares back.

"I grew up in Westfall," I say, my heart squeezing in my chest at the words. "It's a town not too far from here. And they put me out. I'm not sure exactly how long ago. Maybe about a week." Ash looks from me to Caleb and back again. "Have you heard of Westfall?" I ask. I'm pretty sure neither of them is from there. Their faces aren't familiar to me, even vaguely.

"We've heard of it," Caleb says. "We've never had the misfortune of going there."

Ash clucks her tongue at him. "You don't know anything about it."

"I know they chuck girls barely old enough to take care of themselves out into . . . this." His sweeping hand encompasses more than this dusty room, seems to take in the whole wide brutal world beyond these walls. His hand turns into a pointing finger, aimed right at Ash. "And I can't believe you're defending that place."

"My parents were born in Westfall," Ash explains at my questioning look. "They put my mom out when she was sixteen. She refused to marry the person they picked for her. My dad followed her, decided he'd rather take his chances out here with her than live there without her." She tells the story with a kind of well-worn pride, her own personal fairy tale with her parents in the starring roles. My mind wanders to thoughts of Bishop, what it would've been like if he'd come after me, but I sever that idea almost as quickly as I think it. Life is painful enough without my own brain making it worse.

"Is that why you were put out?" Caleb asks me. "Because you wouldn't marry who they chose for you?"

I'm not sure what the right answer is, whether telling them the truth will hurt or help me. For now, it seems better to go with the easiest explanation, the one that they'll immediately understand. "Yes," I say, with a pang that surprises me. I didn't realize until this moment that I was hoping once I left Westfall behind, shed my old life and all the people in it, that my sacrifice would at least leave me free to be honest. Free to end a lifetime of lies and pretending and weighing every word. It's exhausting to know all that deceit has followed me, hundred-pound baggage I can't seem to put down.

Ash tells me that we're going to head out as soon as I'm up and ready to go and then leaves me for a few minutes. "I left some extra water in the bathroom," she says on her way out the door. "If you want to wash up a little bit." She glances at my filthy tank top. "We can find you some clean clothes when we get back to camp."

When I finally roll out of bed, I have to clamp my mouth closed on a groan. My whole body aches, head to toe, as though someone has taken a fist to every inch of flesh. I'm thankful for my long pants, just so I don't have to see what my legs look like. My arms are bad enough, covered with bloody scratches and deep purple bruises. And although my shoulder no longer throbs with pain, I can tell it's still swollen and tender. I clench my jaw and shuffle into the bathroom across the hall, close the door on a screech of rusty hinges.

There's no running water, of course, but true to her word Ash has left a canteen of water balanced on the edge of the chipped porcelain sink. The mirror above the sink is smashed, but a single shard of glass remains, bisecting my face when I peer at my own reflection. It's the first time I've seen myself since I was put out, and it's hard to comprehend the changes that little more than a week have made. My eyes look huge, staring from a sunburned face streaked with dirt and dried blood. My lip is still swollen from Mark's beating, my right eye puffy and dark. Freckles I never knew I had dot my nose and cheeks. I've lost weight, my cheekbones stark and angular. I look older, harder already. What once was soft has been carved away, leaving only what's absolutely necessary behind. I barely recognize myself and find I'm okay with that. I'm not the same girl I was when I believed in my family, when I was Bishop's wife. It's only right that my outside should alter along with everything beneath my skin.

It seems impossible that only miles away Westfall still stands. People right this minute buying jam in the market or feeding ducks in the park. It feels like a different lifetime from where I am now. I close my eyes, my throat muscles fighting a sob. My hands tighten on the sides of the sink. Grief surges through me, memories flowing against my eyelids. Westfall. My family. Bishop. I don't want to think about any of this, any of them, but once the door in my mind is open I'm overcome with fear about what might be happening in my absence, whether Callie has managed to get close to Bishop, whether my father has come up with a new plan to take down President Lattimer, if Bishop is safe and how long he can remain that way. They are questions I will never find answers for; just the asking of them is a type of torture. *Be safe*, I think, wishing there was some way Bishop could hear me across the distance between us. *Be strong. Be happy.*

I open my eyes, push away my thoughts along with a few escaping tears. I give my head a little shake, remind myself that the past is gone for good. Here and now is all that matters.

"You almost done?" Caleb calls from the hallway, making me jump.

"Give me another minute," I call back. I take a deep breath, focus on trying to clean myself up. My hair is caked with dirt and blood, matted into knots I don't know if I'll ever manage to pull free. I leave it alone and instead take the piece of graying rag Ash left next to the canteen and go to work on my face and hands, scrubbing off as much filth as I can. I'm moving a little easier by the time I let myself out of the bathroom, blood rushing to my cramped muscles. I gather my bag from the floor of the bedroom and join Caleb and Ash where they wait in the stripped-down kitchen.

"I'm ready," I tell them. Ash scrambles up from where she's sitting on the floor, grabs her knapsack off the kitchen table. Caleb is already at the back door, probably annoyed it took me so long. I follow behind Ash, let the screen door bang closed behind me. The sun warms my face, my nose full of the scent of dirt and dry grass on the wind. I step off the back porch and into the next chapter of my life.

We head west, back toward the river, negating every hard-earned step I took away from it a few days ago. I tell myself my journey east wasn't wasted; at least I found other people, ones who allowed me to join them. Caleb takes the lead and Ash has fallen back to allow me to walk between them. But strangely, I don't feel boxed in the way I used to when my father and Callie made sure I was always in the middle. Maybe because I sense Caleb would be only too glad to see me break away and disappear forever.

We walk in silence, other than Ash whistling a four-note melody over and over.

"Jesus," Caleb says finally, "give it a rest, would you?"

In response Ash whistles once more, almost a screech, before falling silent.

"Are you guys related or something?" I ask, glancing behind me at Ash. "Siblings?" Although they look nothing alike—one dark, one light—their interactions have the love-hate tone of family.

Caleb grunts something unintelligible, but Ash shakes her head. "Sort of. Not technically."

I'm about to ask what she means when Caleb says, "Her dad found me wandering around out here when I was a kid. Maybe seven or eight?" He hooks a thumb back over his shoulder without turning around. "She was just born."

"So your parents raised both of you?" I ask Ash.

She's pulled abreast of me, and her mouth tightens briefly before she answers. "Just my dad. My mom died having me." I know that giving birth is dangerous, even in Westfall. Women die more often than people like to acknowledge, so it makes sense it would be riskier out here. Ash's father must have been very determined if he managed to keep a newborn alive without her mother.

"Is your dad back at the camp?" I sidestep a hole in the ground, bumping Ash's shoulder as I do.

"No," Ash says. She keeps her eyes on the ground.

"He died." Caleb's voice is quiet, his shoulders and neck stiff. "Last year. Infected leg."

"Oh." I sneak a glance at Ash. "I'm sorry."

"Not your fault," Caleb says, which is probably the nicest thing he's said to me so far.

"So you're on your own?" I ask Ash.

Caleb stops so quickly I almost slam into his back. "She has me," he says. "She's not alone."

"I didn't mean—"

Ash cuts me off, pokes Caleb between the shoulder blades, hard. "Lay off her. God." Once Caleb starts walking again, Ash rolls her eyes at me, making me smile. It's been so long since I've smiled that the stretch of skin feels foreign, like learning a new language.

"You're, what, about sixteen?" Ash asks. "That's still the age they make you get married, right?"

"Yes." I don't look at the green of the trees. I don't think of the rush of the river. "Almost seventeen. How old are you?" She looks older than me, but it's hard to tell by how much. She has the sun-weathered skin of those who spend all day outdoors, her body stripped of everything but essential muscle.

She shrugs. "Around seventeen or eighteen. We don't really pay much attention to that stuff."

Caleb snorts out a laugh, but there's no amusement in it. "No birthday cake and candles around here."

"Yeah, well, my family wasn't big on cake and candles either," I tell him.

It takes us several hours to reach the camp. We could have covered the distance faster, but Ash made us stop every half hour or so to give me more water or a piece of food. I could tell the delays made Caleb impatient, but he only blew out long-suffering sighs, back against an adjacent tree, and waited for Ash and me to get up and moving again.

I can hear the camp before we actually see it. The bustle of humanity, the sounds of voices carried on the warm air, sound all wrong in the world of quiet I've grown used to. I've been desperate for other human voices, but now that I've found Ash and Caleb and I'm no longer alone, the sounds of a larger community bring a hot flush of fear. My heart slams against my ribs, and I don't realize I've slowed to almost a stop until Ash puts a hand on my back, urging me forward. "It's okay," she says. "You'll be safe here. I promise." I want to believe her, but my safety isn't something she can guarantee, no matter how good her intentions. What if Mark has already returned, ready to tell everyone his own self-serving version of what happened between us? Who would Ash and Caleb believe?

We top a small rise and the camp is laid out below us, spread along the banks of the river. There are dozens of mismatched tents, homemade from a variety of materials. I can see a large garden and a cluster of clotheslines strung between the trees on the edge of the camp. People mill around, dodging a few small children who race among the tents. It seems tranquil and unthreatening, which only makes me more uneasy, as if it's all an illusion meant to hide the ugly core underneath.

"Why do you stay here, instead of in a town?" I ask, still not ready to move down the hill and into the camp.

"Some people do stay in town, but most of us prefer it outdoors. I like the freedom. I'm not a big fan of enclosed spaces," Ash says.

"It's safer," Caleb says bluntly, and Ash gives him a warning look. "Not everyone out here is as nice as we are." I glance at him, but there's no hint of irony on his face. "We prefer to be in a large group, able to defend one another. And able to scatter if it comes to that."

"Stop scaring her," Ash says.

"I'm not scared," I tell her. "I didn't think it would be all sunshine and roses out here."

Caleb glances at me, and for the first time I see something other than suspicion in his face. "Come on," he says. "Let's get down there and get you set up."

We start down the small hill, but Ash hangs back a little with me. "You can stay with me, in my tent," she says. "If you want."

"We can find her a tent," Caleb says without turning around. The man has ears like a bat.

"I know that," Ash says, and looks at me. "But if you don't want to be alone, I don't mind the company."

"Sure," I say. "I'd like that." It would be nice to have at least one friendly face close by in this mass of unfamiliar humanity.

"Great," Caleb mutters, "pretty soon you'll be spending all day braiding each other's hair and whispering about boys."

Ash doesn't dignify that comment with a response, so I don't either. Apparently I'm getting used to Caleb and his sharp tongue. Already I sense his bark is worse than his bite. At least when it comes to Ash.

As we make our way into camp, people stop to clap Caleb on the back, pull Ash in for quick one-armed hugs. The eyes on me are curious, but not hostile, and everyone seems to accept that if I'm with Ash and Caleb, I'm welcome among them. There are no formal introductions, but I hear Ash murmur my name from time to time as she greets people, and I nod and give small smiles in return. All the attention is overwhelming, though, and I'm grateful when Ash closes the flap of her tent behind us, shutting out the sights, if not the sounds, of the camp.

Ash is already hard at work, shifting bedding and making room for me on the left side of her tent. "Caleb has an extra cot," she tells me over her shoulder. "I'll have him bring it over here, and I have plenty of bedding." She turns and surveys me. "I'll ask around and find you some clothes. Most of mine aren't going to fit. You're a lot taller and . . . you know . . ." She makes an hourglass motion with her hands. It's so reminiscent of Callie that tears gather on my lashes before I can stop them. I take a deep breath and tilt my head up until they're gone. I don't understand how I can hate Callie and love her all in one breath.

"You okay?" Ash asks, and I force a smile when I meet her eyes.

"Fine," I say, and she doesn't push, which I'm thankful for. I don't know what I'd tell her if she did.

She leaves me alone for a little while, presumably to go round up some clothes, and I take the moment of solitude gratefully. I wander slowly around the interior of the tent, getting used to the space. It's more like a decent-sized room than a tent. There's a cot on the right side, piled high with pillows and blankets, a crate next to it with a lantern and a few books. On the back wall is a small trunk, probably where Ash stores her clothes. The ground is covered with tacked-down oilcloth, and window flaps on both sides let in a hint of a breeze. There's little decoration other than a tattered map of the old United States hanging on the far wall, and I move closer, run my fingers carefully over the fragile paper. There are small dark marks in certain spots on the map, but there's no clue as to what they mean.

"You found our map," Ash says from behind me, and I whirl around. "Sorry," she says, "didn't meant to startle you."

"That's okay." I glance back at the map. "What's it for?"

"It was my dad's," Ash says. "He liked to keep track of where people came from, when they passed through." She moves closer, points at some of the marks near what was once Virginia. "We've had a few groups from this part of the country. They said there's a more centralized government there, but it's harsh. Not much freedom. They wanted out." Her finger trails across the map, all the way to California. "A couple of years ago we had some people all the way from the West Coast. They said there's a fairly big settlement there, near where a city called San Diego used to be. A good place, according to them. They lived with us for the winter before setting out again. They were on a trek to walk from ocean to ocean." She smiles as she speaks, but my heart curls into a painful ball at her words.

"What?" Ash asks, brow furrowed. "What's wrong?"

"Nothing." I clear my throat. "It's nothing. I just knew someone, back in Westfall, who always wanted to see the ocean." I look back at the map, desperate for something else to concentrate on. "Have you ever thought about leaving here? Exploring what else is out there?"

"My dad never wanted to," Ash says. "He thought it was smarter to stay here, where we know there's food and we're familiar with the land. He felt like leaving was too much of a risk. He never wanted to do anything that put Caleb or me in any unnecessary danger."

"But?" I ask, hearing a wary kind of wistfulness behind her words.

Ash shrugs. "But I wouldn't mind seeing what else is out there someday." She holds out the bowl she has in her hand. "You better eat this before it gets cold. Rabbit stew." She gives me an apologetic smile. "We eat a lot of rabbit."

"It smells great," I tell her, meaning every word. "Definitely better than lizards and tree bark." She's brought a hunk of heavy, dark bread as well. I finish it all in huge gulps, and have to resist licking the inside of the bowl when I'm done.

"There's more," Ash says. "But first maybe you want to change clothes? Get cleaned up?"

At her words I realize how itchy I am, from my scalp all the way to my toes. I think there's dirt and blood caked in every crevice of my body. I can't imagine how bad I smell. "Yes, that sounds good."

Ash leads me out of the tent and down toward the river. The sun is starting to set, and the noise of the camp has been reduced to a peaceful buzz, everyone settling in for dinner. We walk along the edge of the river, away from the camp a bit, and Ash points to a spot where the riverbank is flat and even, the water flowing gently. "This is where we wash off," she tells me. "I've heard you have running water in Westfall. Nothing like that out here."

"It's okay," I say. "The river is fine. At this point, I'll just be happy to be clean." I glance around. "What if someone comes along?"

"The men go in that direction"—Ash hooks a thumb back over her shoulder—"so don't worry about prying eyes."

I still stand uncertainly, but Ash doesn't appear to have my reservations. She strips off her clothes in about five seconds flat and splashes into the river in a tangle of sun-browned limbs. She reminds me of a puppy, all big earnest eyes and eager warmth. "Hey, there's soap in my bag, if you want to grab it," she calls back to me.

I tell myself there's nothing to worry about. I'm not embarrassed for Ash to see me naked, but it leaves me feeling vulnerable. But I have to admit it feels good to shed myself of my smelly, dirt-streaked clothes. I leave them in a pile and join Ash in the water, which is surprisingly warm against my bare skin.

The soap is coarse and scratches as much as it cleans, but I scrub hard anyway, suddenly anxious to rid myself of every speck of sweat, blood, and dirt. I dunk my head under the water and work the soap through my tangled hair, too.

"Sorry," I say, passing Ash what's left of the bar of soap. "I used a lot of it."

"We have plenty," Ash says. She pauses in washing and points at my forearm. "How'd you get the scars?"

I glance down at my arm. "Dog bite." I steel myself for her to ask the details, already weighing whether to tell the truth or make up a new version of the story. But Ash only nods, lifts her leg out of the water.

"A wild dog got me right here when I was little," she says, running her hand over a scar on her thigh. "Caleb shot it." She lowers her leg and turns her arm my direction. A web of scar tissue covers her left biceps. "And this is from a mountain lion, just a couple of years ago." She laughs. "I have a bunch more. I'm covered in scars."

"These are my only ones," I say, my fingers sliding over the scars. They don't bother me as much as they used to, not since Bishop changed the way I thought about them.

And I realize from the lack of reaction that to Ash, the scars are just something that happened to me. They aren't me. Not anymore. I look up to find Ash watching me, her head cocked.

"What?" I ask.

"You have sad eyes." Ash makes the observation like it pains her, and I understand why Caleb worried about her wanting to find someone to save. Empathy probably doesn't get you very far out here.

"Not as sad as they were a few days ago," I say, as lightly as I can, but Ash doesn't smile.

"If you ever want to talk about it—"

"Thanks," I say, cutting her off. "I'm going to get out. I'm starting to get cold."

There are towels in Ash's bag, and a change of clothes for both of us. The pants she brought for me are a little short, but I roll them up to midcalf and they work fine. The sleeveless shirt is homespun and worn, but smells clean and fits well.

Woodsmoke dances in the early-evening air as we head back to camp, and Ash points to a bonfire in the distance. "Come on," she says. "We can drop our dirty clothes back at the tent and go sit around the fire." She glances at me. "You don't have to talk to anyone, if you don't want to."

I give her a grateful smile. "It's just a lot . . . getting used to this." I tip my head up, breathe in the scents of river grass and smoke. The stars are starting to come out, faint glitter tossed across the lavender sky. They are the only thing in my whole word that look remotely familiar. "It's like being in a dream you can't wake up from."

"Sounds pretty awful," Ash says.

"Not awful exactly." I don't know how to explain it to her. That what I left behind wasn't so great, either, except for Bishop. "Just very strange."

Ash finds Caleb on the edge of the fire pit and nudges him over so we all can fit on his blanket. He nods to me, which is probably his version of a friendly greeting. I pull my legs up, wrap my arms around them, and rest my chin on my knees. Just a few weeks ago a fire at night would have created nothing but sweat and sticky skin. But with a hint of fall in the air once the sun's set, it's the perfect temperature. Now that I've stopped moving, weariness leaches into my bones, and I wonder if I'll ever feel the buzz of excess energy again.

I notice the way almost everyone stops to greet Caleb as they gather around the fire. "Is Caleb in charge here?" I ask Ash, careful to time the question when Caleb is talking to someone else.

Ash smiles. "No one's in charge. It's not like Westfall." She glances at Caleb. "But people respect his opinion. Just like they did my dad's. But everyone's free to make their own decisions, so long as they don't hurt the group."

I nod, although it's hard for me to fathom a place where the final say in everything you do isn't dictated by someone else. In Westfall the hierarchy was so well-defined: President Lattimer, my father, Callie, Bishop . . . and finally, me, always last to be given a voice. Even though Bishop didn't play by those rules, it didn't change the fact that I was on the bottom rung of the totem pole in everyone else's eyes. It will take time to adjust to making decisions based solely on what I want, not on what is expected of me, on what other people think is best.

I let my eyes roam around the ring of faces, none of them familiar although I know at least some of them have to be from Westfall originally. I don't see Mark or the two men who were put out with him. The three of them were the only people sentenced after I married Bishop, so there's no one here who can contradict my story about why I was forced to leave Westfall. Maybe there will come a time when I'll feel safe enough to tell Ash the truth. But it's too big a risk to take now.

"Have most of these people been with your group a long time?" I ask Ash.

"It's a mix," Ash says. She's cutting into an apple and holds out a slice for me. "Some have been here since before I was born, some are from Westfall originally, and some come from other places."

My gaze falls on an older couple next to us, and the man gives me a friendly smile but the woman only stares. I turn back toward Ash, but I can still feel the woman's eyes on me.

"Who is that?" I whisper to Ash, tilting my head toward the woman.

"Who?" Ash leans back and looks to my right. "Oh, that's Elizabeth. She's from Westfall, too."

Just as Ash's words register, the woman, Elizabeth, calls out. "You're a Westfall, aren't you?"

I pretend I don't hear her, my heart slamming against my ribs as I keep my gaze on the dancing flames. There's a rustle of cloth as Elizabeth stands, the shuffle of feet through grass as she moves closer. Around us the voices have grown quiet. "You're Justin Westfall's daughter," Elizabeth says. "The youngest one."

Ash looks at me, and I meet her eyes. "Ivy Westfall?" Ash whispers.

I nod because I can't find my voice.

"She was supposed to marry the president's son," Elizabeth says and my head jerks toward her. She must have been put out in the last few years if she knows that.

"That's why they put you out?" Caleb says from my left. "Because you wouldn't marry him?"

"I already told you that," I say, voice harsh. "Remember?"

"Yeah, I remember," Caleb says. "But you left out your last name. And who your groom was supposed to be."

"What does it matter?" I say, turning to look at him. His eyes are bright in the glow of the fire, watching me. I can feel that old reckless side of me starting to wake up, waiting for Caleb to push me into saying something I won't be able to take back. A part of me hopes he will.

I startle when I feel a hand on my head, whip around too fast and almost send Elizabeth spilling backward from where she's crouching next to me. She reaches forward again and her hand smooths down my hair. It's a gentle touch, what I imagine a mother's touch must be like.

"You sweet girl," she says softly. "Such a brave, sweet girl." She leans forward and enfolds me in her arms, kisses my cheek. I catch a glimpse of Ash's smile as I close my eyes and allow myself to be held by this stranger. So now I know the answer. Maybe my father gave me something worth having after all, because being Ivy Westfall is to my advantage here.

The fact that I'm actually a Lattimer is just one more secret I will have to keep.

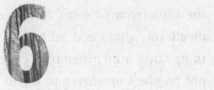

6

I've been living in Ash's tent for five days, and I'm still confused every time I open my eyes. It takes me a second, my mind scrolling through the possibilities: my childhood bedroom, my bed with Bishop, the hard ground and long grass, the empty house in Birch Tree, before settling on the correct one. And every morning, when I figure out where I am, the pain hits all over again, a violent punch right to my heart.

Growing up, our next-door neighbor lost her six-year-old son to the flu one particularly harsh January. I lay in bed on those ice-blue winter mornings and listened to her scream out her grief. Each rising of the sun reopening her wound. Now I understand—how sleep allows you to forget, but your pain wakes with the dawn, worse because for a split second you don't remember what you've suffered. It's a trick made even crueler by the fact that it happens over and over again. I can't stop the hurt from washing over me, but I don't let myself dwell on what, and who, I've lost. I don't hope for things that aren't meant to be mine. I tell myself *never*, not *maybe someday*, and try to remember that it won't always hurt this much—one day the pain will fade to the mellow ache of memory.

Today Ash is already gone, but she's left a bowl of berries and a hunk of corn bread next to my cot. She always brings me breakfast, whether I'm awake or not. Always greets me with a smile and glowing eyes. She is probably the most open, kindest person I've ever known. It's no wonder Caleb hovers, worried her kindness might be her downfall. I wish I could be honest with her, tell her my true story, especially when late at night she speaks about her childhood, the pain of her father dying, her fear of losing Caleb, too. But I don't know if there's a limit to her goodness. Maybe her affection for me ends where my allegiance to Bishop Lattimer begins.

I eat my breakfast while pulling on my clothes. Over the past few days, Ash has managed to gather up a respectable pile of clothing for me, including a second pair of shoes. I untangle my hair with the brush we share and tie it back in a ponytail. This morning we're helping to wash clothes down at the river, a task that caused Ash to wrinkle her nose when she told me about it. But she promised that tomorrow we'd do something more exciting, like Caleb teaching me how to snare small game. I'm not sure about spending a day with Caleb, but being able to catch my own dinner, something beyond lizards, is a skill I'd like to have.

Although fall is tiptoeing up on us, the daytime temperatures don't yet reflect the change, and the air is already thick and sticky when I step out of the tent, pausing to stretch my good arm high above my head. I don't feel comfortable here yet. Maybe it won't ever happen. Maybe no place will ever feel like home to me again. But I'm slowly learning the rhythms of this life, the way everyone follows the cues of sun and moon, how tasks are divvied up based on what needs doing, not the gender of those doing the work, how people are accepted so long as they don't cause trouble and they pull their own weight. It's a harder life than the one I knew, but in a lot of ways it's a freer one, too.

Caleb's tent is right next to ours, and as I pass, raised voices drift out from inside it. Caleb's and another man's. I take a step closer, not eavesdropping exactly, but definitely curious. I hear Caleb's voice. "I'm just telling you what she said."

"Well, she's lying," the other man says. Before the sound of his voice can register, Caleb's front tent flap is thrown open and I'm once again face-to-face with Mark Laird.

I stumble back a step and we stare at each other. It feels like those first few seconds by the riverbank, only this time he's not smiling. And his face and hair are still streaked and matted with clumps of dried blood, his temple a mottled purple. I glance down and see shredded, bloody socks. All of which sends a thrill of brutal satisfaction through me. Belatedly, I notice that he has his bag gripped in one hand. Caleb took it from me when we got to camp, said he would return it to its rightful owner if he ever showed up again. Mark lifts the bag and shakes it in my direction. "Told him you found this?"

"Yes," I say, holding his eyes. "I did find it."

Caleb pushes out of his tent behind Mark, gaze swinging between the two of us. "Mark says you couldn't have found his bag the way you say you did, Ivy." He doesn't sound like he's outright accusing me of anything, at least not yet. He's positioned equally distant between the two of us. Giving the impression that he's not taking sides. Or that he wants to be able to get in between us fast if all hell breaks loose.

"Ivy," Marks says, a kind of slithery whisper. "Told him your name, did you?" And there's his cunning smile. "Your whole name?"

My stomach drops to my feet, my heart tripping in my chest. But Mark's forgetting I know things about him as well, things I'm guessing Caleb has no idea about. "Does Caleb know why you were put out?" I throw back at Mark, and his lips press together in a thin white line.

"You two know each other?" Caleb asks, eyes narrowing.

"From Westfall," Mark says without taking his eyes off me. "I think Ivy and I need to have a private conversation." My first instinct is to say hell no and punch him in the face, but we both have something the other needs: our silence.

"Ivy?" Caleb asks.

"It's fine," I say, gaze never leaving Mark.

After a second, Caleb nods. "Okay. I'll be in my tent if either of you need me." He pauses to look at each of us in turn. "It would be better for everyone if you could find a way to work this out between you."

I hate the thought of Mark stepping into the place where Ash and I sleep, but we need some privacy to talk, and there's no way I'm leaving camp with him. I turn on my heel and walk back into my tent, while he limps after me. I stand on the far side of the tent, but when the flap falls closed behind him, he still feels too close.

"So, I'm guessing you never told them why you're here," I say. I want this over with, one way or the other.

"No," Mark says, eyes sliding around the tent. "Just like you never said who your husband is." His eyes finally stop moving, settle on me.

"I didn't tell them I'm married," I say, voice quiet.

Mark nods. "Smart . . . considering." He takes a step closer to me and I shift backward.

"Don't come near me."

Mark raises both hands, huffs out a little laugh. Like I'm completely overreacting, as if he hadn't tried to rape and kill me a week ago.

"We both want to stay here, right?"

"Right," I say.

"Well, then, if we keep our mouths shut, there's no reason that can't work out."

"You don't deserve to be here. Not after what you've done."

Mark's eyes grow even colder, the pale blue fading to ice. "And you do?"

"I didn't rape a little girl," I remind him.

"*Keep your voice down.*"

I lower my voice to just above a whisper. "I didn't kill a woman who couldn't defend herself."

Mark blows out a dismissive breath. "She was practically dead already. Who cares?"

"You're disgusting."

"Maybe. But you're just as bad." He shakes his finger at me, like I'm a naughty child. "You married a Lattimer."

I open my mouth to protest, and he stops me with a raised hand, a hissed reply. "And don't give me any bullshit about how you had to marry him. I saw the way you looked at him that day in the woods. I saw the way he held your hand. And I'll be happy to tell everyone all about it." He gestures wide with both hands, including the whole camp within his palms. "There are plenty of people out there who blame every bad thing in their lives on the Lattimers. To them what you did is the worst betrayal of all."

My stomach sinks as I realize my chance to be honest with Caleb and Ash about Mark has come and gone. I waited too long. Now that he's back, I can't risk angering him, can't allow him to tell the truth about my relationship with Bishop. So I swallow past the rock of fear and regret that's lodged in my throat and speak. "Fine. You don't say anything, and I won't either. And stay away from me."

Mark nods. "I knew we could reach an agreement." He turns to leave and throws me a glance over his shoulder, his eyes full of a knowing delight that makes me want to vomit. "We're not so different after all, Ivy."

I want to cross the tent and rake his face with my nails, grab a rock and hit him again. Only this time I won't stop until he's dead. "We are *nothing* alike," I tell him.

"Really?" He smiles at me, the smirk that is quickly becoming the star of all my nightmares. "'Cause you seem just as concerned as me with saving your own skin."

He is gone, the tent flap snapping shut in his wake, before I can think of a reply.

"Try it again," Caleb says. "Don't push so hard with the knife." He grips my wrist and turns it slightly so the blade is angled to the side instead of straight down. "That way it's easier to separate the skin from the meat."

I ignore the slide of sweat down my face, the sun beating down on my bent neck like an open flame. "Like this?" I cut the dead rabbit's fur away. Not as cleanly as Caleb or Ash, but better than the last time I tried.

"You're getting there," Caleb says, rewarding me with a half smile.

Ash is sitting under a nearby tree, and she tosses a small twig at Caleb's head. "When is this lesson going to be done? I'm drowning in my own sweat over here."

Caleb throws the twig back, a direct hit to the middle of Ash's forehead. "You're in the shade," he reminds her. He looks back at me, flickering his eyes to the rabbit. "Finish it up."

"Yes, sir," I say, and Ash hoots.

"You want to learn or not?" Caleb says, his smile fading.

"Yes," I say. "Sorry." I roll my shoulders, the muscles tight from being hunched over the small carcass.

When I'm done, I hold up the skin for Caleb's inspection. "I've seen better." He bumps my shoulder with his. "I've seen worse."

I grin at him and raise my eyebrows at Ash. "Careful, Caleb," she says, rolling her eyes. "You're turning into a big softy."

Caleb takes the rabbit, along with the half dozen he skinned while waiting for me, and puts them in his bag. I give Ash back her knife, and the three of us head toward the river without speaking of our destination. We all need the relief of water. As we pass a small group working in the garden, one of the men calls out, "How many today?"

"Seven," Caleb says.

The man smiles. I think his name is Andrew. Or maybe Albert. "Not bad." He looks at me. "Caleb teaching you the tricks of the trade?"

"He's trying."

"She's holding her own," Caleb says.

The man nods, leans his weight on his hoe. "Doesn't surprise me. Any daughter of Justin Westfall's has gotta be a quick learner. Your daddy's a great man."

I remember the way my father sat and watched me be dragged out of the courtroom, destined to be put out beyond the fence, and didn't say a single word in my defense. The way he wanted me to kill an innocent boy. "Yes," I say.

"Must've been hard on him, watching you be put out."

"Yes," I say again, voice a low rasp. It's the only word I can find.

The man shakes his head. "Surprised he didn't follow you out."

I duck my head, bite the inside of my cheek to keep the tears at bay. Caleb's probing gaze on my bare neck burns as hot as any sun.

"Come on," Ash says, pulling at my hand. "We're heading for the river," she tells the man. "Need to wash off the rabbit guts."

I let her lead me away, put one foot in front of the other, and pretend I don't feel Caleb's eyes on me every step of the way.

I'm trying to be quiet as I follow Caleb and Ash through the woods, but every few seconds I snag a branch or snap a twig beneath my feet, and finally Caleb rounds on me, eyes narrowed.

"Sorry," I whisper.

"Don't. Talk," he bites out through a clenched jaw, and I realize this is not just an exercise, that we are tracking something, or someone, who is a genuine danger. When we'd started the return walk to camp after setting a series of snares and Caleb had veered off, mumbling about following a trail only he could see, I hadn't thought much of it. Just assumed he was teaching me more about tracking, although even straining until my eyes hurt I couldn't see the signs he was following. I should have noticed the way Ash got quieter and quieter as we moved deeper into the trees, her shoulders tensing up, her hand hovering above her knife.

Now I make an effort to be more careful, falling slightly behind as I pick my way gingerly across the ground, which suddenly seems strewn with objects put there just to thwart my stealthiness. Ahead, I hear the murmur of voices, and my head whips up, my body freezing in place. Caleb drops down to a crouch, and Ash and I follow, the three of us hidden behind a stand of bushes.

Craning my neck, I can just make out two men sitting together in a small clearing. One of them is drawing something in the dirt with a stick. "Here," he says, using the stick to mark a spot on his crude map. "We'll go in here, once it's dark. Take as much food as we can, any weapons we see, and get back out fast."

"There are going to be people around," the other man says, "even if we wait until the middle of the night."

The first man shrugs. "Then we'll take care of them."

While I'm wondering what Caleb will do with this information, whether he'll set up additional people on watch around the camp or maybe move the food supplies, he's already moving away from us. I glance over at him, startled, and he gives Ash a quick motion with his hand. She nods, puts her own hand down flat between us, gesturing for me to stay where I am, before creeping off in the opposite direction from Caleb, leaving me alone.

My heart is beating so loud I'm surprised the men can't hear it from where they sit. My thighs ache, but I don't dare adjust my position. I know which way Caleb went, but when my eyes scan the tree line I can't find any hint of him. I would feel better if I knew what Ash and Caleb were doing, how long I might have to wait here, and what I should do if the men turn in my direction.

The man with the stick suddenly stops talking, holding up a finger to silence the man next to him. I hold my breath, move my eyes just to the left of them, as though my gaze is what drew their attention and looking away will solve the problem. Both of the men stand, one of them swiveling his head toward my hiding place. I don't know whether he's spotted me, if it's wiser to hold my ground or flee. Every muscle in my body tenses, ready to spring up and away if he moves closer. But before the man can even take a step, something whistles through the trees and he crumples to the ground. One of Caleb's bolts protrudes from his eye. I suck in a breath, my legs suddenly numb. I have to put a hand down to steady myself, my fingers sinking into the warm dirt at my side.

I hear Caleb's voice from a distance, but can't make out his words, my gaze pinned on the dead man. His companion stumbles backward, eyes swinging from the body to the woods where Caleb is hiding. He has some kind of sword in his hand, but doesn't seem to know where to aim it with no visible adversary. He turns toward the sound of Caleb's voice, and Ash streaks out of the trees behind him, buries her knife in the base of his skull, and pulls it free again before his body even hits the ground.

My ears ring, my breath coming in panting gasps, like I've suffered a blow to the head or been smothered in a thick blanket, everything muffled and distant. Sound returns slowly—the faint buzz of flower-drunk bees, a gurgle of blood erupting from the mouth of the man Ash killed, the crack of Caleb's footsteps through the trees. I fall forward on my hands and knees, my view of the carnage partially blocked by tangles of my own hair. Ash stands between the bodies, blood dripping from her knife, her face hard and remorseless. Caleb emerges from the trees to my left, crossbow held loosely in his hand.

"You all right?" he asks me, not waiting for my answer before he steps around me to meet Ash in the clearing. He pulls his bolt from the dead man's eye socket with a wet squelch that pushes my stomach up into my throat. I thought I was tougher now, had grown a thicker skin. But I am still too innocent; part of me has remained sheltered, even here beyond the fence, from what really happens when the world falls apart.

I lever myself to standing, stumble into the clearing after Caleb. Ash glances at me as she wipes her knife on the pants of the man prone at her feet. Her eyes are kind, but hold no apology. She does not seem like a friendly puppy now. She looks as quick and deadly as I imagined her to be that morning I first spied the knife on her hip. A shiver ripples up my spine as I think what she could have done to me back in Birch Tree if I'd been any type of threat instead of half dead already.

"Guess you figured they weren't worth saving," I say, my voice high and giddy, like I might burst into laughter at any second. Or tears.

Caleb looks at me. "We don't do second chances out here. Not with people like this. You protect you and yours the first time. Because that might be the only chance you get. You waste time asking questions, second-guessing when you already know the answers, and you end up dead."

I nod, force myself to look at the bodies, blood seeping into the dirt in black-red halos around their heads. The air is heavy with the metallic tang of death. Bishop once told me that the world we lived in was brutal and that we tried to pretend otherwise by hiding behind normality, scared to face the truth. No one here is pretending. Caleb told me life beyond the fence was dangerous, and now I've seen it firsthand. No one's sugarcoating the reality, trying to convince me things are better than they seem. There's a relief in that, an honesty that makes this brutality somehow more bearable than the kind cloaked in wedding dresses and courtroom trials.

"Now what?" I ask, straightening my shoulders. "Do we bury them?"

Ash glances at Caleb. "No," she says. "It's too much work. And we're far enough away from camp that even if the bodies draw predators, it won't put the camp in any danger."

"Okay," I say. My voice already sounds more my own. Stronger. I point to the knife in Ash's hand. "I need one of those. And lessons on how to use it."

Ash and I practice with our knives every afternoon. Luckily for me, she is a more patient teacher than Caleb. I'm quick to learn how to properly hold the knife and how to thrust with it, but throwing it is a whole other story. After days of practice, I still haven't hit the tree by the river we are using as our target, let alone the bull's-eye painted on its bark. Caleb would probably have stabbed me with my own knife by this point, just to save himself the aggravation.

"Aaargh!" I scream when my knife flies through the air only to hit the ground and bounce. "I'm never going to get this."

"Yes, you will," Ash says with a smile. She releases her own knife with a quick flick of her wrist, and it buries itself in the center of the bull's-eye with a quiet smack.

"Now you're just showing off," I tell her as I walk to retrieve my knife.

"It takes time, but you'll get it. You have to. Sometimes there's no way to get in close, so throwing is your only option."

"Where do I aim, exactly?"

"Not the heart," Ash says, matter-of-fact. "It's too hard to get the knife positioned right. You don't want it hitting a rib and not doing any major damage." She makes a fist and presses it to the middle of her chest, right into the soft hollow in the middle of her rib cage. "Here. Hit them here and they'll go down. They might not die as fast, but they won't have much fight left in them."

"Have you had to do it a lot?" I ask her, eyes on the tree. "Kill people?"

Ash yanks her knife from the target. "Enough," she says. "It's just a reality."

Lately, every time I close my eyes at night, those men dying at Caleb's and Ash's hands plays like a movie against my eyelids. It's not horror I feel or fear; more of a realization that life has a way of coming full circle. I refused to murder Bishop, dropped the rock rather than kill Mark. But this world may turn me into a killer regardless. But if I'm going to survive, I know Ash is right: I have to learn how to defend myself, and I can't be afraid to use the lessons she teaches me.

"Those men we killed the other day?" Ash says, like she's a mind reader. "That's how my dad died."

"I thought he died of an infection."

"He did. But it was from a wound. He was stabbed in the leg. We tried to heal it, but . . ."

I remember the remorseless look on Ash's face, the way her blade sank into that man's neck without hesitation. "Men like that?" I ask. "They're the ones who hurt him?"

"Yes. But a bigger group." The word comes out on an uneven exhale. "We made a mistake. Not killing them as soon as we were sure of their intentions, and my dad paid the price."

"I'm surprised you didn't kill me when you first saw me," I say. "Caleb probably wanted to."

"No. He wanted to leave you, though. But I wouldn't let him."

"Why not?"

Ash shrugs, her eyes on the knife in her hand.

"Caleb said you were looking for someone to save," I say carefully. "Was that because of your dad?"

Ash looks up from her knife, her eyes shiny with unshed tears. "I made my dad a promise. When he was dying. He always said following my mom out here, saving Caleb, raising me . . . those were the things he was most proud of. I tried so hard to save him, but nothing worked." She hurls her knife hard at the tree, buries it to the hilt in the bark. "So yeah, after he was gone, maybe I was looking for someone to help, someone I could save the way I couldn't save him. Do something good to honor his memory the way he did so many good things in his life. And when I saw you passed out in the road, half dead . . ." She shakes her hair out of her eyes, swipes the back of her hand down her cheek to brush away a tear. "I thought of my dad, and I knew I couldn't just leave you there."

"I would've died if not for you," I tell her. "I'd gone as far as I could on my own."

"Nobody can make it out here alone, Ivy." Ash smiles at me. "Except maybe Caleb."

I smile back. "He is kind of inhuman sometimes."

"Don't let him fool you," Ash says. "He's tough, but not as tough as he pretends to be."

"I bet he could hit the damn tree with the knife," I mutter.

Ash slings her arm around my shoulders. "Sure he can. But he couldn't at the beginning either, no matter what he claims." She takes her free hand and closes it over mine, around the hilt of my knife. "Now, stop stalling and start throwing."

It takes little more than a month for my pact to stay out of Mark's way and keep my mouth shut to evaporate. I've kept busy, helping in the garden, washing clothes in the river with Ash, learning to track and set snares with Caleb, who is uncharacteristically patient given the fact that my still-healing shoulder makes me a slow student. I can skin and gut a rabbit or squirrel almost as fast as Ash. I'm settling into my life here. Accepting that this is who I am now, that Ash and Caleb are the closest thing to family I have. It's a careful kind of affection, the type that won't hurt me too much if it ends, but it's something, at least.

I'm not sure I'm destined for happiness, but I think this is a life I can make work. Except for Mark. The deal I've made with him sits in my stomach like a meal of jagged rocks. I tell myself that I'm not doing anything wrong. I'm keeping myself safe, and Mark will have to conform to the morals of the group in order to stay, so there's no harm done. But I don't believe it. Every time I see him gather around the fire in the evening, share a bowl of stew with the person next to him, laugh at something Caleb says, the shards in my stomach cut through me. Remind me of who he really is, and who I am to have traded my own safety for his. I remember Caleb's words about not giving people a second chance to hurt you and know I made a mistake that day on the riverbank.

It's an early afternoon in late September when I'm returning from bathing in the river, twisting my hair to wring water out of it as I walk. The last days of Indian summer are upon us, sky blue and crisp as a sheet of glass, wispy white clouds floating on a mild breeze. We need blankets at night now, and Ash says we'll be packing up to move into town in a few weeks. I will be sad to leave the camp behind; I've grown used to living outside of four walls, just like Ash.

Mark's tent is not near ours, but I pass it every time I leave camp, and I can't resist looking as I walk past. It's rare that I actually see him during the day, but today is different. He is sitting on the ground in front of his tent, a little girl on his lap. His arms are around her, and he's helping her make some kind of doll out of sticks.

I stop midstride, go still as death. I can feel my pulse in my fingertips and behind my eyes. Mark looks up, as if the force of my shock has called to him. He gives me a lazy smile, and goes back to talking to the girl. I drop my bundle of dirty clothes where I stand. The little girl looks startled when I crouch down next to them, slap Mark's arms away from her.

"You need to go home," I tell her. My voice is hoarse. I sound on the edge of tears, but what I really feel is a clawing, tearing rage. "Go find your mom."

The girl looks back at Mark, her eyes wide. She is scared of me. Of *me*. Which would be funny if it weren't so horrible. "Go!" I say again, louder, and she's off. Probably to tell her mother about the mean girl who yelled at her. I don't really care if it gets her away from him.

"Well," Mark says, "that wasn't very nice." He doesn't bother trying to hide his laugh.

I carry a knife in a sheath on my belt now. One very much like the blade I watched Ash kill a man with not so long ago. My hand finds the hilt without me even thinking about it, another thing Caleb has taught me. Too late, Mark catches the movement, and his smile dries up on his face. I don't pull the knife. Not yet. It's enough to watch his eyes go wide before narrowing, his pulse speeding up in his neck. Enough to know he is scared.

"Remember that day by the river?" I ask him, still crouched down beside him. "Remember how I let you live?"

He doesn't answer me. Anger radiates off him; I can feel it like the blast from an oven against my face. He hates that I got the best of him, that I'm not turning to bones on the riverbank and I'm here to throw my triumph back in his face.

"If I see you even talking to another child, *looking* at one, I'll finish what I started that day, you sick bastard." I've never talked this way before in my life. My words have always been almost uncontrollable when my temper flares, but not like this. I've never threatened someone. It's like ever since Mark returned there's been a balloon expanding in my chest, making it hard for me to breathe, and today it finally popped, leaving me with room to fill my lungs. I have an insane urge to cackle with something very close to glee.

Mark looks from my hand on the knife to me. "No, you won't," he says, finding his voice. "Because I'll tell them about you. Who you are. Who you love." His blue eyes twinkle. I can understand how a child would be fooled by them; it takes experience to recognize the evil lurking in those blue pools. "They'll rip you apart."

I shake my head. "I don't think so. I think they're good people. Better people than you, that's for sure. But it doesn't matter. I don't even care if you're right. It'll be worth it. Just to slide this knife between your ribs. Just to watch you die first." Whatever he sees in my face must convince him it's better to shut up than keep talking. I stand and look down at him. "I'm not scared of you." It's not exactly the truth, but it's the closest I can get in words. I'm still frightened by him; I'd be a fool not to be. But it's not enough to be scared anymore, not enough to stop me or silence me.

Mark mumbles something under his breath, but it doesn't matter what he says. He can't meet my eyes, his shoulders slumped. I'm not stupid enough to think it's over between us, but I'll take this victory.

I turn and walk away, head high, heart thumping, hand still curled around my knife.

"Okay, you were right. This is definitely my least favorite chore." I throw a just-rinsed shirt onto the growing pile on the riverbank.

"It took you this long to figure that out?"

"I was giving it a fair chance."

Ash's expression tells me what she thinks of that idea. "I've always hated it," she says. She is knee-deep in the river, scrubbing a pair of overalls with soap.

"At least we only have to do it once a week." I frown at my raw fingers.

"Even that's too much. I'd rather be out hunting. Or gardening. Or something."

"Me, too," I say with a sigh, reaching for another shirt in the thankfully dwindling mound of dirty clothes.

"Glad to hear it," Caleb says. "Because tomorrow that's what we're doing. Hunting."

"Really?" Ash asks, head snapping up. "Real hunting? Not just snaring?"

"Yep."

I look over to where he's appeared, shading my eyes against the sinking sun. He nods at me, gives Ash a smile.

"Wanna help?" Ash calls, splashing water in his direction. Caleb steps back, easily avoiding getting wet.

"Nope. I'm going on a walk."

I catch Ash's eye and look down, trying to swallow my smile. She's told me that Caleb goes on "walks" when he wants to be alone with a girl.

"Who is it this week?" Ash asks, not bothering to hide her grin.

"None of your damn business," Caleb throws back. "You two stick together tonight."

"Why? You planning on being gone until morning?" Ash asks, all mock innocence, and this time I can't bite back my laughter.

Caleb points at me. "Watch it." Which just sets Ash off, too. Both of us smothering giggles behind handfuls of wet cloth.

"Jesus," Caleb huffs. "You two are pitiful."

"Have fun!" I call as he walks away.

"Don't knock her up!" Ash yells at his retreating back.

Caleb throws a rude gesture over his shoulder, but doesn't turn around.

When our laughter has faded away, I look at Ash with raised eyebrows. "So, who is it this week?"

Ash shrugs. "Not sure. I think it's Laurel."

I still don't have names for all the faces in camp. But I think I know who Laurel is, a petite girl with dishwater-blond hair and a lopsided smile. "She's pretty." I wring out the pants I'm holding. "Do you think he likes her?"

Ash rolls her eyes. "Who could tell? He *likes* all of them."

I snort out another laugh. "Almost done," I say, pulling the last shirt from the pile.

"Thank God," Ash says. "What about you?"

"What about me?"

"Did you like anyone back in Westfall? A boy?"

My heart somersaults in my chest. I shake my head, hoping the setting sun hides the roses on my cheeks.

"What about that guy you were supposed to marry, the president's son, did you know him?"

I concentrate on scrubbing the shirt, keep my gaze focused on the faded cotton. "No. Not really."

"What was his name?"

I close my eyes, take a deep breath. "Bishop." Strange how the sound of a single word can hurt more than a ruined shoulder, cut deeper than a bloody gash.

"Weird name," Ash says.

"Hmmm . . ." I look up at her, but she's busy beating the hell out of a pair of pants. "I think it was his mother's maiden name."

"My dad used to talk about the president of Westfall. I guess that would have been Bishop's grandpa back then." She swipes a cluster of suds off her forehead with the back of her hand. "You did the right thing, refusing to marry him. He's probably as horrible as the rest of the Lattimers."

I stumble away from her. "I'll start hanging the clean stuff." My throat is so tight I can barely speak, tears caught trembling on my eyelashes. I remember coming home to Bishop washing our clothes. Hanging them together in the backyard. He was never horrible. Not for a single second. And I can't even defend him, can't open my mouth to speak of him at all.

I'm on watch a couple of nights later when Caleb finds me. At night, there are always people on guard around the perimeter of the camp. After a few weeks, my name was put in the rotation. Probably after Caleb figured I could be trusted. I have a love-hate relationship with watch. As much as I like Ash, it's nice to have a few hours by myself. But being alone in the quiet dark, with only the chilly moonlight and shadows for company, leaves me with too much time to think. And after my talk with Ash at the river the other day, my mind invariably turns to Bishop, the impossible green of his eyes, his real smile—the one I earned over time—his long fingers holding a photograph of the ocean. His good and patient heart. For the most part, I have been able to put away my father and

Callie, Westfall and my childhood. But Bishop refuses to stay in the box I've made for him, always clawing his way out and demanding to be seen.

Tonight I can't stop picturing his face on the night he told me he trusted me. Held me in his arms and let me cry over my dead mother, his warm hand on my neck. I blow out a wobbly breath, press the heels of my hands hard against my closed eyes, trying to force his image to fade. I wonder if it will be a relief or a new kind of heartbreak when the day comes I can no longer remember exactly what he looked like, bring to mind every shifting expression on his face.

"You okay?"

I jerk my hands away from my eyes, spin around where I'm sitting, and almost slam into Caleb, who's crouched down behind me. He holds up both hands, gives me a small smile. "Sorry. Didn't mean to scare you."

"Then stop sneaking up on me," I say, using irritation to cover my fear.

"Duly noted." Caleb holds out a canteen. "Ash was worried you'd get thirsty out here." I expect him to head straight back to camp, but instead he sits down beside me.

I'm not used to Caleb wanting to spend time with me, not unless he's teaching me something or keeping Ash company. His gaze is heavy on me, like a spotlight in the darkness. "What?" I ask, glancing in his direction. The moon glints off his face, forms tiny silver starbursts in his eyes.

"You've been keeping secrets," he says.

I was right to be nervous. My heart races, but I steady my breathing. I open my mouth to deny what he's said, but stop myself at the last second. Caleb's not someone who will easily accept a lie, especially not a lie from me. "Everyone has secrets," I say finally.

"True." A branch breaks in the distance, and we both whip our heads in that direction. It's nothing, probably an animal out searching for dinner, but I'm glad for the distraction. Caleb, however, isn't going to be put off. "But your secrets involve Mark Laird."

I drag a small stick through the dirt beside me, draw a circle, fill it with lines. "Why do you say that?"

"I saw you, Ivy,"

I don't look up. "Saw me what?"

"With your hand on your knife." He pauses. "And murder on your face."

Now I do look at him. I had no idea he was around when I had my confrontation with Mark. I doubt it would've stopped me. I doubt anything would have. But it would've been good information to have.

"I remember those bruises on your arms when we found you," Caleb says. "I know what finger marks look like."

I shrug. "Like you said, it can be tough out here. Alone."

"What did he do?" Caleb asks quietly. "What is he holding over you?"

I want so badly to tell him. To tell someone. To just let all my secrets tumble out and disappear on the wind. But I trusted my father and Callie. And look where that got me. They were my blood, and in the end, they had no trouble cutting me loose. Why would Caleb or Ash or any of these people who've known me only a few weeks do better by me? So I clench my jaw and shake my head.

"Who are you?" Caleb asks, and my blood runs cold, my heart stumbling in my chest. "Who are you really?"

"Ivy Westfall," I say. "You already know that."

"Daughter of Justin," Caleb says with a slight nod. "The great man."

"Yes."

Caleb's eyes catch mine before I can turn away. "Is that why you flinch every time someone says his name?"

I stare at him for a long moment, keep my mouth shut. Because there's nothing I can say. No answer I can give him that will both satisfy him and save me.

Caleb sighs, rubs a hand over the top of his close-cropped hair. "There aren't a lot of people I really care about," he says. "A handful, maybe. And that's probably a high estimate." His face is serious, his gaze intense. "You're one of them. Let me help you."

I'm so surprised I don't know what to say, all my words momentarily dried up on my tongue. "Why?" I ask, finally.

Caleb makes an impatient sound, which is more recognizably Caleb. "Because you need it. I think you're in over your head, and I don't want you to get hurt."

"No. Why do you care about me?"

Caleb shakes his head, like he's not even sure of the answer himself. "Because Ash loves you already. And I love Ash. Because you make her smile. Because you've worked hard here. You've been tougher than I thought you would be. Because you can gut a squirrel in ten seconds flat." I roll my eyes but he doesn't smile. "You're a part of us now."

"So is Mark," I say, voice flat.

"I don't care about Mark."

"You were sure worried about how I got his bag," I remind him.

"That was before. I didn't know you then. Now I do." He pauses, nudges me with his shoulder. "Now I know you're worth saving."

His words take me back to that dusty room in the ruined house, when having a conversation like this with Caleb seemed as distant as the moon. That moment feels like just yesterday and a million years ago, both at the same time. I never imagined a future where sitting next to Caleb would be anything close to comfortable. If I were still a girl who hoped for things, I might wish that Caleb could truly take the place of the family I lost, become the brother I never had and someday love me the same way he loves Ash. But I've stopped making wishes that aren't ever going to come true. I learned that lesson the hard way.

"Let me help you," Caleb repeats. "Please."

I've never heard him say that word before. The sincerity in his voice breaks my heart a little. I didn't even know my heart was capable of that anymore. I can feel the truth pressing against the backs of my teeth, searching for the slightest crack in my resistance. "I can't," I manage to get out.

Caleb blows out a breath, pushes himself to standing with his hands on his thighs. Frustration rolls off him, his jaw tight. But his voice is still gentler than I'm used to when he speaks. "If you don't want help or don't want to tell me the truth, that's your choice. But whatever happens from here on out, it's on you, Ivy." He points at me. "It's on you."

"I know that," I say, ignoring the hollow pit in my stomach, the urge to pull him back down beside me and confide everything. "It always has been."

It's one of our last nights around the bonfire. Ash tells me that in a few days we're going to begin dismantling the camp and we'll move back to town within a week or so.

"It takes a while," she says, around a mouthful of bread. "To get everything into town."

"How far is it?" I ask, picking at my deer meat.

"A few miles that way." She points to the south. "Along the river."

"Where will I live?" I ask. I don't want to assume I'll still be living with her, don't want her to feel like I'm a burden she has to constantly shoulder. Maybe she's ready to go back to how things used to be. It will be enough to be part of the group; I don't have to be right next to Caleb and Ash to survive.

Ash kicks at my foot with hers. "With us, of course. Caleb and I share a house. There's an extra bedroom."

I can't help the grin that slides across my face, and Ash grins back. "Like I'm going to let you get away now that I have you," she scoffs, making me laugh.

"Where is Caleb?" I ask, looking around the ring of faces. "Out on another walk?" Lately when Caleb looks at me, I think I see disappointment in his eyes. But I still like it better when he's here, with his impatient groans and teasing voice.

Ash snickers. "No. He and Mark and a few other people went out hunting earlier. I don't know if they'll be back tonight or not."

I definitely don't like the thought of Mark and Caleb together. Caleb can handle himself, and I don't think Mark would ever break and tell Caleb anything, but the possibility still makes me nervous.

"Caleb said they might stay out an extra day or two," Ash continues. "There's been more activity in the woods than normal, and he wants to check it out."

"What do you mean?"

"Just signs that more people than usual have been passing through. It happens sometimes, probably nothing to worry about."

"Are they coming from Westfall?" I ask, my mind tripping over itself wondering what might be causing people to leave.

Ash shrugs. "They could be, I guess. We don't really know."

I take a calming breath, remind myself that whatever is, or isn't, happening in Westfall no longer has anything to do with me. My part in the Westfall drama is over. But the worry remains, nibbling away at me.

We sit in front of the bonfire until it's burned down to half its original size, huddled under a blanket together. Ash leans her head on my shoulder and something inside me rolls over. How can this girl who barely knows me love me more than the sister who spent every second with me from the moment I was born? And how am I supposed to guard my emotions against someone who is so free and easy with her own?

"You almost ready?" Ash says. She yawns, her jaw stretching against my arm.

"Yes," I say, but don't move. The firelight is hypnotic, the way the flames jump and dance, the smoke weaving into the chilly night air. "I'm going to miss these bonfires."

Before Ash can answer, a shout comes from the far side of the fire. Followed closely by another. Ash's head comes off my shoulder like a shot, both of us up and throwing the blanket behind us. Ash's hand goes instantly to her knife, and mine is only a second behind.

"What is it?" I ask.

Ash shakes her head, eyes locked on the direction of the sounds. All around us people are standing, bodies tense. I can still hear loud voices. And someone calling my name. Which makes no sense. I look at Ash and she looks back, eyes wide.

Mark comes around the edge of the fire, a wild smile on his face. He has blood smeared across his lips and his shirt is torn. "Ivy!" he yells. "Just the girl we were looking for."

I stiffen, hand clutching my knife so hard I know my knuckles are white.

"What's going on?" Ash asks.

"We found something for Ivy," Mark says, moving closer. His eyes gleam in the firelight, his cheeks flushed. My whole body goes cold, the deer meat I ate earlier threatening to come right back up. I don't know what he's talking about, but I know it's bad. I know it's nothing I want to see.

"Where's Caleb?" Ash takes a step toward Mark.

"Right here, Ash." Caleb's voice floats from the far side of the fire, and Ash's shoulders relax. I let out a breath that's been bottled up in my throat.

Caleb and another man step into the light. They are both injured like Mark, Caleb sporting what's going to be a serious black eye, the other man with a bloody, dripping nose. They are dragging a third man between them. He must be unconscious, his dark head hanging down, his long legs limp on the ground, shoes leaving trails through the dry grass. My eyes know what they are seeing, but my brain refuses to make sense of the image. A sound bursts out of my throat, something between a sob and a scream.

Caleb looks only at me as he drags the man forward. I hear his voice in my head, *"It's on you, Ivy. It's on you."* But how could I have known? How could I have known it would come to this?

"We brought you a present!" Mark shouts, practically vibrating with vicious joy.

Caleb takes one final step and drops Bishop's body at my feet.

8

"Oh my God, oh my God . . ." I repeat it like a chant, a prayer I'm not sure anyone will hear. I drop to my knees next to Bishop. He has to be alive; he has to be. I run my hands over his face, sticky with blood, the planes of his cheeks, the line of his jaw still so familiar to me. "Bishop?" I whisper. "Bishop . . . please." I put one hand on his chest, feel the beat of his heart against my palm. My own heart stutters in response, something coiled tight slowly loosening in my chest.

"What did you do to him?" I ask, looking up at Caleb. "What did you do?"

"Beat the hell out of him," Caleb says, face grim.

"Why?" My hands fist in Bishop's shirt, my voice spiraling up into hysteria.

"Because he wouldn't do what we told him," Mark says with a grin.

"I don't . . ." I shake my head, trying to clear away the jumble of thoughts crowding my mind. "I don't understand what he's doing here."

"Who is he?" Ash asks, kneeling down beside me. Her eyes are round with worry, skipping between Caleb and me.

"Bishop Lattimer," Caleb says. I ignore the startled sounds from the people gathered around us, the heated murmurs. "Right?" Caleb asks me. His voice sounds like the old Caleb, the one who didn't want me here. The one who wasn't sure I was worth saving.

I nod, my gaze returning to Bishop's beaten face. I take my sleeve and wipe away the blood that's oozing from a gash in his cheekbone. His upper lip is split open, his nostrils ringed with blood. More blood, dark and thick, is matted in his hair. All I want to do is lie down beside him and weep, bury my face in his neck and breathe him in until my lungs are so full there's no room for anything else.

"But you said you didn't know him," Ash says. "You said . . ." Her voice trails off, and I can't look at her. I know what I'll see: the eyes of someone who understands they've been deceived. The same look Bishop gave me when he realized I couldn't be trusted. I know that look and it hurts too much; I can't bear to see it again.

"I think she should kill him," Mark says conversationally. I rock back on my heels like he's slapped me. "You've got that knife in your belt, always so quick to put your hand on it." He gestures at Bishop. "He's a Lattimer. He's nothing to you." Mark's eyes dare me to contradict him. "So kill him. Make a statement."

"I'm not . . . I can't . . ." My lips are numb, my tongue stumbling over the words. Behind me a few people are taking up Mark's suggestion, the quiet rumble of their voices turning into a rising chorus of vengeance.

"Come on, Ivy," Mark taunts. "Now's your chance to get back at President Lattimer for what's he's done to you." His gaze leaves mine and moves to the larger group. "To all of us."

Someone behind me gives a yell of agreement, and I can feel the press of bodies moving forward. Soon the mob mentality will take over, and if I don't do the job, they'll be happy to step into the void. "No," I cry out, bending over Bishop. And now my hand *is* on my knife, ready to use it on anyone who comes near him.

"Stop it!" Caleb's voice rings out. He shoulders Mark back, away from Bishop. "No one's killing anyone."

"But—"

"I said stop!" Caleb shouts at Mark. "Enough!" He scrubs at his face with one hand, and the firelight illuminates the cuts on his bruised knuckles, injuries he got beating Bishop. My stomach heaves. "We're not killing him." He speaks to the whole group, but his eyes are on Mark.

"You don't get to decide for everyone," Mark says. "You're not in charge here. Right?" he calls out. "I think this guy"—he kicks Bishop's leg—"needs to pay for what his father's done."

There's a collective roar behind me, and I know Caleb and I aren't going to be enough to hold them off for much longer. I stand up, careful to keep my body between the crowd and Bishop. The darkness and fading firelight throw uneven shadows across everyone's faces, turning these people I've lived with the past weeks into strangers. A mob with blood on their minds.

"Please," I say. "He doesn't deserve this. He's a good person."

"He's a Lattimer!" someone yells.

"But he's not President Lattimer!" I yell back.

Someone separates from the crowd, and I raise my knife. "But you were put out because you wouldn't marry him," Elizabeth says. She looks more confused than angry. "Why are you defending him?"

I glance over my shoulder at Caleb, his gaze serious on mine. I look back at Elizabeth. "I did marry him," I tell her, fighting to keep my voice even. "He's my husband." A ripple of shock goes through the crowd, although I can't tell if my admission makes their anger stronger or weaker. "It wasn't my choice, but he was always good to me. He never hurt me."

"It doesn't matter!" a voice yells from the back of the crowd. "He's still a Lattimer."

"Wait!" another voice cries. An older man pushes toward the front. "I know him. I remember him. When I was put out, he came to the fence. He brought me food and water. Told me which way to go to find the river. He saved my life."

"Mine, too," a woman's voice calls.

"You can't kill him," I say, looking at the older man. "You can't." I turn my attention to the crowd. "You'll have to kill me, too."

Behind me I hear movement, and Caleb shoves Mark out of the way to come stand beside me. "We're done here," he says, voice firm. "I'm vouching for him. He's not a threat to us. We aren't animals. We aren't going to kill him. You'll have to go through me to do it."

There's some grumbling from the crowd, but people slowly begin to move back. "Come on," Caleb says, voice low. "Let's get him into a tent."

"Don't look at me," Mark says. "I'm not helping." He gives me one last glance before turning and fading into the darkness.

"The three of us can carry him," Ash says.

Caleb takes Bishop's shoulders, and Ash and I each grab a leg. It's awkward moving him; he's so tall, and his lifeless limbs keep slipping from our grasp. No one else offers to help, but they don't interfere, either.

"We can take him to our tent," Ash says. Caleb opens his mouth to protest, but Ash just gives him a quick, tight-lipped shake of her head.

"Put him on my cot," I say once we're through the entryway. The tent feels too small with all four of us inside, all the unspoken accusations taking up as much room as our bodies.

"I'll go get some water," Ash says, ducking out again before I can even say a word.

Caleb sinks down on Ash's cot. His eyes, one glowing gold, the other virtually swollen shut, never leave me as I sit next to Bishop, brush his bloody hair off his forehead. "Is he going to wake up?" I whisper.

"Yeah," Caleb says. "Although he may be sorry when he does." He sighs. "He's going to be hurting. He may have some broken ribs. And he took a pretty good knock to the head."

I tear my eyes away from Bishop. "You didn't have to do this to him."

Caleb's sitting slumped over, like he's so exhausted he can't even manage to remain upright. But at my words he straightens, points at me. "Don't," he says, voice harsh. "He wouldn't listen to us. Wouldn't do what we said. Just kept going after Mark, asking for you. Screaming your name."

"He knows Mark, knows what he—"

"I asked you to tell me the truth, Ivy. I practically begged you." He looks from me to Bishop. "I only had Mark's word to go on out there, in the dark, with a strange man coming at us. I did what I had to do." He pauses. "I could have killed him. I probably should have. But I wanted to hear what you had to say first."

I want to be angry at Caleb, but I can't blame him, not really. The one I'm really upset with is myself. I wonder when I'm going to stop making decisions that end up hurting Bishop.

"You ready to tell me the whole truth now?" Caleb asks. It's a question, but I know there can only be one right answer this time.

"Yes," I say. And so I do. In the dim glow of the lantern, I tell him every sordid, sad detail. I don't spare my father or Callie or myself. My throat aches with the need to cry, but not a single tear falls. When I finish, I listen to Bishop's breathing, hold his warm hand in my own, until I can look up without falling apart.

"Jesus, Ivy," Caleb says when all my words are used up. "Why didn't you tell me earlier?"

I shake my head. "I didn't know how," I whisper. "At first, I wasn't sure how close you were to Mark. And then, later, I was scared you'd make me leave if you knew the truth about my relationship with Bishop. I didn't want to be alone again."

Caleb's eyes hold a kind of pity that I don't want to accept. But there's warmth there, too, so I'll have to find a way to live with it. Maybe from Caleb I can't have one without the other. "Everyone from Westfall who ends up here has been given a second chance," Caleb says. "Why did you think we wouldn't give you one?"

I don't know how to make him understand. My whole life, I trusted my family without question. And in the end, they betrayed me. "I didn't know whether I could trust you," I say finally.

"Do you think we can trust *him*?" Caleb asks, eyes shifting to Bishop.

"Yes." I don't even have to think about it. "He's not like me. He doesn't lie."

Before Caleb can respond, Ash comes back in to the tent carrying a small bucket of water and some rags. "I got some medicine from Carol," she says. "For the pain."

"Thanks," I tell her.

Ash nods at me, but won't quite meet my eyes. The medicine is a powder made from herbs, and Ash says if we can get Bishop to wash it down with some water, it should work. Caleb holds Bishop's head up, slapping his uninjured cheek lightly. After a few seconds, Bishop moans low in his throat, one arm jerking upward to bat Caleb away. He doesn't open his eyes, but just seeing him move is enough to send relief rocketing through me.

I manage to get his jaw open enough for Ash to spoon in the medicine, and I pour some water into his mouth, making him cough and gag.

"Do you think he actually swallowed any?" I ask.

"Hard to know," Caleb says. "But it's the best we can do right now."

I take one of the rags Ash brought and dip it into the water. As gently as I can, I begin washing the dried blood off Bishop's face. The tent is very quiet while I work; I can feel Caleb's and Ash's eyes on me, watching the way my fingers trace every line of Bishop's face as I clean. But it doesn't matter who is a witness. I can't make myself stop touching him, reassuring myself that he's here and he's alive.

"We'll have to talk more in the morning," Caleb says finally. "Once he's awake."

"Okay," I say, my gaze not leaving Bishop. "And I have to tell you some things about Mark. But not tonight." I don't have the energy to say anything more, don't want to take my focus off Bishop.

"I'm not going to like it, am I?" Caleb asks wearily.

"No." I wring out the rag, Bishop's blood flowing over my fingers. I look at Caleb. "You're not going to like it. It's ugly."

Caleb's face tightens. "Did he hurt you?"

I think of my shoulder, still sore sometimes but mostly healed. The weight of Mark's body pressing me into the dirt. The dead girl by the fence. And the little girl in Westfall. "Not as badly as he hurt other people."

Caleb only nods, his eyes hard. He puts a hand on Ash's shoulder. "Come on. You can sleep in my tent tonight."

"She doesn't have to leave." I smile at Ash, or at least give it my best attempt. She doesn't smile back.

"It's fine," she says. "I'll go with Caleb."

Once they're gone, I finish washing the blood off Bishop's face and neck. I can't get his hair clean, but I run the damp rag through it anyway, push it back from his forehead. His face is pale, but the rest of him is more golden than the last time I saw him, his lips slightly chapped, his fingers rough with calluses he didn't have before. He's been out here for a while. But he still looks strong, even with a battered face.

I know we'd both probably be more comfortable if I slept in Ash's cot, but I can't bear to leave him. I kick off my shoes and take off Bishop's, too, and blow out the lantern. Then I climb over him as carefully as I can and stretch out in the small space between his body and the tent wall.

It takes my eyes a few moments to adjust, moonlight spilling in through the thin material of the tent and illuminating Bishop's face. I can't believe he's here. I can't make sense of it. Was he put out? Did he follow me? I entwine my hand with his and push my face into the hollow of his neck and shoulder. He smells of blood and sweat and, as always, a faint hint of sunshine. If not for that, I might think I was dreaming. I wonder what it means that I'm glad he's not awake, that I can have him next to me without having to actually face him. I match my breathing to his and let the rhythm lull me into sleep.

I wake with my head on Bishop's shoulder, my hand flat on his chest, right over his thrumming heart. It takes me a second to realize he's awake as well, his fingers twining through the ends of my hair. My heart stops and then races. I don't move, but my breathing must give me away.

"Ivy." The soft rush of air from his mouth slides across my temple. "I know you're awake." His voice is hoarse, deeper than I remember.

After I was put out, in the few stolen moments I allowed myself to imagine seeing him again, I pictured racing toward him, grabbing him and never letting go. But now that the moment is here, I am frozen. It seems impossible for us to go back to what we were, not with everything that's come before. I gather my courage in both hands and lift myself up on my elbow so I can see his face. I want to say something, words that will explain my deceit or express my sorrow or beg his forgiveness, but one look in his steady green eyes, eyes I told myself I'd never see again, and everything inside me clenches, clamps down so that nothing can escape.

He just stares at me, his gaze taking in every inch of my face, skimming over cheeks and lips and finally settling on my eyes. I drink him in the same way, wince at the raw cut on his cheek, the bruise blooming on his jaw. My hand hovers and falls away. I don't know how to touch him anymore, not when he's watching me.

"How are you feeling?" I ask. It is the most unimportant thing I could possibly ask him and the only thing I can think of to say.

"I've been better," he says. "But I'll live."

"They brought you here, after . . ." My voice trails off.

"Friends of yours?" Bishop asks.

I nod.

"The one with the crossbow really knows how to pack a punch." Bishop pushes his fingers lightly against his jaw. "Guess I should count myself lucky he didn't just go ahead and skewer me."

The conversation is so mundane, so ridiculous given the circumstances, that it makes me want to weep or scream or laugh hysterically, every possible emotion rising rapidly to the surface. "What..." I duck my head, have to look away for a moment to gather myself. "What are you doing out here?"

His fingers tighten in my hair, not pulling, just urging me to look at him again. I do. We study each other in the stillness. In some ways he seems more a stranger to me than he did when we were first married. He has to be angry, bitter, but I can't see it in his face. Only that familiar, calm acceptance in his eyes.

"You didn't believe me," I whisper finally.

"I didn't believe you," he confirms with the slightest lift of his lips. "Or at least, I didn't believe you for long."

Of course he didn't. I don't know why I'm surprised. He always could read me like a book.

"It was my father's idea," I tell him. I want to hide my face again, don't want to say these words with his eyes on me, but force myself not to be a coward. And part of being brave is admitting my own culpability. It would be so easy to let Callie and my father take all the blame. But I was a willing participant, for far longer than I should have been. "But I went along with it. The whole time we were married, even before that. It was always the plan." I notice my hand has curled into a fist in his shirt, and I make my fingers relax. "But I couldn't do it. Not to you."

"I know," he says, and I marvel all over again at the faith he's always had in me. The sheer belief that somehow hurts worse than doubt. His hand leaves my hair and settles against my neck, his thumb fanning across my cheek. I lean into his touch without thinking about it, heat exploding low in my belly. "Your hair is lighter," he says softly. His hand moves, his thumb skating over my bottom lip. "You have more freckles."

The air between us is suddenly so thick I cannot breathe, my chest aching with pressure. "It's the sun," I say on a strangled exhale.

He nods. Pulls me forward with gentle pressure until my forehead rests against his. I close my eyes against the burning sting of tears. His breath feathers across my cheek, heating the skin like a flame.

"Did they put you out?" I whisper against his mouth. I can't imagine why they would, but I don't know why else he'd be here.

"No. I came to find you."

I shake my head a little, negating his words. It makes no sense to me that he would take this risk, when my own father and sister, my blood, would not. "How did you even know where to look?"

"I'm the president's son, remember? I'd heard rumors about a group near the river, southeast of Westfall. I figured it was as good a place to start as any."

"Why?" I draw back. "Why would you do that?"

"Remember what I told you once?" He pauses. His fingers graze the sensitive skin of my waist underneath my shirt. "About not giving up on you?"

His voice is gentle, but the words hit me like a punch right between the eyes, like a bullet tearing through all my most vulnerable organs, leaving me gasping and undone. After everything I've done to him, he can't possibly be the same Bishop who once loved me, who held my hand and became my best friend. I know I am not the same Ivy. I feel like one of the rabbits I've learned to gut, my insides ripped out, everything I've locked away, tried so hard to forget, in danger of gushing out of me. I'm gripped with a terror not so different from what I felt on the riverbank with Mark, raw and primitive, as if my very survival is at stake.

I jerk out of his grasp, scramble backward off the cot, away from him. My knee connects with his side, and he jackknifes forward.

"I'm sorry," I pant. "I'm sorry. Is it your ribs? I can get you some more medicine."

"Ivy—"

I grab my shoes and practically fall out of the tent. I stand in the gentle morning sunlight, struggling for breath, muscles clenched, air hitching out of my lungs. I don't understand how the pain of losing him can be a pale shadow in comparison to the pain of finding him again.

9

I stop by Carol's tent for some more medicine for Bishop and take the time to gather some breakfast for him as well. When I get back to my tent, Caleb and Ash are waiting outside for me.

"How's he doing?" Caleb asks me.

I hold open the tent flap. "See for yourself."

I follow Caleb and Ash inside, then move around them to hand Bishop the hunk of bread and canteen of water. I put the packet of medicine on the edge of the cot. "Take this after you eat. It will help with the pain."

"Thanks," Bishop says. I know he wants me to look at him, but I avoid his eyes, train my gaze on anything but his face.

"This is Caleb," I say, pointing. "And Ash."

"Your ribs must not be broken, if you're sitting up," Caleb says. He doesn't offer his hand to Bishop.

"Probably just bruised," Bishop agrees. His hand stays at his side, too.

Caleb nods. "Sorry about last night. Couldn't be helped." He points to his swollen, purple-ringed eye. "If it makes you feel any better, you gave almost as good as you got."

Ash is perched on the edge of her cot, and I sit down next to her. Caleb squats down on the ground between the cots. I don't know how he can sit like that for minutes on end, but it never seems to bother him.

"So, you're Ivy's husband," Caleb says after a pause that's gone on too long, everyone waiting for someone else to start the conversation.

"No," Bishop says. I watch his fingers tear into the bread. He is still wearing his wedding ring. "Not anymore."

Now my gaze does fly to his. "What do you mean?"

"They dissolved the marriage. After you were put out."

So I'm not Ivy Lattimer anymore. I don't know why that fact leaves me with a pang of regret. Maybe because it means I don't belong to anyone anymore, neither the West-falls nor the Lattimers willing to claim me as their own.

"Ivy told you everything, I'm guessing?" Bishop continues.

"Not at first," Caleb says. "Only after you got here."

Bishop huffs out a small laugh. "Well, telling the truth isn't Ivy's strong suit." And there it is, the anger I've been waiting for. Just a hint of it, but there all the same. I wonder when it will come roaring out of him, if I'll be ready for it when it does.

"But you still came looking for her," Ash says, not quite a question.

"Yes."

Caleb is twirling a small stick around and around his fingers. "Took you long enough."

Bishop swings his gaze away from me, thoughtful eyes taking Caleb's measure. "They kept a close watch on me. I couldn't get away. I think my mother suspected I'd go after Ivy as soon as I could." I can only imagine how that must have eaten at Erin, knowing her only son would side with me over his family. Just one more Lattimer man who chose another woman over her.

"And now what?" Caleb asks. "You want to stay here?"

"That's up to Ivy," Bishop says.

Caleb turns his head toward me. "Is that what you want?"

I swallow. Just because I'm not sure how to live with Bishop anymore, doesn't mean I want to live without him. Maybe I am as selfish as Callie once accused me of being. "Yes," I say, barely a whisper. Even from across the tent, I can feel some of the tension drain out of Bishop.

"I'm not saying it's going to be easy," Caleb says. "A lot of our people are out here because of your father."

"I'm not my father," Bishop says.

Caleb stares at him. "Some may not see the distinction."

Bishop gives a slight nod, then asks, with a raise of his eyebrows, "The same way I might lump Mark Laird and you together?"

"Fair point," Caleb says after a second's hesitation. I think I catch a glimpse of respect in his eyes when he looks at Bishop. "I'm not making any promises, but I'll talk to everyone, urge them to give you a chance."

"That's all I'm asking for," Bishop says.

Caleb nods, glances from Bishop to me. "We've put it off long enough. I need to know the story on Mark."

"Bishop can tell it," I say. I find I don't want any more words about Mark on my tongue, as if even speaking of him is infecting me somehow.

Bishop is matter-of-fact in his recitation, beginning with my work in the jail and the crime that caused Mark to be put out, up through the girl he killed on the other side of the fence. When he's done, Caleb looks at Ash with sorry eyes, and I know he's beating himself up for letting someone like Mark near her. He turns those regret-filled eyes to me.

"He's the one who hurt you, isn't he?"

Bishop shifts on the cot across from me, but I don't take my eyes off Caleb. "Yes."

"What did he do to you?" Bishop asks. His voice is steady, but raw, like he's fighting hard to keep it that way.

I glance at him and then at the ground. "It was my second day out. He found me. He attacked me . . ."

"Bashed her face in pretty good. Dislocated her shoulder," Ash says. No one speaks, everyone unwilling to voice the question they must all be thinking.

"Did he rape you?" Bishop asks finally.

"No," I say, looking up into his drawn face. "He would have. But I hit him in the head with a rock until he was unconscious."

"Should have hit him harder," Caleb mutters.

"Should have killed him," Bishop says and the two of them share grim smiles.

"I knew you would say that," I tell Bishop, with a tiny smile of my own. "I wanted to. I knew I should. But I just ... couldn't."

"Still," Bishop says, "sounds like you kicked his ass."

"From here to next Tuesday," I say, my smile widening. His eyes lose some of their graveness, warming as we stare at each other, remembering another day in another place. From the corner of my eye I can see Ash glancing between us, and I turn my attention back to her, even as heat spreads along my neck and races into my cheeks.

"So what now?" Ash asks. "What should we do about Mark?"

"Nothing to do," Caleb says with a sigh. "He's gone."

"What do you mean, gone?" I ask.

"Went by his tent this morning and it's cleaned out." Caleb shrugs. "He must have figured you were going to tell us the truth and he made a run for it."

"Good riddance," Ash says.

"Yeah, for now," Bishop says.

Caleb catches his eye again. It's like the two of them are already working out some kind of unspoken guy language. "Exactly. I doubt he's gone for good. He doesn't seem like the type who can survive the winter out here alone."

"Then we'll have to keep an eye out for him," Ash says.

Caleb stands with a grunt, points at Bishop. "For now, you need to rest. Get healed up. We're moving camp soon." Caleb pauses. "Let me ask you something. Were things all right in Westfall when you left?"

Bishop's eyebrows go up. "Why do you ask?"

"No real reason," Caleb says. "I've just noticed signs in the woods, tracks, more people coming this way. Trying to figure out why and where they're from."

"Everything was fine when I left." Bishop pauses. "Well, maybe not fine. People were a little more on edge than usual, ever since Ivy was put out, but no real unrest." Bishop's eyes find mine. Worry, tempered with the knowledge that whatever happens in Westfall is beyond our control, flows between us.

"Okay," Caleb says, pushing open the tent flap. "Just thought I'd check."

Ash scoots around me. "I can handle the washing today, Ivy," she says, voice clipped. "There are plenty of other people to help."

"No, it's okay. I'll come," I tell her.

After Caleb and Ash are gone, I busy myself tying my hair up in a ponytail, my back to Bishop.

"Are you ever going to talk to me?"

I turn. "We're talking. We've been talking."

Bishop sighs. "What about looking at me? Can you bring yourself to do that, at least?"

The truth is, I barely can. I glance at him, but keep my gaze unfocused, my heart beating triple time in my chest. "What?" I ask, wishing he would stop staring at me.

He doesn't answer, just continues to watch me. My blood buzzes; my whole body tingles. I want to peel out of my own skin to escape. "I didn't need you to come save me," I tell him. I don't even know what I'm saying, or why I'm saying it, words hurling out of my mouth like weapons. "I was doing fine on my own." Which is so far from the truth. Apparently lying still comes as easily to me as breathing.

His head jerks back just a little. "I know that," he says. "I'm not here to save you. That's not why I came."

"Then why are you here? What do you want from me?" And oh, I'm being so unfair. Maybe I hope I'll push him to anger, if only so I don't have to face some even more dangerous emotion.

"What do I *want* from you?" Bishop asks, like I've lost my mind.

"Yes. What do you want?" I realize this is a question I've needed an answer to from the time we met. The suspicious part of me, birthed and nurtured by my father, still can't truly believe Bishop doesn't have some type of ulterior motive, even after all the times he's proved otherwise. Nobody ever wants me solely for me.

Bishop's jaw tightens, but he only sounds incredibly tired when he says, "I just want to be with you. Walk next to you, Ivy, wherever you're headed. That's all."

My stomach drops. My heart twists into a tiny ball. "I have to go. Ash is waiting." I leave him there, alone in the tent, running as far and fast as my fear can take me.

Ash and I don't talk much as we work, other than the basics: *Can you pass the soap? I'll rinse that one. We're almost done.* When we've finished hanging the last of the clothes, I sink down on the riverbank, cross my arms over my upturned knees, and rest my chin on my forearms. At some point, the sound and smell of the river have become soothing to me. I understand now why Bishop spent so much time here. Bishop. Who, by now, probably wishes he'd never bothered coming after me. Just more time wasted on a girl who will never deserve him.

Ash lowers herself next to me. "So," she says, "that's Bishop."

"That's Bishop." I turn my head so I can see her, my cheek resting on my folded arms. "Do you hate him?"

Ash's eyes open wide, like I've slapped her. "Why would I?"

"Because he's a Lattimer. And his family put your mother out."

"He wasn't even born then, Ivy," Ash says. "And you obviously care about him, so he must be a good guy."

A sobbing little laugh escapes me. "Mark said no one here would forgive me for caring about a Lattimer."

Ash rolls her eyes. "And you believed *him*?"

"I was scared not to."

Ash doesn't have a response for that, and we both sit quietly for a few minutes, watching the river roll by. "Bishop must love you a lot," Ash says finally. "Coming out here to find you."

"Yes." It takes me a second to continue. "I think he did."

Ash shakes her head. "Not did, Ivy. Does."

"I don't know why he would," I say, voice quiet. "I've hurt him. Over and over again."

Ash's face softens, her eyes warm. "That's what love is, though, isn't it? You don't stop loving someone just because they disappoint you."

I've always thought of myself as older than Ash, though her years probably outnumber mine. With her quick smile and easy laugh, her steadfast belief in the good left in this world, she's always seemed more innocent and hopeful than I'll ever be again, even after that day in the woods with those dead men at our feet. But now for the first time I feel like the younger one, tongue-tied in the face of her superior knowledge.

"I don't know," I say finally. "I don't know if I understand what it means to love someone. Not really."

Ash gives me a tender smile, so different from her usual broad grins. "Caleb told me about what happened to you in Westfall. About your family."

"They weren't the best teachers." Probably the biggest understatement of my life.

"No." Ash tucks an errant strand of hair back behind my ear. "But that doesn't mean you can't still learn. It's not an excuse for not trying."

The sun is out, but it has the weak, watery quality of autumn, clear and bright in the sky, but not carrying much warmth by the time it hits your skin. I sit up straight and pull the sleeves of my sweater down, tuck my river-pruned fingers inside.

"I'm sorry," I say, "that I wasn't honest with you from the beginning."

"I forgive you. I know you must've been afraid. But no more secrets, okay?" She lays her hand over my forearm and squeezes.

"I'll try," I say. "It's something else I have to learn. How to trust people. How to stop lying to them." I wonder if it's even possible for me; maybe deceit is something I carry in my blood, passed down from my father without my consent.

"It's probably none of my business, but you seem mad at him," Ash says after we've watched the water flow for a while.

I shake my head, and Ash makes a clucking noise with her tongue. "You don't have to tell me, if you don't want to. But you just promised not to lie anymore."

I sigh. She's right. I'm so, so angry. When I close my eyes and breathe, it flows through me like acid, making my stomach boil and my fingers ache to clench, rip into something too hard and leave damage behind. "I'm angry," I admit, voice low. "Not with Bishop, not really, but . . ."

"But he's here? And they're not?" There's no judgment in Ash's voice, none in her eyes when they meet mine. "I get it," she says. "When my dad died, I was furious. At the whole world, I guess. I mean, I'd never had a mom, and then I lost my dad, too? The only person I had left?" She breathes out a tiny, bitter laugh. "I took it out on Caleb. For longer than I should have."

"He probably didn't mind," I say, thinking of the way Caleb protects her, worries over her like a mother hen.

"Oh, he minded," Ash says, with a roll of her eyes. "He's not the most patient guy in the world. He got sick of it pretty quick. But I worked it out eventually." She smiles at me. "You will, too."

But it's not just anger that's keeping me away from Bishop. There's the snapping, snarling fear that's even stronger. A fear I don't understand or really want to examine, not sure what it will tell me about myself. About us.

Ash stands up. "You heading back?"

"No, I think I'll stay here a little longer."

"Okay." Ash takes a few steps before stopping to glance back at me. "Your eyes are still sad," she tells me. "But your whole face lights up when you look at him."

I manage to keep away from the tent for most of the day. Ash takes Bishop lunch, and from a distance, I watch Carol enter the tent midafternoon, bringing Bishop more medicine for the pain. At dinnertime, I ask Caleb to take Bishop a plate, and he does after only a slight hesitation. I linger outside the tent when he goes in, expecting him to come right back out and give me a report. Instead, I hear the low murmur of their voices and after a while, a laugh from Caleb. So unexpected it makes me jerk a little where I stand. Less than twenty-four hours and Bishop's gotten a genuine laugh out of Caleb, something I have yet to accomplish in more than two months. It makes me smile to imagine the two of them, Caleb squatting on the floor, Bishop leaning back against the tent pole, although I can't come up with any idea of what they might be talking about. But they both need a friend, someone they can count on but don't feel responsible for; maybe they will be good for each other.

After Caleb finally emerges from the tent, I trail behind him to the bonfire. He gives me a questioning look when I sit down next to him, but doesn't ask why I'm out here instead of in my tent with Bishop. There are times Caleb's silences can be oppressive, but the flip side is he always knows when to leave well enough alone.

I stay outside after Ash and Caleb have left for his tent. After most of the other people have melted away. After the last of the glowing fire has been covered and extinguished.

Only then do I rise and make my slow way toward my tent. I take a deep breath before I duck inside, but the tent is dark, the only sound Bishop's slow, even breathing.

I slip off my shoes and clothes as quietly as I can, leaving on only my underwear and tank top. I tug the band out of my hair and run my fingers through the tangled strands. Ash's cot is empty, just waiting for my weary body. But as if I'm watching from outside myself, I climb gingerly over Bishop, settle into the small space I occupied last night. I turn on my side to face the tent, my back to his sleeping body.

The night air is chilly and I shiver, reaching down to pull up the blankets that are puddled at our feet. As I lay back again, Bishop turns onto his side, closer to me. I freeze, not sure what to do. I feel caught, but lack any real desire to escape. Not here in the dark, where we can pretend nothing's changed. His arm snakes around me, guiding me back against him. My body goes willingly, like it's sinking into a long-remembered home. I take his hand in mine, bring it up to my lips. Not kissing, but close enough to my mouth that I can smell his skin, imagine the taste of his fingers on my tongue. His lips graze my shoulder, his exhales raising goose bumps along the back of my neck. He doesn't speak, and neither do I, content to leave the communicating to our touch-starved bodies.

10

Bishop's been here for a little over a week, and his assimilation has gone better than I expected. Most of the blood lust left along with Mark Laird. Granted, there are people who give him hostile looks, grumble that he doesn't belong, but there are also those who remember the boy who came to the fence with water and food after they were put out. Others lived in Westfall back when he was a child and remember him as simply a little boy, born into a family he didn't choose. They are open-minded enough to understand that who he came from doesn't necessarily define who he is. I wish it were a pardon I could offer to myself, but my family's bad deeds still feel like my own.

It's actually my relationship with Bishop that's causing more raised eyebrows than his being here in the first place. I know that people are confused. They remember the way I threw myself across his body to protect him, but they also notice the fact that I never meet his eyes, that I go out of my way to find things to do during the day that keep me far from him. They know he left Westfall to try to find me, and they see us disappear into the same tent together every night. But every morning we head our different directions, barely speaking. No one seems to know how to put all the disparate pieces together to make a coherent picture. Least of all me.

Bishop's injuries are healing fast, the bruises on his face fading to streaks of sickly yellow and his ribs, although still tender, not so sore that he can't be up and moving around. His willingness to help out whoever needs it, regardless of his injuries, has also gone a long way toward easing his transition into the group.

Today is our last day at the camp. Most everyone has already moved to town. There are just a few final tents to take down, a couple last loads of supplies to be transported. Caleb and Ash left this morning and will be back by afternoon to escort Bishop and me. In the meantime, we're taking down my tent, packing up the last of my belongings.

I tried to switch places with Ash, so I wouldn't have to be here alone with Bishop, but she shrugged off my offer. I think she's as tired of the awful, grinding tension as anyone. Hoping, maybe, that leaving us alone will force us to confront it. But I'm more unsure and tentative than

I was in those first few days of our marriage. At least then I knew why there were walls between us, understood my own reluctance to close the distance. Now I am a mystery, even to myself.

As I watch, Bishop reaches up to try to unclasp the top of the tent from the wooden pole, but stretching so far must aggravate his ribs because he yanks his arm back to his side with a wince before he can get the tent down.

"Here," I say, stepping in front of him. "Let me do it." Standing on my tiptoes I can reach it easily, managing to unclasp the tent with one hand. As I step back, my foot tangles in a half-packed bag, and I stumble. Before I can fall, Bishop is there, catching my body with his own.

I suck in a breath as his hand curls into my stomach, my body pressed against his from shoulders to feet. He doesn't let go or move back. His other hand finds the curve of my hip, resting against the bone.

"You all right?" he asks. He's so close his lips move against the top of my ear. I try not to shiver and fail.

"Uh-huh," I manage. I can't find air, my chest rising and falling like I've been running a race. He's warm and strong, his heart pounding against my back. His fingers spread on my stomach, his thumb coming to rest right below my breasts, his pinky nudging the waistband of my pants. My insides coil and twist; my blood simmers. I wouldn't be surprised to see steam rise out of my pores. It's the first time he's touched me outside the darkness of our tent. It's the first time I've let him.

He runs his other hand over my hip bone, up and down, up and down, a slow, simple rhythm. "You've lost weight," he says, voice quiet.

He sounds concerned, not critical, but I latch onto his words as a way to escape the fire in my belly, the weakness that makes me want to turn in his arms and meet his mouth with mine. It takes all my willpower, but I pivot away from him, chest heaving. "Disappointed my curves aren't quite as curvy?" I mock, balling my hands into fists to stop their trembling. I hate the sneering sound of my voice. My back feels cold without him. My heart feels empty.

Bishop takes a deep breath, then shakes his head, shoves his hands into his pockets. "It was never about the way you look, Ivy," he says. "You have to know that."

I do know that. Which only makes it worse. I don't know how to stop hurting him; I wish I did. I raise both hands and let them drop. "What are you doing here with me, Bishop?" I ask. "You should be with some other girl. Some girl who makes you happy."

"I don't want a girl who makes me happy," he says. "I want you."

My eyes fly to his, and I can't help the laugh that tumbles out of me. Bishop's slow smile makes my heart flip-flop in my chest. We stand there, watching each other, the unstrung tent billowing in the breeze between us.

"We should finish up," I say, suddenly anxious to have something to do with my hands. Bishop doesn't move, even as I bend down to begin folding the tent. "Are you angry with me?" he asks, reading something on my face I didn't know was there.

I swallow hard, my throat working. "Why would I be mad at you?" As I ask the question I remember being attacked by Mark, how anger helped me win that battle. And how some of that anger was directed at Bishop. Even Ash thought I was angry with him. "That wouldn't be fair."

Bishop shrugs. "I don't think fair really enters into it. You feel what you feel."

"I don't blame you for what happened, Bishop. How could I? None of it was your fault."

"Maybe you're angry because I did believe you, even for a minute."

I toss the tent down with a snap. "I wanted you to believe me!"

"It still had to hurt," Bishop says. I don't know what to say to that. I can hardly claim a right to pain after everything I've put him through. And he's already so close to the truth of it, edging right around the way my heart broke when he finally believed I was capable of all the terrible things everyone else already took for granted. "Maybe because if not for me, you'd be with your family right now," Bishop continues. "All of Westfall at your feet."

My body goes cold. "I never wanted that," I whisper.

"I know. But it might have been easier."

I shake my head. "That would never have been easier."

"I knew you were lying," he says after a long moment. "I think I knew the whole time. Even at the end. But I was so hurt, so angry. I let myself believe you were really going to kill me, because in some ways that was easier than believing you still didn't trust me."

"It wasn't about not trusting you," I say. Unshed tears burn in my throat. "I was trying to protect you." I pause and Bishop just waits, his eyes searching my face. I'd forgotten what it was like to have all that focus solely on me, to be the recipient of such undivided attention. My chest aches from the fierce pounding of my heart. "I don't . . . I don't want to talk about this anymore," I say.

"We have to, Ivy,"

I shake my head. "Not now. Not yet."

"All right," Bishop says. "But soon." Even with a hint of frustration weaving through his voice, his patient acceptance stabs at me. That he should be so forgiving after everything when my own family was not, condemning me as easily as they would a stranger.

"They let me be thrown out," I say, my voice thin. Somehow my mouth is making decisions my brain has not approved. "Like I was garbage."

I can see the moment he catches up, my words slotting into place. Sadness passes across his face, bleeds into his eyes. Not pity, though, just an understanding. Like what happened to me, happened to him. And maybe that's love, too—feeling the other person's hurts like your own.

"Yes," he says simply. I'm glad he doesn't try to make excuses for them or convince me it's not as bad as it seems. I would think less of him if he did. "But that says everything about them, Ivy. And nothing about you."

I know he's right, but knowing the truth of something, deep down, doesn't lessen its impact. Doesn't stop that little voice telling me that maybe if I'd been a different kind of girl, maybe if I'd been able to change, they would have loved me enough to fight for me.

"Did they ever, after I was gone . . ." I look away, clear my throat. "Did they ever talk about me?" I keep my gaze on the empty camp, the spots where tents used to stand, and the grass is trampled flat and dry. I tell myself my eyes sting because of the wind.

"I didn't see your dad much," Bishop says. "Callie came around a lot. At first." He pauses. "She talked about you."

"None of it good, I'm guessing."

"No, not much of it. She tried to talk about you with me. But I didn't want to hear what she had to say. I knew none of it was true."

"Some of it probably was," I say, thinking of the day I married him, how I spoke my vows knowing I planned to kill him. How I smiled at him with murder in my heart. "She was trying to get close to you."

"Yes," he says again.

I swing my eyes back to him, my stomach hollow. "Did it work?" I remember Callie's hand on his arm, her pretty face tipped up to his. I know firsthand the power of Callie's persuasion, the tricks she uses to get what she wants, so slick and sneaky you don't realize what you've given up until she's already holding it in her hand.

He gives me a small smile, his eyebrows cocked. "What do you think?"

Selfish relief flows through me. "I think you hated each other." I know for a fact Callie hated him, probably was thrilled I was out of the picture so she could finally have her chance to ruin him. And I think he probably figured her out fast. Bishop's so good at seeing what's behind the surface. And once you really know Callie, there isn't much to love.

He takes a step closer to me. "She was a pretty good actress. But I'm better at reading people than she is at faking it. And I didn't have any interest in playing her game. All I cared about was finding you."

The breeze lifts his dark hair off his forehead. He moves even closer, reaches out, and runs his knuckles across my cheek. Before I have to decide what to do, step closer or move away, he drops his hand, bends and begins gathering up the tent. We work together to fold it. Bishop stacks the wooden tent poles while I pack the last of my clothes. Once we're done, we sit in the cool sunlight and wait for what comes next.

11

I'd almost forgotten what it's like to live within four walls. To not fall asleep to cicada song and the wind in the trees. To not wake with the chatter of birds and the sun already burning through the thin material of a tent. The town Caleb and Ash and the rest of the camp move to in winter is situated almost on the banks of the river. A small collection of houses strung out like weather-beaten rocks, their clapboard exteriors all faded to a uniform, dreary gray. The stores that once ringed the tiny town square are in even worse shape; only what was once probably a restaurant is used at all. It still has a counter with a few intact stools, and Caleb says people gather there sometimes when spending another snowbound day in their own houses is too much to bear.

The house that Caleb and Ash share is on the outer edge of town, which doesn't surprise me. Same as with the tents, Caleb likes the ability to move fast, to be the first one to sense a threat or sound the alarm. None of the houses in the town can be considered in good shape, but they are all more sound and welcoming than the ones in Birch Tree.

It takes us a good two days of cleaning to get the house free of dust, aired out and ready for living. Some of the upstairs windows are still intact, but downstairs Caleb has fashioned shutters over the empty holes. There's not a lot of natural light, but the shutters will keep us safe and protect us from wind and snow come winter. The kitchen is used mainly for storage, but the fireplace in the living room is large, and Ash tells me that's where they cook most of their meals. In the winter, meals aren't communal, although everyone is willing to share food if necessity demands it. Caleb's bedroom is off the living room, and there are two additional bedrooms upstairs. One for Ash and one that Bishop and I share. Ash never offered to let me sleep in her room, and I never suggested it. It never occurred to me to sleep anywhere other than next to Bishop, which considering the state of our relationship is probably strange. The bed Bishop and I share is bigger than the cot, but we sleep curled even closer to each other, most of the extra space left empty.

The first few weeks in town are spent preparing for the coming winter, each morning just slightly colder than the one before. We all go out hunting some days; others just one or two of us go and the rest stay behind and can fruit or make jerky from earlier catches. At night we gather around the fire in the living room, huddled on the ancient sofas, their dust-encrusted surfaces covered with blankets we brought from camp, and talk. Well, Ash does most of the talking. And Bishop joins in. Some nights I think Caleb and I don't manage to say a word, the two of them filling the awkward conversational gaps that Caleb and I leave behind.

Bishop's frustration has become a palpable presence between us, his patience stretching thinner with every passing day. He rarely mentions Westfall or his family, but I know he must miss them, worry about them now that he's gone. I wonder if he balances what he's gained against what he's lost. I hope not, because I doubt the end result would weigh in my favor.

Today, Caleb and Ash have gone out to set more snares, and Bishop and I are working side by side in the kitchen, wrapping up jerky for the winter ahead. Bishop cuts the jerky into strips and I roll the strips in cloth, tying the ends tightly. We don't talk as we work, and the silence isn't easy. It boils and crackles with all our unsaid words. The air between us is thick with tension, a powder keg of emotion that I know is set to explode no matter how hard I try to defuse it.

I concentrate on our task, my eyes lowered. Dim sunlight flows in through a crack in the shutters and lands on Bishop's hand, lighting up the gold band on his finger. "Why are you still wearing that?" I ask.

Bishop looks over at me, follows my eyes to his wedding band. "Does it bother you?"

I shrug, but I can feel the tightness in my shoulders. "We're not married anymore."

"I know that," he says. He glances at my bare finger. "Where's yours?"

"I threw it away," I say, voice sharp. "It didn't mean anything. Not out here." I reach over and grab the jerky. "It didn't really mean anything in Westfall, either." Not because I didn't love him by the end, but because every vow I made to him was based on a lie. But I can't find the words to make the distinction clear.

Bishop doesn't move, even as I begin wrapping the jerky. "It meant something to me," he says. "It still does."

I keep my eyes on my hands, Bishop's gaze heavy on the side of my face. "The guard they had watching me after you were put out carried a gun," Bishop says. I glance at him, startled, unsure where this revelation is going. "I tried to get away from him constantly. Took off every time he turned his back. God, he hated me. I made it as far as the fence once. I got halfway up before he caught me."

"But the razor wire . . ." I say, not wanting to imagine the damage it would have done to him if he'd gone over the top.

Bishop shakes his head. "I didn't care. But he said he'd shoot me if I tried it. My mom had given him permission to shoot me in the leg, if it came down to that." He cuts into a piece of jerky, knuckles tense around the knife. "I almost did it anyway. I was *desperate*, Ivy. Desperate to get to you." He pauses. "I thought you'd be desperate, too."

Almost against my will, I look at him. His face is drawn, hurt and anger swirling in his eyes. "I couldn't afford to be desperate," I whisper. "I was trying to survive." I remember how hard I fought not to remember him during those first weeks beyond the fence. How every time he entered my mind it felt like a weakness that had the power to kill me, my still-beating heart ripped right out of my chest.

"What about now?" Bishop demands. "You seem to be surviving just fine." His laugh is dry and humorless. "Maybe you can teach me your trick. How you manage to move on like it's the easiest thing in the world. Like nothing that happened before even matters." I hate the bitterness threading through his voice, especially because I know I'm the one who put it there.

"Of course it matters. And it's not easy." I have to force the words out through a tight throat. "None of this has been easy."

Bishop blows out a breath. "That's not how it looks from where I'm standing."

I open my mouth, not even sure what I'm going to say. Probably something that will drive him further away, but he doesn't give me a chance. The knife falls from his hand, clatters to the counter. He crowds me back against the wall with his body, pressing against me, shoulders to hips.

He's already breathing hard, but I can barely hear him over the whoosh of blood roaring in my ears. One of his hands tightens in my hair, the other pushing up under the hem of my shirt. I close my eyes as his mouth lowers to mine, loop my arms around his neck even as every survival instinct I have is shouting at me to shove him away.

We have not kissed in all these weeks beyond the fence. We touch in the dark, hold each other close, but our mouths never meet. I was so sure I'd never have this again—his lips on mine, the scratch of his stubble and the slide of his tongue—that I've barely allowed myself to imagine it, to remember how good it is. The weight of his body pins me against the wall. His calloused fingers glide over the hollow of my waist, my ribs, move higher to cup my breast, his thumb fanning across the bare skin above my bra. I am all sensation, bolts of energy running between every point of contact.

I can't focus, my body lit up in a dozen different spots, so it takes me longer than it should to realize these kisses are different from any we've shared before. I can still feel his love for me, his desire, but now also his pain. And it breaks my heart. I turn my head, pulling my mouth from his, but he doesn't move back. He has one hand wrapped behind my neck and he uses his thumb to tilt my jaw upward, his lips falling to my throat, trailing wet, hot kisses against my skin. My stomach knots and rolls, fire licking through my veins.

"Bishop," I breathe. "Stop. This doesn't fix anything." I clutch his wrist, his pulse hammering against my fingertips. "*Stop*."

He does, instantly. He drops his forehead against the wall beside my head, his chest heaving. I close my eyes and fight to get my own breathing back under control. Slowly, he pushes away from me. He grabs my left hand, his fingers sliding over the empty patch of skin where my wedding ring once was.

"I can't believe you threw it away," he says, voice husky. I open my eyes, and we stare at each other.

I pull my hand back. "It hurt too much to look at it," I say, because I owe him this, at least, this little bit of truth. "It was a reminder of what wasn't mine anymore."

The anger in his eyes fades. "Ivy . . ."

The front door bangs open, Caleb's voice booming into the silence. I slip out from between Bishop's body and the wall, move away from his grasp, ignoring his hand still reaching out for me.

We feast on fresh venison for dinner after Caleb and Bishop return home with a buck strung between them. We're going to have to spend the next week turning it into jerky to help us make it through the winter, but Caleb cuts four fat steaks for dinner. One last hurrah before months of dried meat and mealy potatoes.

After, Ash and Bishop sit on the couch playing a game of cards while Caleb works on making more bolts for his crossbow. It's my turn to clean the dishes and I'm taking my time rinsing our plates in the sink, using a bucket of water Caleb brought in earlier. I've avoided the kitchen since Bishop and I kissed here last week. My eyes keep skipping to where he pressed me against the wall, my body remembering the warm weight of his.

I can hear Ash's laughter rising from the living room, the low murmur of Bishop's voice. Usually it's comforting listening to them, reminding me that I'm not alone, but tonight it scrapes against my nerves, setting up a sharp thrum under my skin. Everything has been irritating me the last few days, as if the routines of my new life are a splinter I can't dig out, ever-present and always aggravating.

Caleb looks up when I enter the living room, gives me a small smile. Ash and Bishop barely glance at me. Ash is digging her toes into Bishop's leg as she accuses him of cheating at their card game.

I set the empty bucket down with a too-loud clatter and reach for my sweater hanging on the back of a dining room chair. "I'm going to get some more water," I announce.

"I can get it," Bishop offers, but I shake my head without looking at him.

"I've got it," I say, shoving my arms into my sweater. None of them speak as I cross the room, but I feel their eyes on my back. I put too much force into opening the front door, barely catching it before it bangs into the wall. I'm slightly more careful when I close it behind me, but only slightly, the wood shaking against the frame. Not quite a slam.

The night air is cold, the stars like tiny ice chips in the black velvet of the sky. I smell smoke from dozens of fireplaces, see warm lantern light glowing from behind cracks in curtains and shutters. But the only sound is the faint rush of the river, the rustle of wind-tossed branches, everyone else already hunkered down for the night. I gather my sweater more securely around me and step off the porch, headed toward the river. My eyes sting, and a hot, bitter ache has settled underneath my ribs.

When I reach the river, the water is running fast and black, only the surface turned a shimmery silver in the moonlight. My fingers are numb in seconds, the water icy cold. Already it's hard for me to imagine how frigid it will be once winter arrives in earnest, cobwebs of ice greeting each dawn. I should head back to the house now that I've filled the bucket. My hands are frozen, and my breath puffs out of me in steamy clouds.

But I sink to my knees instead, not caring that the ground isn't much warmer than the water. I suddenly don't have the energy to face Bishop, to watch him smile at Ash and make easy jokes with Caleb. I know it's unfair of me to be jealous when I'm the one creating the distance between us, my silence a wedge I force into the space where our words used to be. But recognizing the ridiculousness of an emotion and being able to master it are two very different things, I'm finding.

A branch breaks behind me, and I scramble to my feet, almost overturning the bucket in my haste. I'm already reaching for my knife when Bishop appears; I know even his silhouette so well I can pick him out of the near-darkness.

"I said I didn't need any help," I tell him, my hand falling away from my knife.

"I figured I'd give you a hand anyway," he says, reaching for the bucket. I swing it away from him and turn back toward the house.

"I'm surprised you were willing to leave your card game," I say. Even as I'm speaking, I'm telling myself to shut up, but my mouth is one step ahead of my brain. Apparently that hasn't changed. "You and Ash seemed to be having a great time. Very cozy." Just hearing the words makes me cringe. I never wanted to be this kind of girl. I never thought I was.

Bishop's hand snakes forward and grabs the handle of the bucket, forcing me to stop. "Are you done?" he asks. He sounds utterly exhausted, worn beyond the point of endurance.

I shrug, keeping my back to him.

"You honestly believe I'm falling for Ash?" he asks me. "That we would ever look at each other that way?"

"No," I say on a whisper. I know that's not how they feel about each other, just as I know neither one of them would ever hurt me intentionally.

"Then say what you mean," he demands, giving the bucket a slight shake. "Or just"—he blows out a breath—"shut up."

I whirl on him, forcing him to loosen his grip on the bucket. Water sloshes over the side and down my leg, soaking my pants. "Shut up? *Shut up?*"

He stares at me, his eyes a cool, glowing green in the moonlight. "We can't keep doing this, Ivy," he says. "*I* can't keep doing this."

"Doing what?" I ask and feel an immediate flush of shame. I'm the one playing games now, no better than Callie.

"Don't do that," he says. "Don't pretend you don't know what I'm talking about."

"Then maybe you should leave," I say, even as my heart protests the words. "Go back to Westfall. I know you probably want to." Just the thought of waking up to-morrow and not seeing his face makes panic rise up in my chest, squeezing my heart like a cold fist.

"Why would you say that?" His eyes bore into mine, his jaw tight. He is teetering right on the edge of losing his temper; one hard nudge from me and he'll fall.

"I know you're angry with me, Bishop. When are you going to admit it?"

"Of course I'm angry," he says, taking a step toward me. I take a step back to compensate. "I've never denied it. Is that what you want to hear?"

"Maybe." My heart knocks against my ribs. I'm terrified suddenly of where this is leading, whether I'm brave enough to make my own admissions in return. I wish I'd kept my mouth shut, gone back to the house and crawled into bed. But how many more nights can we do that before he turns away instead of holding me, before I wake up one morning and he really is gone?

"Okay, then," Bishop says, voice rising, "I'm angry that the entire time I was falling in love with you, you were figuring out ways to kill me!"

My mouth drops open. "I didn't ... that's not ..."

"I'm angry that when you had the chance to tell me the truth, you lied instead!" He has closed the distance between us faster than I can move backward so we're standing almost chest to chest. "And I'm angry because now that we have a second chance, you still won't be honest with me!"

"Were you planning to say any of this?" I ask, heat flooding my cheeks.

Bishop lifts his dark eyebrows. "I would have, if you ever stayed in one spot long enough for us to have an actual conversation."

The fear is rising in me, the same desperation I've felt every time he's near me since we found each other again. I start to turn away from him, and he grabs the bucket, holds it tight in his hand so I can't leave.

"Let go," I say through clenched teeth, my suddenly sweaty fingers slipping against the bucket handle. And the moment might be funny if I weren't on the verge of tears, if I weren't petrified of where this will end.

"No," he says, voice hard. "Neither one of us is leaving until we figure this out ... one way or the other."

I tilt my head up to his, take in the tension in his jaw, the determined crease of his brow. Bishop's capacity for patience, at least where I'm concerned, has always seemed almost infinite. All those days and nights we spent together in Westfall when he never forced me to give more than I was ready to offer, never demanded emotions from me that I wasn't yet able to admit feeling. But along with his patience, there is also an underlying firmness, a wall that marks a point at which he will no longer bend. I witnessed it firsthand when he shoved Dylan off the roof. Have the evidence right in front of me now—the very fact that he came beyond the fence to find me.

Once Bishop has reached the limit of his patience, he is done holding back. And I think that tonight, on this dark riverbank, I have pushed him as far as he's willing to go. I know he would never put his hands on me in violence. But he's not above forcing me to confront what I've been running from, face the distance I've created between us. And maybe that's what I've been waiting for all along, for Bishop to corner me into admitting things my mind tells me are better left unexamined.

"I know you're scared, Ivy," he says. "But if we don't talk about this, it's going to ruin us."

I drop my hold on the bucket and lurch away from him. "Stop telling me how I feel!" I practically shout.

"Then you tell me!" Bishop yells back, startling me. He tosses the bucket away, river water gushing out into the grass. "Tell me why you crawl into bed with me every night and then act like I don't exist once the sun rises! Tell me why you say you want me here, but can barely bring yourself to be in the same room with me!"

"I thought you liked me complicated," I throw back at him. "I thought that's what fascinated you in the first place."

Bishop looks away, takes a deep breath. "Really? You're going to use that against me now?" When he looks back at me, I have to drop my gaze from the hurt in his eyes. "You say you're not angry. You deny being scared. So what is it then? Tell me why you're acting this way."

"I don't know what to say." I shake my head. "I don't know what you want me to say."

"How about the truth," Bishop suggests, voice icy. "Can you manage that for once?"

And in an instant all my fear boils over into rage. Every dark, ugly thought I've had since the day I was put out comes writhing to the surface. "I lost everything!" I scream, so loud and shrill my throat aches. I wish I still had the bucket so I could throw it at him. "My family! My home! My best friend! The person I loved most in the world!" My chest feels like it's going to explode, too much emotion confined in too small a space. My hands are curled into fists so tight my fingernails threaten to burst through my palms. "I had everything ripped away from me! Do you have any idea what that's like?"

Bishop's whole face is clenched, like he's fighting his own battle beneath his skin. "Yeah," he says, voice low. "I have a pretty good idea what that's like."

And that's so typical of Bishop, to remind me I'm not the only one to suffer. Only right now I don't want to hear it. My anger is like a balm, soothing over all the tender spots I don't want to examine too closely. "You didn't have to come after me. You had a choice."

"You think I had a choice?" Bishop demands. "What choice? I'm not like your father or Callie, Ivy. I was never going to just let you go. I love you. There was never any choice."

His words stop me cold. For the first time it really hits me, what it means that Bishop is here, that he came to find me. He's the only person in my entire life who hasn't failed me. As quickly as it descended, the anger swirls out of me, like a black cloud lifting up and away. But it leaves all my open wounds exposed with no way to protect them. I cross my arms and dig my fingers into my elbows. I feel like if I don't hold on to something, I will disappear.

"Talk to me," Bishop says, quieter. "We used to be so good at that. Please . . . just talk to me."

It's like we're back in the basement of the courthouse, separated by the iron bars of a cell. That time, I chose to lie in hopes that it would spare him. This time, if I lie it will be out of pure cowardice. And he is right; it will ruin us. There's a limit to how many lies I can tell him before he stops caring about the truth.

My father, Callie, President Lattimer—they have already taken so much from me. Am I going to let them take Bishop, too? I want to reach for him, pull him close and whisper my secrets against his skin. In so many ways I am stronger than when I was put out. But my heart has grown timid, constantly trying to protect itself from a fatal blow. I know now that I can survive out here. The question is whether I have the strength to really live.

The silence looms between us. Even the wind in the trees has fallen silent as if it, too, is waiting to see what will happen next. "I'm scared," I manage to get out, my voice a thin wire. "You're right. I'm so scared."

Bishop takes a step toward me, stops when I hold up a hand. If he touches me now, I will break apart. "Okay," he says, careful, like finally we're getting somewhere. "Scared of what?"

"Of you!" I choke out. "I'm scared of losing you again," I whisper, tears stinging against the backs of my eyes.

"Ivy . . ."

"I can't . . ." I breathe in slowly, try to calm my heart so that I can speak without my voice shaking. "I couldn't stand that again. I had to lock you away. Pretend you never existed. I tried so hard to forget you." Despite my best effort my voice breaks, my words turn watery. "That's the only way I could make it out here. And then you were back, right in front of me. And it was almost worse than not having you. The thought that I might have to suffer it all over again."

Bishop's eyes never leave me as I speak. That same look in them I remember so well, like he's seeing right to the heart of me. "I can't promise that I'll never hurt you, Ivy. Or that I'll always be here. Every day is a risk. There are no guarantees. Especially not in this life."

"I know that," I whisper. I give him a wobbly smile. "That's kind of the problem."

He closes the distance between us, not touching me, but right there in front of me. Solid and warm and strong and everything I told myself I could never have again. "I'm here now." He takes the final step and hooks a hand around my waist, pulling me in tight. "I'm exactly where I want to be."

Being so close to him startles the breath from my lungs, sends a tear trailing down my cheek. Bishop cups my face with his free hand, wipes away the tear with his thumb. "I'm still yours, Ivy," he whispers. "I always have been." His body is warm. His jacket smells like autumn, brittle-backed leaves and chilly sunlight. I watch my hands come up and flatten against his chest. My hands climb higher, skimming over his neck and face, fisting into his hair. My tears are coming faster now, streaming out of me like they haven't since the day I let go of the fence and stepped into this new world. I drop my head and rest my forehead against his shoulder. My tears soak into his jacket, sting my chapped lips.

"I'm sorry," I whisper on a hitched breath. "I'm so sorry." The words sound small to my ears, this apology that can never be big enough to encompass all the ways I've wronged him.

Bishop doesn't speak, but I can feel his uneven breaths against my hair, his hands rubbing my arms. My sweater slips off one shoulder, and his fingers find bare skin. The night air is cold and his hand is warm and my whole body catches fire. I turn my head and run my lips up his neck, kiss the line of his jaw until I find his mouth. Our kisses taste like salt and forgiveness, and I've never been so thankful for his arms around me, supporting me, holding me, weaving us together.

I feel hollowed out, but not empty. All my lies and secrets and fears are finally flowing out of me, leaving me floating. I'm light with the knowledge that Bishop and I have found our way back to each other. That in the end, we are stronger together than all the forces that tried to pull us apart. We belong to each other now. Not because someone forced us to marry or bound us with lies, but because we've chosen each other. And I understand in a way I never have before that loving someone is always going to feel like flying—the unthinkable drop, the fear of falling, the heart-in-your-throat thrill. It is always going to be impossible until the moment that it's not and you're soaring on pure faith, your altitude completely dependent upon something you can't control.

I pull back slightly, a breathless laugh when his lips chase mine. I trail my fingers over his face, the curve of his cheekbones, the line of his brow. For the first time since he got here, his eyes are twinkling with that barely suppressed amusement I remember so well.

I hold his face between my palms, stare into his eyes. "I love you, Bishop. I never stopped." It's the first time I've really told him how I feel, the sentiment not disguised as something else or hidden between lies. They are not easy words for me. They don't flow effortlessly off my tongue. My family taught me to keep them clutched tight, always stingy with the things that matter most. It will take work before the words come naturally to my lips, before what's in my heart doesn't feel like something I need to hide. I see the gleam in his eyes and tilt my head, the corners of my mouth lifting even as my tears still flow. "But you already knew that, didn't you?"

Bishop smiles. "Yeah," he says quietly. "I knew."

"How did you know?"

He brushes my hair off my face, touches his lips to my temple, my cheek, the sensitive skin below my ear. My eyes close, my heart beating in my throat. "Because for all the ways you've changed, you're still the same girl, Ivy, deep down. The one who says everything with her eyes, with her face, even when she refuses to speak. And I know that girl is brave enough to love me, no matter what it costs her."

Are most people this lucky? To find someone who really understands them? Someone who accepts all their strange and foreign ways of looking at and approaching the world without constantly trying to change them into someone more like themselves? Letting me be Ivy, when so many others have tried to mold me into a different kind of girl, is the most valuable gift Bishop will ever give me.

12

"I think I might actually prefer washing clothes to this," Ash says, causing me to raise my eyebrows over the deer carcass we're butchering. "I'm serious," she says. "It feels like this is all we've been doing lately."

"That's good, though, right? The more meat now, the easier winter will be."

"Yeah, I know." Ash sighs. "I'm just sick of blood and guts."

I huff out a sympathetic breath, thankful at least that the cold weather has eliminated the flies that used to collect around the dead animals in the heat of late summer. Back in Westfall I never got this close to the food I ate, never had to kill it myself or watch its blood soak into the dirt. Never carved it up and ate it later. I didn't know what hard work it was or how innately satisfying it would be once I got past the gore. Leaning back on my heels, I swipe my hair off my face with the back of my hand.

"When we get done with this, we still need to check the snares," Ash says.

"I'll do it," Bishop says from behind me. He's getting as good at walking quietly as Caleb and Ash.

I look up at him with a smile, shading my eyes from the early winter sun with my bloody knife. "You're finished already?"

"Yep, took down a couple trees and got them chopped up. Caleb's finishing stacking the logs."

"We're almost done here," I tell him. "If you want to wait, I'll go with you."

Bishop crouches down next to me, balancing one hand on his ax. With his free hand he brushes my ponytail off my shoulder, leans over, and kisses the tender skin below my ear. "I want to wait," he says, voice low.

I tell myself it's stupid to blush over a simple kiss even as my cheeks flame. "Okay," I croak, clear my throat. "Give me ten minutes."

"Oh my God," Ash groans. "You two are so disgusting. I think I liked it better when you weren't speaking."

Bishop laughs, pushes himself to standing. "You did not."

Ash smiles. "You're right. I didn't. But don't let Caleb catch you doing that crap. He'll give you an earful."

I go back to carving the deer meat, tell myself I don't still feel the imprint of Bishop's lips on my skin. "He has been grouchy lately."

"I think it's the lack of *walks*," Ash says with a meaningful glance in my direction. "We've been too busy for taking time off." She wiggles her eyebrows up and down and I grin, shaking my head.

"I'm lost," Bishop says. "He's grumpy because he misses walking?"

"I'll fill you in later," I tell him around a smile.

As if on cue, Caleb rounds the side of the house and glares at Ash and me, stabs a pointing finger in our direction. "Less talking, more doing!" he shouts without breaking stride.

I catch Ash's gaze, and we burst into laughter at the same moment. "See what I mean?" Ash says between giggles.

Ten minutes later I meet Bishop at the tree line behind the house, the worst of the blood scrubbed from my hands and an extra sweater layered over the one I'm already wearing. "You going to be warm enough?" Bishop asks.

"Sure. If we walk fast." I'm only half kidding. Caleb's been saying we're going to get an early winter this year, and if the rapidly falling temperatures are any indication, he's right. It's no wonder he's anxious about us stockpiling as much food as possible before the first snows hit. Winters now are harsher than they were before the war.

It's not uncommon for us to get more than a hundred inches of snow in a bad winter, and this one is promising to be bad. All the weather is more extreme since we blew the world apart. Hotter summers, colder winters, raging tornadoes, violent floods, unrelenting drought. I wonder what it used to be like, when the seasons didn't feel like just one more form of violence.

Bishop zips my sweater up all the way to my chin. "We need to get you a warmer coat before it snows."

"We'll find something. Don't worry," I tell him. "Come on." We lace our fingers together and head into the woods. I'm still getting used to the easy way we touch now, the way my hand seems to find his without my even thinking about it. These past few weeks have been the first time we've touched without the burden of secrets or fear. The freedom of it has made me greedy.

"Caleb thinks it's going to snow soon," Bishop says.

I give a little laugh, shake my head. "Westfall's not that far from here. How did we grow up not knowing this much about the weather?"

"Because we didn't have to. We trusted that someone else would take care of what needed doing."

I glance at him. "Someone like your father?"

We walk a few steps before Bishop answers. "I know you don't like him, Ivy. But he did a pretty good job of keeping most of us alive." He squeezes my hand before I can respond. "But he made us lazy, too. Unprepared for handling our own survival."

"You seem to be doing pretty well."

"I learned as much as I could. I tried to talk my father into teaching people the basics, so that they could survive if things ever went bad."

"He didn't like that idea?"

Bishop shrugs. "He thought it would cause people to panic. Think Westfall wasn't safe and secure." He gives a harsh little laugh. "As if anything can be safe and secure nowadays. It's all an illusion anyway."

We walk in silence for a bit, leaves crunching under our feet. I could swear the air smells like snow, although it's probably too early in the season, even with the promise of an early winter. I glance at Bishop. His cheeks glow a faint red in the cold, his alert eyes scanning the woods. He has a rifle slung across his back. Ash didn't speak to Caleb for an entire day after he gave it to Bishop. Just as in Westfall, guns are prized out here. But Caleb said from watching Bishop he knew he'd be patient, wouldn't take any unnecessary shots and waste bullets . . . unlike other people he could name. That's when Ash had stomped off. The rifle already seems like a natural extension of Bishop's lean frame, the same way Caleb's crossbow is a part of his.

"You love it out here, don't you?" I ask him.

He stops walking and turns to face me. "I love that I feel useful."

"You've always been useful," I protest, and he's shaking his head before I can even finish my thought.

"No, I haven't. Not really. We already have a president in Westfall. We don't need one just sitting around, waiting in the wings. Especially when he's not even interested in the position."

"Okay," I say conceding the point. "But it's more than that."

Bishop reaches out and pulls a piece of leaf out of my hair, crumbles it between his fingers. "I used to beg my father to let me have a job in Westfall. I would've been happy with anything. A patrol guard, working in the cotton fields. Anything. But he always said no."

"Why?"

Bishop sighs. "He thought if I worked a regular job, alongside everyone else, they'd start to see me as one of them. And he believed the only way to keep control was for people to look up to the president, see him as someone above them, not an equal." Bishop gives his head a little shake. "I used to sit in those council meetings and look around the room and wonder how I ended up there. No one ever asked me what I wanted. Everyone just assumed I would follow in my father's footsteps and be happy to do it. But I was so bored, restless every second. But out here, I have freedom. Out here, I'm no one's son. No one expects anything of me. I can be exactly who I want to be." He looks at me. "What about you? Is this where you want to stay?"

I'm not sure how to answer that question. I care about Ash and Caleb, more every day. I like living a life that's not filled with lies and is free of having to second-guess my every action for fear I'll give something away. I like making my own choices. But I'm not sure this is where I belong for the rest of my life. I don't know if this is where my story ends. "I feel like this is my life now. But I'm not sure it's my life forever. I'm just not sure what the next step is. Does that make sense?"

"Perfect sense." The sky is a dirty white above Bishop's head, all the trees around us stripped of leaves and their bark the color of ash. It's like the whole world has turned colorless except for Bishop's eyes, bright beacons in the unrelenting gray. "We don't have to have everything planned out. We can take it one season at a time. One day at a time."

My whole life I've been burdened with the knowledge that everything's been planned for me without my consent. The idea that I can just watch things unfurl organically, make decisions without always thinking about the end game, is something I'm still getting used to. Having choices is what I always wanted, but I still hate that it came at the expense of so many other girls' futures.

"Do you think everything's okay in Westfall?" I ask.

Bishop pauses, searching my face. "Do you want it to be?"

He always knows how to get right at the heart of what I'm feeling, slicing through all the unnecessary outer layers to find the kernel of truth. "I still want things to change there," I say. "And I always will. But I don't want anyone to get hurt. And I know my family, Bishop. They won't give up." On me, yes. On their plans, never.

"My father knows that," Bishop says. "I'm sure he's being careful. But we can't protect any of them, Ivy, not from out here. And we can't control what happens."

"I'm sorry you can't be there with your family," I say, guilt coloring my words.

Bishop gives me a small smile and pulls me into his arms. "I'm not. We may not be married anymore, but you're still the most important family I have." He opens his coat to wrap it around me. "You're shivering."

It's like being in a warm cocoon, and my head drops forward, my lips finding the open vee of his shirt. His skin is so hot against my cold mouth it makes my teeth ache, like swallowing fire. My arms are wrapped around his waist, and I ease my hands under his shirt, spread them across his lower back as I press myself even closer against him. He hisses in a breath and I start to draw my arms back. "Hands too cold?" I ask.

He tightens his hold on me. "No," he says. "That's not the problem."

I run my hands farther up his bare back, flatten myself against him. He sucks in another rough breath. Unlike that night in our bed back in Westfall, at least we are fully clothed this time. "Torture?" I ask him on a whisper as a smile slides across my face.

He tips his head down to mine. "The best kind."

It turns out all the snares we checked were full, and we returned with six plump rabbits swinging between us and a wild turkey Bishop shot on the walk back. We cooked one of the rabbits for dinner for the four of us to share. Not really enough meat to fill us up, but all we were willing to spare.

"You know what I miss?" I ask Bishop as we lie in bed after dinner, the small lantern still glowing on the bedside table. We've all been going to bed earlier and earlier as the days get shorter, running out of things to keep us occupied. It's going to be a long winter.

Bishop is sitting back against the headboard, and he tilts his head down and looks at me where I'm sprawled across him. "What?" He seems surprised, maybe because I don't mention Westfall very often, and this makes twice in one day.

"Those oatmeal cookies from the market." I can practically taste one, the mix of butter and oats melting on my tongue. I haven't gone hungry since Ash and Caleb found me, but the food is even more basic than what we had in Westfall. Nothing rich or decadent, nothing that lights up your mouth when you bite into it.

Bishop laughs and I elbow him in the side. "Your turn," I prompt. "Something you miss."

"Showers," Bishop says without skipping a beat.

"Ah, good one." The river isn't a bad place to wash in

warmer weather, but now having to haul water to the house and heat it up whenever we want a bath is exhausting and time-consuming. "Strawberries."

"You can't miss something that's not in season. You couldn't get strawberries in Westfall now, either."

"Hey," I say, "my game, my rules. And I miss strawberries."

Bishop shakes his head with a smile. "I think you're cheating."

"I'm not cheating! But fine, how about electricity? I miss electricity. Even though it didn't work half the time."

"Better," Bishops says. "I miss ice."

"They'll be plenty of that soon enough. Books."

"My grandfather's photo album."

Something in Bishop's voice makes me stop our game. I push myself up and straddle his lap so I can see him better. "You had to leave it behind." Of course he did. It's not like he could drag it along with him when he ventured beyond the fence. Practicality trumps sentimentality out here.

"Kind of hard to carry," he says with a small smile.

I rake my fingers through his hair, let my hand linger. "I miss my dad and Callie," I say. "Or the idea of them, at least." I miss being someone's daughter. Someone's sister. "Even though I probably shouldn't. I doubt they miss me."

"You might be surprised." Bishop runs his fingers over the scar on my forearm, tracing the silvery lines. "You leave a pretty big hole when you disappear." His hand on my waist tightens, pulling me closer. "And I miss my parents, too. But I had to make a choice, and I chose you. They knew what they were doing, Ivy. They knew you were taking the fall for your family, but they had you put out anyway."

"Your father?" I always figured Erin didn't really care about the facts. She just wanted a Westfall punished, and I fit the bill as well as anyone. But I was never sure about President Lattimer, what he really believed.

"I think he felt guilty about it," Bishop says. "After-ward. Putting you out." Bishop's hand moves upward to fiddle with the strap of my tank top, his fingers feathering against my skin, outlining my collarbone. "I think he did it as some sort of twisted gift to my mother."

Bishop's hands on me make it hard for me to concen-trate, hard for me to breathe. "What do you mean?"

"Like putting you out could make up for the fact that he always loved your mother more. Maybe by hurting you he was showing allegiance to my mother instead of yours. But it ate at him. He didn't fight very hard when he found out I was leaving."

"He knew?"

Bishop nods. "I finally told my dad either the guard would have to shoot me or I was going. He didn't try to stop me after that. Told the guard to let me leave." Bishop runs his hand down my arm, entwines our fingers. "He said he remembered what it was like to be in love."

"He said that?" I ask, surprised. It's hard for me to imagine President Lattimer being so open with his feelings.

"He was drunk." Bishop shakes his head slightly. "I'd never seen him like that before. I think he was finally admitting to himself that maybe he made a mistake all those years ago, not marrying your mother. That's how he's lived with it all this time. Telling himself he did the right thing."

"We wouldn't be here if he'd married her," I say. It's funny, when Bishop's father told me the story of my mother I'd thought he'd been a fool to let her go. But Callie and I would never have been born if he had. Bishop wouldn't exist. My mother would probably still be alive, but she wouldn't be my mother.

"No," Bishop says. "We wouldn't." He lifts my hair with one hand, uses the other to trace patterns on the back of my neck. It's like he's painting me with his hands, out-lining every part of me. We have both gotten so much better at touching.

"I've been angry with her," I admit. "With my mother. Ever since I learned the truth about her suicide. Angry that she left me. That she didn't love me enough to stay." Bishop doesn't say anything, just skims his hands down my back, fingers bumping over my spine. "But I'm trying to forgive her."

"She was so young," Bishop says. "And her heart was broken."

I nod. It's easy for me to forget sometimes that she was only nineteen when she died. Not much older than me. With two children already and a husband she didn't love. And the man she did love right there in front of her. Close enough to see but never have. The pain of it must have been unbearable. If it were me in her place, with Bishop just out of reach, I don't know how I would stand it.

"Maybe you and I are their second chance," I say, my own hands falling to rest on his stomach. "Your dad's and my mom's. Or does that sound stupid?"

Bishop shakes his head, pulls me closer with one warm hand around my waist. "Not stupid," he whispers against my mouth.

I wonder if my mother would approve of Bishop and me? Of her daughter giving her heart to the son of the man who broke her own? I like to think she would. Glad at least that President Lattimer's son had the courage to fight for what he wanted, that her own daughter had the strength to endure. Maybe the best way Bishop and I can honor the love between our parents is to try to rewrite a different ending to their story.

For the last few days I've been pretty sure that Bishop and Ash are up to something. Probably Caleb, too, although he's not quite as obvious. Every time I walk into a room, Bishop and Ash stop talking, their voices trailing off and quick glances passing back and forth between them. When I ask what's going on, they both look at me full of mock confusion and deny everything. And tonight cemented my suspicions, when Caleb invited me along with him to go pick something up from a friend of his. All four of us are already feeling the effects of an early winter, stir-crazy at being cooped up together for so many hours a day. Especially Caleb. So there's no way he'd pass up a chance to run an errand alone unless Bishop and Ash asked him to get me out of the house.

"Where are we going?" I ask Caleb as we trudge down the street. It hasn't snowed yet, but I can taste moisture in the air, the sky hanging so low and heavy I swear I can feel clouds pressing against the top of my head.

"I need to pick something up," Caleb says.

"Are you going to be more specific?"

Caleb glances at me. "Nope."

"Right," I say with a sigh. "Of course not." I may live in the same house with Caleb now, he may trust me in a way he didn't before, but he's still not someone who opens up. Getting him to talk sometimes feels like trying to pry open a locked vault with my fingernails. "Well, can you at least tell me what Bishop and Ash are up to?"

This time Caleb doesn't bother looking at me. "I have no idea what you're talking about."

"The whispering? The weird looks? Any of this ringing a bell?"

Caleb turns left when we reach the center of town, down a short street with only a couple of intact houses.

"I don't think they're up to anything," he says. From the tone of his voice I know I'm not getting anything more out of him.

"Fine." I sigh and follow him up the short walk to a house that looks precariously close to toppling over to one side. "Who lives here?" I ask.

"Andrew," Caleb says. "Have you met him?"

"Yeah, once or twice." I don't know Andrew well, but I remember him from when we were camped near the river. He was usually working in the garden, harvesting vegetables and hauling baskets of them for canning.

The front door opens before we knock and Andrew steps out, a large box in his hands. "Got it all ready for you," he says to Caleb. He looks over Caleb's shoulder and grins at me. "Enjoy! But be careful with it!"

"Umm . . . okay," I say with a confused look that only makes Andrew smile wider.

The box is big and unwieldy, but Caleb carries it with ease. My curiosity is killing me, but I don't bother asking what's inside. I already know Caleb won't tell me, and I'm not giving him the satisfaction of refusing my request.

When we get back, Caleb opens the front door and pushes it wide, motions for me to go in ahead of him. Bishop and Ash are standing in front of the roaring fireplace in the living room.

I've barely cleared the doorway when Ash cries, "Happy birthday!" flinging her arms outward. There's a small loaf of dark bread on the table between the couches and next to it what looks like a present, wrapped in printed cloth and tied with a fabric bow.

My eyes fly to Bishop, who is smiling. "Happy birthday, Ivy," he says.

"What?" I say, a grin sliding onto my face. "Is it even my birthday?" I know we're well into November now, but I don't know the exact date. It's almost impossible to keep track, and Caleb and Ash never seem that worried about the day on a calendar. They live by the seasons, the temperature in the air, and the leaves on the trees.

Bishop shrugs. "Right month. I figure we're close enough."

Ash sinks down and kneels in front of the table, pulls a handful of something small from a sack. "We even have birthday candles," she says, delighted. "I traded a rabbit for them. Elizabeth Granger made them special."

Behind me, Caleb has shut the front door, set the box on the floor. I turn and look at him. He's not smiling, not exactly, but his eyes are bright. "Hey," I say, "I thought you said you didn't do birthday cake and candles out here."

"We don't," Caleb says, moving up beside me. "But some besotted fool"—he tilts his head toward Bishop—"assured me this is how birthdays are properly celebrated. Even if it's bread instead of cake." Now he does smile at me, quick and warm. "Happy birthday."

"Thank you," I say, hit with a sudden flash of shyness, not sure where to look with everyone staring at me, unsure what to do.

Caleb gives me a gentle shove. "Get over there, before Ash works herself into a fit."

"Ha ha," Ash says, "very funny." She's stuck the candles into the bread and lit them, little droplets of wax already beginning to run down their sides. "We have to sing fast," she says with a laugh.

"We're singing?" Caleb groans.

Ash shoots him a look. "Yes. We're definitely singing."

Bishop wraps his arms around me from behind, his chest vibrating against me as he sings. Ash stands in front of me holding the bread, her grin big enough to split her face in two. And despite his protests, Caleb is right there next to her, singing loud and slightly off-key.

"Make a wish," Bishop says as I lean forward to blow out the candles.

This. I wish for exactly this. This is more than I ever thought I'd have. It seems greedy to wish for anything more. But there is more. The apple bread. A new-to-me coat, thick and warm with only a few mismatched patches in the wool. And, just when I think the surprises are over, from the box by the door Caleb lifts an ancient phonograph.

I laugh at the sight of it. I've never seen one in real life, only in the pages of book, and to have one appear here, of all places, seems like a kind of magic. Like Caleb has snapped his fingers and pulled a rabbit from a hat.

"It's Andrew's most prized possession," Caleb says. "So if we break it, he *will* kill us."

"He hides it in the summer when we're not here," Ash says with a roll of her eyes.

"Why did he lend it to us?" I ask.

Caleb glances at Bishop. "The besotted fool struck again. Traded him a deer for it."

I round on Bishop, eyes huge. "A whole deer?" I practically screech.

Bishop holds up both hands, laughing. "It wasn't one of ours. I took a separate hunting trip."

"Was that where you were last week? That day you disappeared?"

He nods.

"You shouldn't have given him a whole deer," I say. "That was too much. We—"

"Shhh," Bishop says, stepping into my body, which is pretty effective at shorting out my brain and quieting my protests. "No worrying on your birthday."

Ash is already shifting through the metal cylinders that accompanied the phonograph. "How do we know what's on these?" she asks Caleb.

He shrugs. "We don't. Just pop one on and see."

Ash grabs a cylinder at random and puts it in the phonograph, winds up the handle with careful hands. The music that pours out is scratchy, the voice of the man singing tinny and indistinct. But it's music all the same, and the sound reverberates around our small living room, bouncing off each one of us, hitting ears and skin and pushing smiles onto all our faces.

"Let's dance!" Ash says, her sock-clad feet already shimmying across the floor.

Caleb flops down on one of the sofas. "Not happening. This is where I draw the birthday line. There is no way I am dancing."

"I'm with him on this one," Bishop says, hooking a thumb toward Caleb.

Ash sticks her tongue out at them and grabs my hand, pulls me into the empty space between the front door and the kitchen. We dance like fools, like children, swinging each other back and forth, spinning under each other's arms and giggling, high pitched and ridiculous. We replace each cylinder with a new one when the song is done. Caleb and Bishop watch us, laughing when Ash slips and falls, clapping when we take our final bows, our cheeks flushed and sweat beading our brows. For those few minutes we are not facing a long, uncertain winter. We are not dreading the dreary days ahead. We have not lost anyone we love. We are young, and we are simply and completely happy.

We end the evening sitting quietly in front of the fire, listening to the cylinder spin one last song out into the golden air. Relaxed there, Bishop at my back, the firelight in front of me, the remains of my birthday bread on the table scenting the air with spice, I can feel the changes inside myself. I knew that beyond the fence I would have to become tougher, and those hard edges have been easier to accept than I thought they might. I'll never be Callie; I would never want to be. But I'm comfortable with the heft of a knife in my hand. Some part of me enjoys the backbreaking work it takes to survive each and every day. But there are also spaces inside me that are softer than they've ever been, spots that are now filled with warmth and joy—the sound of Ash's laugh, Bishop's hands on my face, the pure kindness of tonight.

Callie once told me that no revolutions are won without sacrifices, and she was right. She may have been talking about literal war, but the sentiment applies just as well to what's happening within me. I've lost so much, but I've gained something, too. Life beyond the fence is transforming me. Not into a new person, but back into the girl I've always been underneath all the layers my father and Callie built on top of me. Slowly, I am finding myself.

I am becoming Ivy again.

Later, Bishop and I are curled up in bed, the covers practically over our heads to keep out the cold. I kiss my way down the side of his jaw, the column of his neck. "Besotted fool, huh?" I whisper near his ear, unable to keep the laughter out of my voice.

Bishop groans. "I was hoping you forgot that part."

"Nope, no such luck."

He rolls me onto my back, slides his body over mine. I try to keep my eyes open, but they flutter shut, the firm weight of him sucking the air from my lungs.

"I take exception with the fool part," he says, his lips on my neck this time, moving lower. He bites down gently on my shoulder. "But besotted? Yeah, that sounds about right."

13

The strangers arrive with the first winter storm. Ice fell most of the night, tapping against the sides of the house, and even with a fire in our bedroom fireplace and Bishop wrapped around me under our pile of blankets, I wake up shivering. Bishop gets up first, stokes the fire, and ventures downstairs to bring me a warm cup of tea. The rest of the house is quiet, and I suspect Caleb and Ash are taking advantage of the weather to stay snug in their beds as well.

When Bishop returns with my tea, I sit up in bed to drink it, still shrouded in blankets. I'm dreading the moment my feet will hit the frigid floorboards, cold seeping through my socks and numbing my toes in seconds.

"Your nose is pink," Bishop tells me with a smile.

I press a palm to my nose, the tip of it icy against my skin. "I need to put the blankets over my head, I guess."

Bishop laughs, his own cheeks flushed from the morning cold. He pulls back the thick curtain over our bedroom window and peers out. "It's changed over to snow now," he says.

"Coming down hard?"

"Pretty hard."

I sigh. Caleb was right about winter hitting brutal and fast this year. I try to ignore the little bubble of fear in my stomach, the voice in my head that is constantly calculating how much food we have, how many months the cold will last, wondering which will run out first. Winters were bad in Westfall, too, but there I wasn't responsible for feeding myself. There were plenty of winters where food was scarce, where we ate oatmeal or jerky for meal after meal. But somehow I always took for granted that there would be *something* to eat. Now, beyond the fence, with the wind howling around the eaves of the house and snow piling up against its sides, starvation feels like a very real possibility two or three months in the future.

"Hey," Bishop says softly, drawing me out of my own head. "It's going to be okay." He crosses the room and sits down beside me on the bed, wraps his hands around mine on my mug. "*We're* going to be okay. Caleb and Ash know what they're doing. This isn't their first winter out here."

I nod. And he's right; I trust Caleb and Ash with my life. But I've already caught Caleb twice running his hands over the packets of jerky, counting the jars of pickled vegetables in the kitchen cabinets. "But maybe when this storm clears we can set some more snares," I say. "Just to be safe."

Bishop smiles. "Definitely." He takes the mug of tea from my hands and sets it on our bedside table. "But right now, it's too cold to get out of this bed." He lifts the covers and slides in next to me, pulls me down to lie beside him.

I tuck my face into the warmth of his neck, his stubble scratching against my cheek. "What did you have in mind?" I ask, already short of breath. I keep waiting for the day he doesn't have this instant effect on me, my stomach rolling over, my heart racing, my limbs gone limp and languid.

His hands skim down my sides, work their way back up. "Something warm," he says.

"Yes," I breathe out. "Warm sounds good."

Bishop laughs against my neck, causing a whole different kind of shivering. "Ivy?" he whispers.

"Hmmm?"

"Are you happy?"

It takes me a long time to answer. I find I'm reluctant to say the word out loud. Happiness is an emotion I don't fully trust yet. Like love, it's something I have to learn. Feeling it isn't enough. I nod finally, say "yes" in a voice that's lower than a whisper, and even then I feel like I'm tempting fate.

I should have known it could never last.

The day passes in the way I suspect many of our winter days will, the four of us sticking close to the big fireplace in the living room, trying to keep busy with card games and small chores. Things we can accomplish with blankets wrapped around our legs. With the shutters pulled tight against the cold and snow, it's impossible to tell what time of day it is or even to gauge how long we've been awake. I understand now why Caleb is always the first to volunteer to head out into the swirling snow. Too many hours inside this room and I'll go crazy. Only a few days in, and already it's hard to imagine passing an entire winter this way. Frostbitten fingers sounds like the lesser of two evils when the other alternative is insanity.

"We should probably get some more wood for the fire," Ash says, eyeing the dying flames.

"I'll go," I say, before anyone else can speak.

"I'll come with you," Bishop says.

"You don't have to, if you want to stay warm," I tell him.

"No, it's okay," he says. "I need the air." Obviously, I'm not the only one starting to feel the walls closing in.

I pull on my new coat and a pair of boots Ash managed to scavenge for me. She also gave me one of her extra hats and a pair of mittens. Once Bishop and I are bundled up, we head to the front door, but before I can open it someone knocks from the outside, loud and hard against the wood. I freeze, my gaze flying to Bishop and then to

Caleb, who's jolted upright from where he was napping on the couch. People knock on our door almost daily, but this violent pounding speaks of urgency. Or danger.

"Who is it?" Bishop calls, putting one hand out to scoot me behind him.

"Stuart," a man yells. "Stuart Murphy. I need to talk to Caleb."

"It's okay," Caleb says. "Let him in. I know Stuart."

Bishop opens the door and a man stumbles inside, bringing a swirl of snow and icy wind with him. "Caleb," Stuart says. "Three strangers showed up at Elizabeth Granger's house. Two men, one woman."

"Where are they now?" Caleb asks, already shrugging into his coat.

"We took them to the meetinghouse in the town square. They claim to be from Westfall but say they weren't put out." He glances at me and Bishop. "They say they left voluntarily."

"That's a lie," Caleb says. "No one would leave this time of year, face a winter out here alone." His face is grim. "The question is, why would they lie? And what else are they lying about?"

"That's why I came for you," Stuart says. "Figured you could talk to them before we decide what to do."

"We're coming, too," Bishop says. "If they are from Westfall, we may know them. Maybe we can help figure out why they're here."

Caleb nods.

"I'm coming, too," Ash says, and we all wait while she gets into her outdoor gear.

I have to agree with Caleb that there's no way these people are telling the truth. I can't imagine any reason why they would leave the relative safety of Westfall at the beginning of what's promising to be a horrible winter. It would be close to suicide to make such a decision.

The five of us trudge out into the fading daylight. The sky is smoky gray, flat and low. It's no longer snowing, but the wind whips tiny tornadoes of snow at our feet. Above us, a ragged vee of geese crosses the sky, honking to one another as they fly. Even bundled up, the air hits me like a slap in the face, rockets down into my lungs where it spreads frozen fingers under my ribs.

"God, it's cold," Ash breathes, her words turning to steam as she speaks.

Caleb rolls his eyes. "You have a real knack for stating the obvious."

No one laughs, and Ash doesn't respond. We are all too tense, worried about what we're going to find when we reach the town square, to be in the mood for joking. We walk as fast as we can through the snow, and even with the subfreezing temperature, it only takes a few minutes for me to warm up, sweat beading along my hairline under my hat.

The meetinghouse is located in the remains of the old restaurant in the town square. As we get close, I can

see lantern light spilling out through the one intact front
window. Around me, the rest of the group continues
moving forward, but I slow until I've fallen behind. Somewhere deep inside me, a warning bell is ringing, loud and
clear, telling me I don't want to take those final steps. I try
to tell myself I'm being ridiculous, but I can't shake the
feeling that walking into that building will set something
in motion that I will be powerless to stop.

"Ivy?" Bishop has stopped ahead of me. "Are you
okay?"

No, I want to say. *Don't go in.* But it's already too
late. Caleb has pushed the door open, the ancient bell
that hangs above it giving a shrill peal that quiets the
voices inside. I push my fears down, the same way I did
on the day I married Bishop, the same way I did when
I was put out beyond the fence, and follow Bishop into
the house.

The small space is crammed with people, the smell of
wet wool, firewood, and sweat barreling into my nose as
soon as I'm through the door. I pull off my hat and mittens and stuff them into my coat pockets. Already I'm
thinking of the clean, frigid air outside with fondness.

"Where are they?" Caleb asks the crowd.

A few people point to the far end of the room, and a
path opens up in the crowd, allowing us to snake through
toward the fireplace and the three ragged strangers
crouched around its warmth. At first it's hard to tell
which one is the woman. They are all curled over mugs of

stew, their hair thick with dirt and grease, worn blankets thrown over their shoulders.

They look up at us as we approach. The woman and one of the men appear to be in their midtwenties, the other man older by a good twenty years. Caleb stares at them, and then glances at Bishop and me. "Do you know them?" he asks.

Bishop shakes his head. "No."

I look at the woman and the younger man. Their faces are unfamiliar to me. But my eyes return to the older man. To his gaze, which never leaves mine. To his one useless arm, curled up against his chest. I remember taking raspberry jam from his good hand. I remember the feel of the note from Callie, buzzing against my palm. He is waiting for me to speak, waiting to see if I will save him.

"Yes," I say, finally. "I know him."

It turns out the woman is the jam man's daughter and the other man is her husband. They've been out on their own for a few weeks now, this storm the thing that would have killed them all if they hadn't seen the glow of a lantern from Elizabeth Granger's window and followed the beacon up to her porch, where they'd collapsed against her door.

Bishop has pulled a chair up next to them by the fire, but I am still standing, arms crossed and hands tucked protectively over my elbows. "I don't understand why you're out here," Bishop says. "If you weren't put out."

"We left," the woman says.

"But why?" Bishop asks. I want to tell him to stop. I already know I don't want to hear the reason, can tell from the way the jam man—whose name I've learned is Tom—watches me, his gaze a mix of pity and fear.

"Things have gotten bad in Westfall," Tom's son-in-law says. "It's . . . it's all falling apart."

Bishop finds my eyes and we stare at each other, remembering all the people we left behind. I think of my father's need for vengeance, Callie's thirst for power, and wonder what havoc they're wreaking now. Or maybe it's President Lattimer this time. Maybe he's making sure no one has any ideas about hurting his family ever again.

"Ivy," Tom says, and my body jerks, my eyes skipping to his. "Your sister."

Everything inside me freezes, like I left my body out in the cold and the ice is settling in my bones. "What about her?" I manage.

"She got caught, trying to break into the gun safe in the courthouse."

Caught because of me, because I gave her the wrong code. I can actually picture the moment in my mind, Callie's face furious and desperate, the thud of guards' footsteps rounding the corner. Callie left with nowhere to run. I don't realize I'm digging my fingers into my skin until I feel the stinging press of pain and force myself to loosen my grip. "What did they do to her? Are they putting her out?"

Tom looks down into his empty mug. A log slides forward in the fire, a hiss of smoldering bark, an explosion of sparks. "No. They're going to execute her."

I see the air leave Bishop's lungs, his head dropping down, but it's all very far away, like a bad dream, something that's not really happening. Something that maybe I can wake up from if I concentrate hard enough. "When?" I ask. Visions of Callie swinging from a rope, body riddled with bullets, blood staining the street, streak across my vision.

"The end of the month," Tom says. "They're waiting until things calm down. If they ever do. And I think President Lattimer would like to find your father first."

"My father?" I ask, my voice high and thin.

Tom nods. "He's missing. But I'm pretty sure he's still in Westfall. Hiding out in the woods, probably. There have been riots. Someone set fire to President Lattimer's house." Bishop's head whips up at that, but Tom's daughter jumps into the conversation before he can ask the question. "They got out in time," she tells him. "They're all right," and Bishop's body relaxes.

"But everyone's turning on everyone else," Tom's son-in-law says. "Selling out their neighbor in hopes of getting in the good graces of one side or the other. The police are all carrying guns now, arresting people right and left, sometimes just based on rumors."

"Sooner or later someone was going to find out what I did for you," Tom says. "For you and your family. We couldn't take the risk. We had to leave."

"Wait, what?" Bishop says. "What did you do for her?"

I would do anything to not have to answer his question, to not bring a reminder of all the ways I betrayed him back into our lives. But I've made a promise to myself that I won't lie anymore, especially not to Bishop. "He gave me messages from Callie. While we were married," I say, forcing myself to hold his eyes, to accept the quick flash of anger and pain as my due. It is a burden I've earned, so I will have to learn how to carry it.

But Bishop's voice is gentle when he speaks. "It's all right, Ivy."

I try to smile at him because I don't want to cry in front of all these people. But I can feel the weight of sadness pressing down on me. My secret interactions with Tom, the way I came so close to risking Bishop's life, the fact that this man and his family were forced to flee because of me, they all feel like bricks being stacked on my shoulders one by one, burying me under the weight of my own bad decisions.

Behind me the crowd shifts and Caleb moves closer to the fire. "We've found a place for you to stay. At least for now."

"Thank you," Tom says. He looks at me. "Thank you, Ivy."

"Don't thank me," I say, voice harsh. "I'm the reason you're out here at all."

The four of us eat a quick dinner after we return from the town square, and then Caleb and Ash decide to head back to the restaurant. Caleb wants to talk in more detail to the rest of the group about what's happening in West-fall. He is worried that if Westfall completely collapses, then these three strangers will be the first of many who will find their way here this winter. There needs to be some kind of plan to deal with a possible influx of new faces, especially during the lean months. After Caleb and Ash are gone, I leave Bishop to clean the dishes and climb the stairs to our bedroom.

My mind is spinning, random thoughts bouncing off the edges of my brain, making it hard for me to concen-trate. It takes twice as long as it normally would for me to start a fire in our bedroom fireplace, my fingers numb and clumsy. When I finally have it going, heat beginning to radiate out into the icy corners of the room, I sit on the edge of the bed, staring at nothing. Unlike Caleb, whose only concern is how Westfall's potential collapse might affect those of us outside the fence, I can't help but worry about the people still inside.

"Hey," Bishop says from the doorway. "Can I come in?"

I glance at him over my shoulder. "Of course."

He squats in front of me, balancing easily on the balls of his feet. He must have taken lessons from Caleb. My hands are hanging limp between my knees, and he takes them in both of his, presses a soft kiss to the back of my knuckles, first one hand and then the other.

"What are you thinking?" he asks. "What do you want to do?"

That's the question I've been asking myself in a nonstop loop for the last few hours. Balancing all the various options in my mind, thinking about my father and Callie. How they betrayed me. How I can't stop caring about what happens to them even though I wish I could. What leaving them to their fates will do to me. And I think about President and Mrs. Lattimer, too. I love Bishop, which means I owe something to his family; I have an obligation to the people he loves, even if I don't love them myself.

I look at Bishop, his clear green eyes, his beautiful face, his good heart that shines out of him like a beacon. Am I willing to risk hurting him again? Losing him? "I want to stay here," I tell him. "I don't want anything to change." I tighten my fingers on his. "But I need to go back."

"Why?" As always, not demanding, just asking, wanting to know exactly what I'm thinking.

"I hate her," I tell him. "So much of me hates her. For what she did, for what she tried to make me do. And I'm not stupid. I know she wouldn't risk anything for me. But even if I want it to be, my hate isn't big enough to sit back and let her be killed in the town square. Not without at least trying to stop it." I take a deep breath, brain flooded with images of Callie. "She's the first person I ever loved, Bishop. She's my sister." I don't know if he will understand, never having had a sibling, but for me, that's reason enough.

"What about your father?" Bishop asks.

"I want to try to find him, too," I say, "if we can. Maybe I can convince him to leave Westfall and start over again out here." Beyond the fence there is room for my father's dreams, a place where some of his best ideas could be implemented. Maybe, after everything, there's still a way to save my family.

"Do you think we can really help them?" Bishop asks.

I shake my head. "I don't know. And it's probably crazy to try. But it feels like I have to make the attempt. And what about your parents? Aren't you worried about them, if it's as bad in Westfall as they made it sound?"

"Of course I am. But my parents aren't helpless. We all have to take care of what's most important to us." Bishop squeezes my hands. "And for me, that's you."

"I know," I whisper. "It is for me, too."

"But?"

I look down at our joined fingers, his still faintly golden from the summer sun. Sun that seems a lifetime ago, and not just because now it is winter. "I wish it didn't, but this feels like what I'm supposed to do. What I have to do. My family . . . Westfall . . . they feel like unfinished business. Before today, something bad happening in Westfall, something bad happening to our families, was only a theory. But now we know for sure." I pause, searching for a way to explain something I don't even really understand myself. I raise my eyes to his. "You told me you weren't like my father or Callie. That you couldn't just let me go. I'm not like them, either. I can't stay here and let her die. I can't move on without at least trying to help my father."

"If they catch you, Ivy, they'll kill you." Bishop's face pales as he speaks; his throat muscles work. "And I don't know if I'll be able to stop them."

I already know the risks. Bishop can go back to Westfall. I cannot. Not without putting my own head on the chopping block. "Then I guess I better not get caught," I say, with a pathetic attempt at a smile.

He stares at me. I wonder what he sees? I hope it's something good. I hope it's someone he can still love. I'm being so selfish, asking him to be all right with me putting my life on the line for the very people who planned his death. If the situation were reversed, I don't know if I could let him go. I don't know if I could forgive him for asking it of me. "Okay," he says finally. "Then we go back."

I'm already shaking my head before he's done speaking. "No, you don't have—"

"Yes, I do, Ivy," he says, his voice harder, his gaze sharper. "Where you go, I go. We're *together*. And if this is what you need to do, then it's what I need to do, too. That's the only way this is happening." There it is again, that wall of strength in Bishop, that core of steel. The one I know no amount of pushing will crack. His thumb slides over the back of my hand; his fingertips find the rapid pulse of my wrist. "All right?"

"All right," I say. Sometimes I still forget that we are a team now. We have each other's backs, no matter what. I've never had that before, the security of knowing someone will love me even if he doesn't always agree with me. Bishop's love for me isn't dependent on conditions. He doesn't love me because of what I can do for him or what I represent. He loves me. Full stop.

I slide off the edge of the bed and pull him to standing, wrap my arms around his neck, and hold on tight. When he kisses me, it lights me up, just like always. But this time there's something fizzing in my blood, hot and anxious and not eased at all by the feel of his mouth on mine, his hands touching me through layers of clothes. The edge of this hunger is sharp and desperate, and it demands more than I've given it so far.

I pull away from Bishop just enough to yank my sweater and shirt over my head and toss them aside. I unclasp my bra and let it slide down my arms. The chill air plays over my bare skin, and I shiver.

"Ivy . . ." Bishop says, a question in his voice. I silence him by reaching out and grabbing the bottom of his shirt. He doesn't say anything more, keeps his eyes on mine as he lifts his arms, lets me pull off his shirt and drop it next to my own on the floor.

"Remember back in Westfall?" I say, breathless. "When I said I wasn't ready to have sex?"

"Yes," Bishop says, voice low.

"I'm ready now." I take a step closer to him and put my hand on his warm chest. His heart pulses against my palm. "Are you?" I ask, because I'm not the only one with a voice in this conversation. This isn't a decision that's mine alone.

Bishop's mouth curls up a little as he looks at me; his eyes flare. "Yes," he says again. "I'm only human, Ivy, and you're . . . you." He runs both hands up my arms, traces the jutting bones of my collar with his fingers. My head falls back a little, my whole body melting, like my skin is filled with liquid instead of bone and organs. But when I move up against him, he stops me, slides his hands to my waist. I can feel the imprint of each individual finger against my skin. "But why now? Is it because we're going back?"

"Yes," I say, thinking about how if the worst happens, I don't want to die without knowing what it's like to love Bishop in every way I can. "No," I say, so aware that my desire for him, my longing, has nothing to do with a fear of the future. "I don't know. Does it matter?"

"It matters," he says. "I don't want you doing this because you're scared."

"I am scared," I tell him. "I'm going to *be* scared, probably for a while. But that's not why I'm doing this. I'm doing it because I love you. I'm doing it because I want to." I put my other hand next to my first on his chest, run them both up to his neck, push myself forward until our torsos meet, everything between us swirling and sparking like a fresh branch thrown on the fire. Cold seems like a distant memory. "I want to see you naked. I want to touch you. I want you to touch me. I just . . . *want*." And maybe my words should shame or embarrass me, along with the shake in my voice, my breathing high and fast, the sheer need in my tone. But this is Bishop. And he's already stripped me bare in ways that have nothing to do with taking off my clothes.

He doesn't second-guess me after that. And I don't second-guess myself. Neither of us makes the moment, the decision, bigger or smaller than it actually is. Bishop and I together will always be more than what's happening tonight in this bed. But this is also the most intimate thing we've ever done, this act we've chosen to do only with each other. No one else knows the secrets we are sharing with our bodies. Only I know the taste of his skin beneath my tongue. Only he knows the way my back arches as he moves above me. Only I know the sheer joy of watching calm, steady Bishop fall apart under my hands.

14

I'm alone in our bed when I wake in the morning. From downstairs, I can hear Ash's voice, the banging of dishes in the kitchen. And Bishop's deep voice in response, making me remember the things he whispered into my ear last night in this bed. I roll onto my back, trying to fight the ridiculous grin that's spreading across my face, the hot blush racing up my body into my cheeks. I stretch, feeling the pull and give of my muscles. Not sore, exactly, or at least not a soreness that really hurts. Not one I would ever wish away.

There's a fire crackling in our fireplace, but I still take a fortifying breath before I tumble out from underneath the warm pocket of blankets, brace myself for the biting cold against my nakedness. I scramble into clothes as fast as I can, tug on a pair of socks, and knot my hair up on top of my head. I'm at the bottom of the steps when I'm hit with an unexpected wave of shyness. I can still hear Bishop and Ash in the kitchen, and I assume Caleb is in there with them. I know it's silly, but I feel like I have a giant sign on my forehead that Caleb and Ash will be able to read, outlining exactly what Bishop and I were doing last night. It's not like Caleb would even care. He's done the same thing on plenty of his walks, I'm sure. And Ash would probably just squeal and pull me aside for details I'd refuse to give her. But last night feels private in a way that I'm anxious to protect. So few things in my life have been solely mine, and what happened last night belongs to Bishop and me alone.

In the kitchen, Bishop and Ash are leaning against the counter while Caleb sits at the small table, dozens of packets of jerky laid out in front of him. Before I can ask him what that's about, Bishop smiles at me, and Ash holds out a mug of tea.

"Morning, sleepyhead," Bishop says. His eyes are locked on mine, and I can't look away, even as I reach out to take the mug from Ash's hands.

"Good morning," I say, surprised by how hoarse my voice sounds.

Bishop steps closer and leans his face down, presses a tender kiss against my neck.

"Could you not sleep last night?" Ash is asking. "You're usually up before this."

I feel Bishop smile against my skin. "Uh-huh," I manage, heat rising up from my stomach. Bishop pulls back, one arm wrapping around me to rest on my hip. I let my gaze settle on Caleb and the table, which feels like the safest option. "What are you doing with all the jerky?"

Caleb looks at Bishop. "I told them we're going back to Westfall," Bishop says as I lift the mug to my mouth.

"Oh." My sip of tea hits my stomach like a ten-pound rock. I'd almost forgotten about Callie and Westfall, about vowing to return, my mind too occupied with Bishop. Hearing it out loud makes it real, makes it a commitment I'm going to see through. "That's too much jerky for us to take, though," I say. "That's almost all we have, isn't it? You and Ash will need that for the rest of the winter."

Now Caleb looks at Ash. "We're coming with you," he says.

Bishop stiffens next to me, his fingers digging into my hip. "No," I say, before he can. "No, you're not."

"We are," Ash says.

Caleb catches my eye. "We're not asking, Ivy."

Bishop's arm drops from around me as he takes a step closer to the table. "The hell you aren't," he says. "We're not letting you two do this. You have no idea what you're walking into."

Caleb shrugs. "Figure we've handled worse."

"Maybe you have," I say, voice unsteady. "But this isn't your fight. You'd be risking your lives."

"You're our family now," Ash says. "Both of you. You can't expect us to sit back and watch you walk into a bad situation without our help."

I shake my head. My hands are starting to tremble, and I turn to set my mug down on the counter. I thought I'd been so clever, making sure to keep Caleb and Ash at just the right distance. Close enough to feel affection for them, but not close enough to really love. But I was so stupid, because of course I love them. How could I not? They've been more a family to me than the one I was born into. "This is all because of me," I say. "Because of things I did. Or didn't do." I look at Bishop. "It's hard enough knowing that going back puts Bishop at risk. I can't live with it if something happens to anyone else I care about."

Caleb leans back in his chair, crosses his arms. He appears completely unmoved by my words. "Will us being there help you?" he asks. "Will it give you more of a fighting chance?"

"What . . . that's not . . . that's not the point," I stammer.

"Will it?" He's looking at Bishop now, and I can see something passing between them, the silent communication that began from almost the moment they met and has strengthened every day since.

"Yes," Bishop says.

Caleb nods. "Then we're coming. End of story."

"Caleb," I say, "please. You don't need to do this."

Something in Caleb's eyes softens just a bit at my words. He gives me a small smile. "This time it's not on you, Ivy," he says. "It's our choice. And we're not letting you and Bishop go in there alone."

I look at Ash, begging her with my eyes, but she only nods at Caleb's words. "Besides," she says with a grin, "I've always wanted to see Westfall."

We spend the rest of the day preparing. Bishop and Caleb talk for hours with Tom, getting all the information and detail they can about exactly what's happening in Westfall. Bishop returns in the late afternoon looking grim and exhausted, filled with stories about armed men ransacking the houses on my family's side of town, pistol-whipping anyone who gets in their way. Stories of houses burning on his side of town, the powder keg underneath Westfall's calm exterior finally catching fire. And it all started with me, my attempt to kill the president's son. Tom said after I was put out, people allied with President Lattimer suspected my father of having more involvement than he'd admitted. They pushed, harder than they had before, and my father and his allies pushed back. Tensions already high were poised on the edge of boiling over. And then Callie was caught outside the gun safe.

"She's in the cells in the courthouse," Bishop tells me. I wonder if she's in the same one I occupied. Just thinking of those cinder-block walls makes me feel claustrophobic. "Or at least she was." I'm going through our meager collection of clothing, figuring out how much we can carry, what needs to go and what has to stay.

"So how do we get her out?" I ask.

"We have weapons," Bishop says. He faces me across the bed, grabs a sweater to fold. "But it's not like we can just burst into the courthouse, guns ablaze. There are only four of us. Maybe it would have been enough, before, when everything was calm. But now they're going to be on edge, with extra men and guns. They'd take us down before we got ten feet."

I hold up a shirt, debating whether it offers enough warmth to bother taking it with us, before tossing it aside with a sigh. My mind churns. "We need someone to let us in."

Bishop's eyebrows rise. "And who's going to do that? Not even I will be able to talk my dad into that one."

I pause, look up at him. "Victoria. No one knows the courthouse better than she does."

I can see Bishop turning the idea over in his head. "Why would she do that?" he asks finally. "She's no fan of Callie's."

"Who is?" I ask, and we smile at each other, grim and quick. "But I think she might do it anyway. No matter what, I can't imagine Victoria is one hundred percent on board with executing Callie in the town square." I shrug. "Maybe if I talk to her, if *we* talk to her, we can get her to help us."

"It's a risk, Ivy," Bishop says. "What if she blows our cover? What if she tries to kill us herself?"

"This is all a risk," I say, frustrated. More with myself than him. I wish I could talk myself out of going, find some loophole in my conviction that if I don't finish what my family started in Westfall I'll never be able to fully move on, some part of me forever stuck. "But that's the best idea I have. I think it's worth considering."

Bishop nods. "Okay, let's keep it on the table for now. See what develops."

"Before we even get to the point of rescuing Callie, we have to get back inside Westfall," I remind him.

"That's not going to be a problem."

I raise my eyebrows. "It's not?"

"I'm Bishop Lattimer. The president's son. The patrol guard will let me back in."

"What about the rest of us?"

"He lets me in. I bash him over the head, knock him out." Bishop spreads his arms. "You're in."

I can't help the smile that slides across my face, even as I'm shaking my head. "That easy, huh?"

Bishop smiles back, but his voice is serious when he says, "It better be. That's the simplest part of this entire plan."

I look down at the pile of clothes on the bed. I hate being reminded of the risks we are all taking. The risks Bishop is taking for me. But even filled with fear over what's coming, uncertainty about how we're going to attain our goal, I'm suddenly grateful for this moment, this conversation.

"What?" Bishop asks, reading my face as easily as always.

"I was just thinking how different this is, the way we're talking. With my father and Callie, they were always the planners. They made all the decisions without ever asking my opinion. I was expected to keep quiet and do what they said. Sit in the corner like a potted plant until they needed something from me."

Bishop snorts out a laugh. "Which is probably the reason their plan failed so spectacularly."

"You mean because I'm no good at keeping my mouth shut?"

Bishop's smile fades. "No, because you're too smart and too valuable to be a potted plant."

How does he do that? With just a few words, he turns me inside out. My throat knots up, but there's no time for weakness now, no time for tears. His eyes darken as we look at each other, and I would swear the temperature in the room is rising, pure heat radiating off both our bodies. I am suddenly acutely aware of the bed between us.

"Hey," Bishop says. "Last night?"

Images of our tangled bodies flash across my vision. "What about it?" I manage, my voice husky.

Bishop reaches across the bed and cups my cheek in his hand, runs his fingers along my jaw. My breath stutters out of me. "No regrets?"

"Not a single one." I turn and press a kiss against his palm. "Part of me is wondering why we didn't do it sooner." But I know why not; it wouldn't have been the same if we'd come together with lies between us, with the shadow of my father's plan hanging overhead. We needed to be wiped clean before we could start building something new.

Bishop smiles. "Yeah? So does that mean there are better than even odds of it happening again tonight?"

I laugh, the tension that's been enveloping me all day dissolving into happiness. "I think that's a pretty safe bet."

We leave town at daybreak, all four of us burdened with heavy packs across our backs. Caleb's holds blankets and a single large tent that will serve as nighttime shelter as we make our way back to Westfall. The rest of us carry a mix of clothes, food, water, and our scant medical supplies. I double check twice to make sure my knife is in the sheath at my waist, and I see Ash doing the same. Bishop has his rifle, and Caleb isn't going anywhere without his crossbow. We are as ready as we can possibly be, both for Westfall and what we might encounter along the way.

I stop on the edge of town, turn back to watch the curve of the sun inching up over the still-sleeping houses. A few curls of smoke lift up from chimneys, swirl into the gray morning sky. The air is so crystal clear it looks like you could hit it with a fist and it would shatter around you, crisp and thin as glass. Above me, the sharp call of a crow. To my right, the crack of a branch in the river. Behind me, the icy wind creeping into the collar of my coat. I tell myself to remember these things, this moment. Somehow I already know I will not pass this way again.

"Hey," Bishop says. "Are you all right?"

I turn toward him, nod. One look at his face, the way his eyes move from me to the silent houses behind me, and I know he feels it, too. We are saying a final farewell to a place that was good to us. It might never have been home, not quite, but it sheltered us, kept us alive. But we have each other now, and that is enough.

"Come on," I say. I hold out my hand, fingers stiff inside my mitten, and Bishop grasps it with his gloved hand. I don't shed any tears as we walk away, following Caleb's steady pace into the trees. Already I am getting better at letting go.

For most of the first two days, Caleb and Ash take turns leading the way. They seem to effortlessly know the exact path to follow. I'm able to discern the general direction we should be headed, but don't know the terrain well enough to get us back to Westfall by the quickest and easiest route.

The ground is snow-covered in some parts, a soup of slushy mud in others where the sun has done its work. The nights are a mix of relief at being off our feet and sheer misery at lying on the cold ground, wind easing under the edges of the tent no matter how hard we try to seal off all entry points. The first night, after a few hours of trying to give each other a little space, we give up and smash together—Bishop and Caleb on the outside, Ash and me curled around each other in between. I only manage to sleep once I can feel Bishop's heart against my back, Ash's stomach under my arm.

On the morning of the third day, Caleb and Bishop are walking ahead, Ash and I behind them, both of us gnawing on half-frozen pieces of jerky. The air is so frigid it makes my gums throb every time I open my mouth for a bite. "Bet you're wishing you hadn't volunteered for this," I say, breath puffing out of me in frosty clouds of steam.

Ash glances at me, her wool hat pulled all the way down to her eyebrows. It makes her look younger, more vulnerable somehow. "What, you mean because it's cold?" She shrugs. "Cold where we were, too. At least this way we're all together. Beats sitting in that house for another winter with only Caleb to stare at. Last year there were a couple of times I thought I might actually kill him, just for something to do."

I laugh, but her words make me feel small, silly to have questioned her loyalty even in jest. "Thank you," I say quietly.

She bumps her shoulder against me. "For what?"

"For being my friend." I bump her back. "For coming with us."

"It was never even really a question," Ash says, "not for either one of us. For so long, it was just Caleb and me and my dad. I mean, we had everyone else, but they weren't family. And after my dad . . . we still had each other, but we didn't feel quite like a family anymore."

"And then I came crashing into your life," I say with a smile.

Ash smiles back. "Yep. And it's been *good*, Ivy. Bishop and you, you turned us into a family again. And we don't turn our backs on family. There's no way we were letting you two take on Westfall alone."

I look down at the piece of jerky in my hand, no longer hungry, my stomach curling in on itself. I hate that I'm putting Ash in jeopardy to help someone who will never be a tenth of the person she is. "You've already been more of a sister to me than Callie ever was," I say.

"It's okay," Ash says. "You don't have to explain it to me, why you need to go back. It's enough that you do."

We've caught up to Caleb and Bishop, who have stopped walking, both focused on the ground, foreheads furrowed. Ash opens her mouth to speak, and Caleb silences her with one sharp look, points down to our feet. There are footprints in the snow. Bigger than Ash's. Bigger than mine. So probably a man. The footprints veer off into the brush to our right and disappear. Caleb gives

Bishop a look and motions Ash to follow him. Bishop holds back with me for a few seconds before we continue on behind Ash and Caleb.

"What are we doing?" I ask in a whisper.

"Figuring out who that is," Bishop whispers back. "And what they want."

"How—"

"Just keep walking," Bishop says. "Stay with Caleb." Before I can ask him anything else, he's stepped into the trees to our right. Within seconds, he's melted away into the maze of gray branches. I want to follow him, my body turning toward the spot he disappeared, but I force myself to keep walking forward, eyes on Caleb's back. If it were only my life on the line, I would probably crash after him, instructions be damned. But I don't want to do anything to endanger Bishop. My blood is pounding in my chest, my ears straining for any sound of him. I know Bishop can handle himself, that he's as good as Caleb at navigating these woods. He's strong and he has a gun. My brain knows all that. My heart isn't quite getting the message, throbbing painfully against my ribs. The base of my neck is knotted with nerves, like someone is yanking hard against the top of my spine.

We've been walking silently for what feels like an hour but is probably only a quarter of that when I hear branches breaking behind us, something big and thrashing cutting through the trees. Caleb whirls, crossbow already off his back and aimed into the woods in the direction of the sound. Ash and I flank him, knives out of their sheaths, poised and ready to fly.

Bishop crashes out of the woods, Mark Laird stumbling along next to him, his head caught in the crook of Bishop's arm. Seeing Mark doesn't bring even the slightest shock to my system, and I realize I've been prepared for this moment since the day he disappeared. He was never going to stay gone.

My frantic eyes look for damage, but all they can find on Bishop is a split lip, and I'm able to take a full breath for the first time since he walked into the trees. Mark, on the other hand, is looking worse for wear, and not only from the beating Bishop has obviously given him. He's much thinner than the last time I saw him, his cheeks hollow and eyes sunken, hair matted with dirt. His clothes are shredded to almost nothing; it's a wonder he hasn't frozen to death already. He doesn't look like a sweet cherub doll anymore. He looks rabid, like if I waved a hand in front of his mouth, he'd tear the flesh from my bones.

"He was following us," Bishops says, out of breath, but not loosening his hold on Mark's neck. "He'd circled back around."

Caleb takes a few steps closer to Mark, and Ash and I do the same. "All this time," Caleb says, "you've just been waiting instead of finding shelter, a new place to live? You're even dumber than I thought."

Mark raises his eyes to Caleb, a thread of bloody saliva hanging off his lower lip. "You aren't going to beat me," he says, voice a harsh rasp. His eyes skip over to me. "That bitch doesn't get to win."

Bishop's arm jerks against Mark's neck, hard, and Mark gasps out a choking moan, his hands flying up to try to pull Bishop's arm away. "Shut up," Bishop says in that same flat voice I heard when he talked to Mark through the fence. "And guess what? You're the one trapped and bleeding, so I think we've already won."

"This time," Mark says. He's not getting enough air, his words weak and reedy. "Just this time."

There's a beat of silence that lengthens into hours, fat and ripe with possibility. And then Bishop says, even and quiet, "This is the last time."

My whole body goes still at his words at the same time that Mark begins to fight, flailing and kicking, desperate, the meaning behind what Bishop's said sinking in. But Bishop holds on, gives a slight grunt when Mark catches him in the ribs with an elbow, but doesn't loosen his grip. It takes less than a minute for Mark to wear himself out, head hanging low, air gusting out of him in uneven bellows. Blood drips off his face into the dirty snow at his feet.

Bishop looks at Ash, looks at Caleb, looks at me. Waits. He's reading our faces, searching for a sign that we want him to stop. Waiting for a sign I won't give him. Because I know what has to happen. Mark's already had more than one second chance. He's earned this ultimate punishment, earned it through pain he's doled out, lives he's taken, innocence he's stolen. And if I'd finished what I started that night on the riverbank, then Bishop wouldn't have to be the one doing it now. So I keep my gaze on Bishop when he jerks the arm he has around Mark's neck upward, tightens it against Mark's throat. I center myself with Bishop's unflinching eyes as Mark's life is choked out of him—his gasping breaths eventually fading into silence, his drumming feet slowing to a stop. I don't look away when Bishop finally lets go, Mark's body crumpling to the ground.

We leave Mark's body where it fell and keep moving. We don't have the tools to dig him a grave in the frozen earth, even if he were worth the effort. None of us talks much the rest of the day. Bishop takes up the rear of the procession, and I can tell he wants to walk alone. It reminds me of the night he pushed Dylan from the roof, the solitary walk he needed to come to terms with what he'd done. So I give him space and walk silently in front of him, hoping in some small way that the simple fact of my presence will bring him comfort.

When we stop for the night, Caleb manages to catch two small rabbits, and while Bishop and Ash set up the tent, I gut them and cook them over the fire. Almost as soon as we're done eating, Ash and Caleb retreat to the tent, Ash mumbling something about being extra tired. It's not a particularly convincing excuse, but I'm grateful for it anyway. Neither Ash nor Caleb seems affected by Mark's death. They are practical about this world we live in. Out here we don't always have the luxury of making moral judgments like right or wrong. Sometimes it is simply kill or be killed. But I think they want to give Bishop and me a chance to talk privately. Caleb lays his hand briefly on my shoulder as he passes, squeezes once, before disappearing behind Ash into the tent.

The fire we used to cook the rabbits is dying down, but still gives off some warmth. I scoot closer to Bishop, watch the way the firelight plays over the line of his jaw. He turns to look at me, his face grim.

"I killed him," he says. They're the first words he's spoken since Mark. He holds his arms out in front of him, fingers splayed. "With my bare hands." He laughs, a hollow rasp. "Well, with my bare arm, if we're being technical."

I suck in a breath. I don't want to say the wrong thing, don't want to blurt out something that's going to hurt instead of heal. I take his hands and fold them between mine. "They're good hands," I say, remembering all the ways he's touched me with those long fingers, all the ways he's used those hands to comfort and love me. "You're a good person, Bishop."

He flinches just a little. "I don't know if you can still say that after today." When he tries to draw his hands back, I hold on, tighten my fingers.

"Yes, I can."

He stops fighting my grip. "You want to know the worst part?" he asks, eyes back on the fire. "I don't even regret it. I'm just glad he's one less thing I have to worry about.

I never have to think about him hurting someone else. Never have to worry that he's going to hurt you again."

"That doesn't make you a bad person. It's like you told me back in Westfall—the world is brutal now. It's *hard*, and sometimes we have to be hard, too, just to live in it." He turns to look at me, and I let go of his hands so I can run my fingers lightly over the swollen corner of his mouth. "And it's going to change us. There's no way it won't. But what you did today, it doesn't alter what's at the heart of you, Bishop. You're still the best person I've ever known."

He doesn't speak, just leans toward me and kisses me. I shift and pull him closer, thread my fingers through his hair. When we move apart, I put my head on his shoulder, watch the dying flames dance in the wind.

"What happened with Mark," Bishop says, "it made me think about where we're headed, what we're going to do when we get there." He kisses the top of my head, leaves his lips against my hair as he speaks. "And I can't see it ending any differently than today."

I shift my head so I can see him. "You're going to strangle my sister?"

Bishop laughs, and I'm not sure what it says about the people we are becoming that we can make light of what happened so soon. All I know is I'm thankful for the sound of Bishop's laughter, the smile that lifts all the way to his eyes. "Don't think I haven't considered it," he says. "But no." He wraps a strand of my hair around his finger, gives it a gentle pull. "I just mean, even if we're able to help her, even if we do this for her, I don't think she's going to be any different, Ivy. Some people ... some people never change, even when they should."

"I know," I say, because he's probably right.

"It's like when I gave that food to Mark when he was first put out. Looking back now it was so stupid and pointless —"

"It wasn't," I protest.

"It *was*," Bishop says. "A guy like that, a person like that, he's never going to change. No matter how much other people did for him or how many chances he got, he was always going to be the same terrible person. And I don't think Callie's any different."

It seems unfair somehow, the sharp stab of pain his words brings. As if I should be beyond feeling such grief over Callie. He's not telling me anything I don't already know. Not telling me anything I didn't already figure out myself that day in the courtroom when I saw Callie talking to Bishop, already trying to work her way into his good graces.

"I think my needing to go back has more to do with me than it does with Callie," I tell him. "Or my father."

"What do you mean?"

"I could go on with my life, our life, out here. Leave Callie and my father to their fates, the same way they did with me. And I'd probably be okay with that, actually. For a while at least." I sigh, push the toe of my boot against a blackened stick that's fallen from the fire, watch it crumble to ash. "But it would eat at me. I wouldn't be able to forget it. Just letting Callie be killed, not at least trying to stop it? Not making the attempt to help my father? It would leave a little rotten spot, right here." I push my fist into the soft space beneath my rib cage. "Something that would only get bigger and darker with time." I shake my head, hating the wobble in my voice. "And I don't want to live with something like that inside me."

I slide my eyes toward Bishop, sure I sound crazy to his ears. I sound halfway crazy to my own. But his gaze is tender, heating my skin far more than the fire.

"I love you," he says quietly.

I want to take his words, the truth of them I can see on his face, and cup them in my hands like a glowing coal from the fire. Keep them with me warm and bright, a talisman.

"I love you, too," I tell him, thinking about each word as I say it, putting everything I feel into each syllable. I hope I'm giving him back what he's just given me. Something to hold on to. A touchstone against the darkness we are walking toward.

16

The dead girl's bones are covered in snow. But not completely. I can see a flash of bone sticking up through the icy crust; a rounded lump up above that is probably her skull. I don't point it out to anyone, but I know from the stiffening of Bishop's shoulders that he's seen her, too. The four of us are crouched in the trees, the gate in the fence directly in front of us, the early-morning sun painting the ground with gold and pink.

"Is this where they put you out?" Bishop asks me.

I can feel Ash watching me as I answer. "No. It was another gate. Farther west."

Bishop nods. "They don't use that one as much."

"Probably hoping if they put me farther from the river I'd die before I found water."

Caleb makes a disgusted noise at the back of his throat, but his eyes remain on the gate. "Now what?" he asks.

We're all exhausted, hungry, and worn down, and I wish there were some way for us to regroup, have a few days of warmth and good food before we walk back into Westfall. But that's never going to happen, so the best thing to do is push on before we use up even more of our reserves.

"The patrols come along here every day," Bishop says, nodding toward the fence.

"How many men?" Ash asks.

"Sometimes two. Sometimes just one. I'm guessing with everything going on inside Westfall, they won't want to spare two men out here checking the fence. When the patrol comes around, I'll get him to let me back inside."

We linger in the shadows of the trees, eating jerky and sharing water from our two canteens. I don't ask Bishop if he's sure about the plan or tell him to be careful; he knows what he's doing, and from now on we'll all be as careful as we can be. When I'm just at the point where I think I'll need to move or go insane, I hear the crunch of boots over snow. Caleb holds up a hand, even though we're silent already.

Bishop grabs my hand, squeezes it once, and lets go. He moves out of the trees and toward the gate as I shift onto my knees, torso pressed against the tree in front of me, eyes glued on his back. He reaches the gate at the exact moment a patrol guard steps into sight on the Westfall side of the fence. He almost pinwheels backward at the sight of Bishop, hand falling to his gun.

"Hey," Bishop says, keeping his voice calm and even. "I'm Bishop Lattimer. I need to get back in."

The guard hasn't moved, and his hand hasn't left his gun, either. Next to me I feel Caleb slide his crossbow off his back. He does it without making a single sound.

"I thought you were gone," the guard says. It's hard to tell how old he is. He's bundled up against the cold in a hat and a dark scarf wrapped around his face, tiny ice pellets embedded in the wool. But he sounds young. Young makes me nervous, makes me think unpredictable and scared.

Bishop must hear it, too, because when he speaks his voice has gotten even deeper, more adult. Trying to show the kid who's in charge here. "I left. Now I'm back. I need you to let me in."

Still the guard hesitates, and my heart is beginning to throb, my pulse jackhammering in my neck. Next to me, the air shifts as Caleb fits a bolt into his crossbow. Ash lays a hand on my back, trying to calm me.

The guard moves closer, finally. "Take off your hat," he tells Bishop.

Bishop does as he asks, his dark hair blowing in the stiff wind. The guard peers at him through slitted eyes. "Why'd you come back?" he asks.

"Heard what was happening in there," Bishop says, jerking his head toward the guard. "Wanted to come back and help my family."

"Some people thought maybe you left to go find that wife of yours," the guard says.

"No," Bishop says. "And she's not my wife anymore." He shifts slightly, and the guard tenses up. "Listen, I'd love to stand out here all day and chat, but it's freezing and I'd really like to see my family. I'm not sure how thrilled my father will be if he hears you made me wait."

That gets the guard moving. "Just have to be safe," he says, pulling a ring of keys from his pocket.

"Of course," Bishop says, "totally understand."

The gate opens and Bishop steps through, claps the guard on the upper arm. "Thanks."

"No problem." The guard pushes the gate closed again and Bishop steps behind him, swings his rifle off his back in one fluid motion, and brings the butt of it down hard against the guard's head with a *crack*. So fast the guard never saw it coming.

The three of us are up and racing toward the gate as Bishop grabs the guard's legs and drags him out of the way. Once we're through the gate, Bishop takes the keys from the guard's limp hand and locks it behind us. We stand and stare at one another, all breathing hard.

"Nice work," Caleb says.

Bishop looks at me, cups my cheek briefly in his hand. "Piece of cake, right?"

"Right," I say. I tell myself that it's fine. That the guard was never going to hurt him. But the thought that this is the easiest test we'll have sits in my gut, hard and heavy.

"So what do we do with him?" Ash asks, toeing the guard's shoulder. "We can't put him outside the fence without a weapon, and we can't exactly take him with us."

"We leave him here," Bishop says. "Tie him to the fence. Eventually someone will come looking for him. But we should have a good day or so with everything else going on. Plenty of time for us to get in and out."

"Won't he freeze?" I ask.

"Nah," Caleb says. "He's got a thick coat, boots. He'll be okay."

"What if he yells?" Ash asks.

Bishop squats down, hand on the guard's scarf. "We gag him. Won't be the best day he's ever spent. But he'll live."

I use my knife to cut the scarf in two, and Bishop uses half of it as a gag. Caleb takes the other half and winds it around the guard's wrists behind his back and then ties the ends through the fence.

"Think it'll hold?" Bishop asks, eyes on Caleb.

"For a while, at least," Caleb says. "If he does get loose, he's just going to be screaming about you. He didn't see the rest of us. So that gives us some room to maneuver."

Bishop nods at him, satisfied. He lifts the guard's coat before he stands, plucks the gun from the holster at his waist, and hands it to me.

I take it gingerly in my fingers, surprised at how heavy it is. "What do you want me to do with it?" I ask.

Bishop is concentrating on unbuckling the holster from around the guard's waist. "Carry it," he says. He looks up at me, eyes dark and serious. "Use it if you need to."

"I don't even know how," I protest.

"It's pretty simple," Caleb says. He takes the gun from my hand. "This is the safety. You want to press it off before you fire. Then it's just aim and pull the trigger. You miss, fire again. Like I said, simple."

He hands the gun back to me, and I raise my arms while Bishop fastens the holster around my waist, below my knife sheath. The gun doesn't feel simple to me. It feels dangerous, like a snake hissed and coiling in my hand. Bishop's rifle has never bothered me. I've always wanted to learn how to use a gun, even back before I was outside the fence. So I don't understand the way my skin crawls at the feel of this one in my palm. Except that from the second Bishop handed it to me, something clicked into place, one more step on this journey slotting into position.

I don't really believe in fate or destiny. Or at least I don't believe that fate can't be altered. I'm living proof. I altered my own. If that weren't possible, I'd most likely be ruling Westfall now along with my family, Bishop and his father dead at our feet. But regardless of what I believe, or don't believe, something inside me recognizes this gun, already understands that it's going to have a part to play in what's to come.

I wait while Bishop finishes fastening the holster and slides the gun onto my hip, making sure I can easily get to my knife as well. He is staring at me, head tilted, a little smile on his lips.

"What?" I ask.

He reaches out and winds a strand of my hair around his finger. "You need to cover this up," he says. "One look at it and people will know who you are."

I slip my hands from my mittens and roll my hair into a quick knot, tuck it up inside my hat. "Better?" I ask.

"No," Caleb says. "But it covers your hair."

I roll my eyes at him, and he and Bishop share a grin.

"If you two are done being idiots, we should get moving," Ash says, and now it's our turn to share a smile.

"We'll head through the woods," Bishop says. "Come out as close to my side of town as we can."

"Where are we going first?" Caleb asks.

Bishop looks at me. "I used to work with a woman named Victoria," I say. "I think she might help us get to Callie."

"And if she doesn't?" Caleb asks.

"Then we deal with it when it happens," Bishop says. "Once we're in town, we're going to stand out." He gestures at our weapons. "But I'm hoping things are chaotic enough, or people are scared enough, that we can escape too much notice." He pauses. "But if something happens, if Ivy and I get separated from the two of you, do what you have to do. Get out." He tosses the guard's ring of keys at Caleb, who catches them easily in one hand.

"We're not leaving you behind," Ash says. She has her determined face on, a little crinkle between her brows, her mouth drawn tight.

Bishop glances at Caleb. "I mean it. If they catch us, you two aren't going to be able to do anything but get your-selves killed if you stick around. Find a way and get out."

Caleb's and Bishop's gazes lock for a moment. Caleb nods. "We will," he says. He slides the ring of keys into his pocket and lays a hand on Ash's arm when she opens her mouth to protest. "If it comes to that, we will."

"Okay," Bishop says, and I can see some of the tension in his face ease, the same way I feel my own shoulders relax. Caleb is here for us, but Ash will always come first for him. If he has to leave us behind to save her, then he will. Strangely enough, the thought comforts more than it stings.

The woods we travel don't seem familiar at all, al-though I walked them more than once with Bishop in the months we were married. Instead of a humid green canopy above our heads, the bare branches stretch gray and gnarled into the equally gray sky, making it impos-sible for me to get my bearings. Even the river is quieter now, the surface most likely choked with muting ice. But Bishop knows these woods better than anyone, could probably navigate them blindfolded and with both arms tied behind his back.

It's the smell of fire that first tells me we're getting close to the populated sections of town. Bishop doesn't speak, just points a finger toward the sky where plumes of black smoke are rising. When we finally emerge from the winter-bare trees, we're on the gravel road I recognize from the times Bishop and I made the trek to the fence. We are the only people in sight, which eases the tightness in my chest just a little.

Even with no one else around, Bishop keeps his voice pitched low. "When we get closer to town, I'm going to move fast. Stay with me."

"Do you know where Victoria lives?" I ask him, because I have no idea, other than somewhere on Bishop's side of town.

He nods, and we set off at a brisk pace, facing into the biting wind. The acrid smell gets stronger the closer we get to town, smoke burning the lining of my nostrils. My eyes sting, but I don't know if it's from the wind or the remnants of fire. Bishop doesn't slow when we step off the gravel onto the regular paved road, the first houses visible in front of us. I keep my head down, shielding my face, and keep pace with his footfalls in front of me. From the corner of my eye, I can see that three houses have burned on this street alone, their blackened frames still smoldering. I don't see any people, but I can feel eyes on us, have to fight the urge to take off at a dead run.

"How far?" I whisper.

"Not far," Bishop whispers back, but I can hear the tension in his voice, his words pulled taut. Caleb and Ash have bunched up beside me, doing their best to protect me from curious eyes.

"We've got company," Caleb says, voice low, and I glance up, see the way Bishop's back stiffens. He doesn't turn around.

"Where?" Bishop asks.

"Behind," Caleb says. "To our right. Coming fast."

It's too early to engage, not if we can find any way to avoid it. If someone recognizes me at this stage, then even if we escape, they will know why I'm here and we'll never get to Callie, with or without Victoria's help.

"Get ready to move," Bishop says. He veers left, three steps to take off and he's running, weaving between houses, long legs jumping over the debris from a fire. I'm right on his heels, can hear Ash and Caleb behind me.

"Hey!" a man yells behind us. "Stop! Get back here! Where'd you get those weapons?"

Bishop vaults over a low chain-link fence and I don't stop to think about it, just grasp the top with my mittened hand and leap. I don't land as gracefully as he did, rolling onto my side, but adrenaline has me bouncing up to my feet like a spring and Bishop grins at me. I'm terrified, but I grin back. There is power in what we're doing, in taking control, in making our own choices, even if they're dangerous or maybe even foolish.

"Let's go," Caleb hisses as soon as Ash hits the ground, and we take off again, following Bishop through an alley between two brick buildings and out onto a residential street. In the near distance, I can see the remains of President Lattimer's house, but Bishop doesn't even spare it a glance, just leads us across the street and down the driveway between two small bungalows. The house on the left is dark blue, with a lopsided back stoop. Bishop leaps up the stairs and tries the doorknob. Locked. The top half of the back door is a series of small glass panes and Bishop uses his elbow to smash in the one closest to the doorknob, reaches in and turns the lock.

"Go, go, go!" he says to us. I can hear the sound of footsteps pounding down the driveway. We slip inside and Bishop closes the door, all four of us pressed up against the wall of the narrow hallway.

From outside the sound of men's voices, at least two of them, maybe three. They pause in the backyard and I hold my breath, willing them to keep moving. After a few endless seconds, they do, the crash of bushes as they cross into the neighboring yard. A relieved breath gusts out of me, and Bishop leans forward, his hands on his knees.

"Are you okay?" I ask, one hand on his elbow. "Did the glass cut you?"

"I'm fine," he says, twisting his head to look at me. There's a noise from the end of the hall, a sharp, sudden inhale and we all spin, our bodies crowding out the light coming from the door and throwing the far end of the hallway into shadow. Even so, I can see that it's Victoria standing there, frozen.

"Victoria," I manage around my heartbeat in my throat, my fear-choked voice.

Her mouth opens, a wide O of shock.

From beside me, Caleb moves, brings his crossbow up, and points it right at Victoria's head. "Don't scream," he says.

17

Victoria doesn't scream. I didn't think she would. She's too practical for that, too levelheaded. In fact, she barely seems to notice Caleb at all. Her eyes bounce back and forth between Bishop and me.

"Ivy?" she says finally, taking a step closer.

Caleb's arm tightens and I put a hand on it, pushing lightly. "It's okay," I tell him. "She's okay."

He doesn't take his eyes off Victoria, but Caleb relaxes a little, the crossbow still raised but no longer aimed at her head.

"Yeah," I say, pulling off my hat. "It's me."

I'm not sure what I expected from her, but a hug wasn't one of the possibilities on my list. But she rushes forward, enfolds me in her arms. I'm so stunned it takes me a minute to respond before I embrace her in return. She smells like soap and the apple tea she always drank, and I close my eyes in an effort to keep them dry.

After a minute, Victoria pulls back and I do, too, neither one of us quite sure what to do with our hands now that we're no longer hugging. "I can't believe you're alive," she says. "I can't believe you're here." She glances at Bishop, reaches out and grasps his hand. "It's so good to see you both."

She ushers us into the kitchen, taking a second to pull the curtains shut on the window above the sink. We introduce Caleb and Ash while she points us to her kitchen table. "Are you hungry?" she asks, setting a kettle on her stove.

I'm about to say no; eating seems like a waste of valuable time, but Caleb answers before I can. "Yes," he says simply. "We're hungry." He looks at Bishop and me with a shrug. "We have to eat. It might be a while before we're able to again." His words remind me once again why he's survived beyond the fence. Basic needs come first.

Victoria slices a loaf of bread, thick with nuts and raisins, and slathers the pieces with butter. She pours us all warm tea as we eat. I try to remember my manners and not just stuff the bread in my mouth like an animal, but it's been more than a week since we've had much beyond jerky. The rabbits on the fire are only a faint memory on my tongue.

Victoria sits with us, but she doesn't eat. Her fingers wrap around a mug of tea she doesn't drink. "Ivy," she says finally, "you can't be here."

I glance at her. "I know. We'll leave. I don't want to put you in danger. More than we already have."

Victoria shakes her head. "No, that's not what I mean. You can't be in Westfall at all. They'll kill you." She pauses. "The way things are now, there are people who will kill you the second they see you, no questions asked."

"How are things now?" Bishop asks. "We've heard about what's going on, but how bad is it, really?"

Victoria looks at him. "Not as bad as it was a few weeks ago. But still bad. Ivy's dad disappeared right after they arrested Callie. Some people think your father had him killed, Bishop. Others think he's hiding out somewhere orchestrating the rebellion."

I try to pretend she's talking about a stranger and not my father. Not the man who taught me to read at the same time he taught me to hate. "Do you think he's dead?"

"No." Victoria pushes her mug away. "Everything is still too angry. I think if your father were dead, it would have died down with him."

"So he's still got a hand in it?" Bishop asks.

"Probably," Victoria says. "But things haven't been blameless on your father's side either, Bishop."

Bishop's jaw tightens. "I never thought they would be."

"He's clamping down on everyone he suspects of disagreeing with him. Even people who were just friendly with Ivy's family."

No wonder the jam man ran when he had the chance.

"I still don't understand what you're doing back here," Victoria says to me. "You survived out there. You found each other." She glances at Ash and Caleb. "You found other people. Why come back?"

I take a sip of tea, delaying the moment when I'm going to have to speak her name, watch the judgment in Victoria's eyes. "Callie," I say finally.

Victoria stares at me. I don't see judgment in her eyes after all, just a weary disbelief. "You can't save her," she says. "I can't believe you'd even want to try."

"She's my sister."

"She's poison," Victoria says without hesitation. "The same as that vial she gave you." She holds up a hand. "Don't try to deny it. That was never you, Ivy. It was always her."

I don't even realize my fingers are biting into my thigh until I feel Bishop's warm hand over mine, his fingers gentling my grip, giving me something else to hold. "Everything you say may be true," I tell Victoria. "I'm not defending her or what she did." I squeeze Bishop's hand. "What she tried to get me to do. But she's still my sister, and I can't let them kill her."

"How do you think you're going to stop it, Ivy? Not even Bishop can stop it."

I take a deep breath. "You can stop it."

Victoria sucks in a laugh. "Me? How do you figure that?"

"Let us into the courthouse," Bishop says. "That's all you have to do. We'll take it from there."

The screech of Victoria's chair against the floor is loud in the silence. She pushes back from the table, stands and crosses to the doorway, turns back, pacing. Caleb looks at Bishop and me in turn, asking the question with his eyes: *what's she going to do?* Bishop raises just his fingers from the table, telling Caleb to wait.

"How can you even ask that of me?" Victoria says. She's not yelling, but her voice has the hard edge I used to hear when she talked to prisoners. "She was trying to get to the guns!"

"But she didn't get to them. She was never going to. I gave my father the wrong code."

Victoria's eyebrows go up at the same time Bishop makes a startled noise in his throat. One more detail I never gave him. Sometimes all the secrets I've held feel like the layers of an onion; peel and peel and there is always one more waiting. "Regardless," Victoria says, "her intention was to get the guns."

"But she didn't. She didn't get them," I repeat. "She doesn't deserve to die for the attempt."

"That's the worst logic I've ever heard," Victoria snaps. "So because we were able to stop her before she actually killed anyone, she gets a free pass?"

"No one's saying she gets a free pass," Bishop says. "We'll get her out of here, but then she'll be beyond the fence, just like us. Believe me, that's not a free pass."

Victoria shakes her head, a humorless smile on her lips. "And how's that going to work? The three of you are going to be a happy family? You think Callie's going to bounce your babies on her knee someday? Be a doting aunt?"

I've already thought about what happens after, and I know Callie can't stay with us. It would never work. And she would never want to, anyway. "No," I say. "Once we get her out, then we'll go our own ways." I stand up and cross to where Victoria is standing near the doorway. "I know you don't like her. I know you don't understand why I'm doing this."

"You're right, I don't."

"But I also know you aren't bloodthirsty, Victoria. You don't really think her punishment fits the crime."

Victoria closes her eyes, pinches the bridge of her nose. "So what are you thinking? I let you in and you waltz out of there with her?"

Just the fact that she's asking the question tells me she's going to do it. But I keep my voice calm when I answer. "All you have to do is unlock the basement door. And tell me where to find a key to her cell. That's it. We'll get her out."

Victoria opens her eyes, pins me with her gaze. "Without hurting anyone."

I nod. "Okay. Without hurting anyone."

"Ivy," Bishop says, from his seat at the table, "we can't promise that. We may—"

"I'm not doing it otherwise," Victoria says. "I'm not putting other people's lives on the line for Callie."

I look back at Bishop. "All right," he says. "We won't kill anyone. That I can promise."

Victoria blows out a breath. "I can't believe I'm agreeing to this."

"Thank you," I say.

"I'm doing it for you, Ivy. Not for her. I'm doing it because I feel like I let you down, when they put you out. I should have done more, tried harder to stop it."

I'm already shaking my head before she's done speaking. "That wasn't your fault. It was my choice. I don't blame you."

Victoria's smile is small and bittersweet. "I'll unlock the door in an hour. Be ready. The cell key will be on the top of the doorway. She's in the very first cell."

My heart is starting to pound harder just listening to her words. By the time we get to the courthouse it will be raging in my chest. "Okay."

"Once you get her out, you need to go, Ivy. Get out of Westfall. Fast."

"I want to try to find my father, too," I say, "if I can. But I promise we won't stay long. And we won't get caught. No one will ever know you helped us."

Victoria nods. "Okay then," she says, voice brisk. "Let's get this done."

Before we left Victoria's, she gave me a scarf to wrap around the lower part of my face. She also tried to convince Bishop and Caleb to leave the rifle and crossbow at her house, saying they made us too conspicuous, but they both refused. After living beyond the fence, going anywhere without a weapon makes us all feel naked. Better to take our chances being singled out because we have weapons than to go out on the streets unarmed.

Victoria leaves before we do, tells us to follow half an hour behind. While we're waiting, anxious eyes on the clock on her kitchen wall, Caleb asks how far it is to the courthouse.

"It's pretty close," Bishops says. "We can stick to backyards and stay off the streets as much as possible."

When it's time to leave, Bishop pauses at Victoria's back door. "Listen," he says, looking at Caleb, "when we get there I want you and Ash to stay outside."

"What? No!" Ash protests.

"What if something goes wrong?" Bishop says. "What if we need your help to get out? Or what if there's no point in helping us? I want you to be able to get away."

"Makes sense," Caleb says.

"How about you give us twenty minutes?" I say.

"If we're not back by then, you can come looking," Bishop says. "Or you can take off if things have turned a corner."

Ash huffs out a breath. "Doesn't anybody care what I think about this?"

Bishop smiles. "Not if it means putting yourself in more danger than you are already."

"Just knowing that you're going to be waiting for us makes me feel better," I tell her.

"Fine," Ash grumbles. "God forbid I get in on any of the action."

The walk to the courthouse goes faster and more smoothly than getting to Victoria's house. We don't see another person, although a few times I see curtains twitch in windows as we pass through empty backyards. But no one tries to stop us or comes out to ask what we're doing, probably thankful we just keep moving.

Luckily the rear of the courthouse backs up to a small stand of trees, no other buildings visible. The last time I stood on the other side of this door, Victoria and I were watching Mark Laird and the other prisoners starting their walk to the fence. The Ivy I was then could never have imagined this day, the twists and turns my life has taken since. I glance over at Bishop, let my eyes linger on his profile. I am thankful all over again for every choice that's led me here, to him.

He must feel my eyes on him because he turns his head, gives me a quick smile. "Ready?"

"Yes."

"We'll be here," Caleb says. He and Ash are on the edge of the trees, bodies tense and eyes watchful.

Ash grabs my hand as I start for the door. "Be safe," she whispers. "Come back."

I squeeze her hand. "We will."

I have a split-second thought that Victoria will have changed her mind and the door won't be unlocked, but when I give the handle a yank the door swings open, and Bishop and I slip inside. At first I'm disoriented because the lights are off, and as the door shuts behind us we are shrouded in shadows. But it only takes a moment for my eyes to adjust.

"They must be saving electricity," Bishop whispers.

"Or something's wrong with the power grid," I say. It wouldn't surprise me if that's something my father tried to sabotage.

"You know your way around here better than I do," Bishop says. "I'll follow your lead."

We slide to the end of the short hallway and pause, listening. There's no sound at all, which only makes my nerves worse. I poke my head around the corner. The hallway that ends at the cells is empty as well.

"It's clear," I whisper.

We round the corner and walk fast but silent down the hall. The door that leads to the cells is closed and I reach up, feel along the rim of the doorframe for the cell key. It's not there. My fingers sweep frantically across the edge of the wood, my heart throbbing harder with each passing second. "There's no key," I whisper.

"Here," Bishop says, "let me." His hand brushes along the wood, and when he's almost to the end of the door-frame a silver key slides into view, falling to the floor before I can catch it. The sound is as loud as a gunshot to my ears, and I drop down toward the floor, frantic to have the key in my hand.

"Someone's coming," Bishop says, just above a whisper. My head jerks up, and I hear the sound of footsteps approaching from behind the door to the cells. Bishop grabs my hand and yanks me down the hall, pulls me into the first open doorway and smashes us both up against the wall. There's no time to shut the door, the footsteps already out into the hall we just vacated. I push my mouth against Bishop's shoulder, try to muffle the sound of my own ragged breathing. Bishop's hand comes up and curls around the back of my neck, steadying me.

I close my eyes as the footsteps pass by our hiding place. If whoever it is glances behind him, looks into this room, then it's all over. But the slap of his shoes against the tile doesn't slow. I blow out an unsteady exhale as the footsteps fade. I can feel Bishop's heart pounding even through both our coats, and the hand I have clenched around his wrist is trembling.

"I think I may have just had a heart attack," Bishop whispers, and I smother a laugh into his neck. It's nervous laughter, but it still feels good to release it. Almost as good as having Bishop pressed up against me. We've barely had time to talk, much less touch, the last few days. "You okay?" he asks, pushing away from me slowly. "Still have the key?"

I hold up my clenched fist. I can feel the key pulsing against my palm. This time we don't hesitate, just slip out into the hallway, open the door to the cells and keep moving. As Victoria promised, Callie is in the first cell; the one I occupied during my time here and separate from the other prisoners. Unlike me, she isn't curled up on the cot. She is sitting on the floor, back against the cinder-block wall, and even with her head bent and eyes closed, she looks determined. She hasn't given up. A wave of anger washes over me at the sight of her, but I don't have time for it now. Emotion will have to come later, once we're all safe.

"Callie," I whisper.

She looks up, her dark eyes moving slowly from me to Bishop and back again. "Ivy?" She doesn't sound all that surprised. Her time in this cell, the knowledge of her impending death, hasn't taken anything from her. She is as fierce as ever.

"It's me," I say. I step forward and grasp the cell bars. "You have to hurry. We're getting you out of here."

Callie doesn't waste time asking questions. She shoves herself upright with no hesitation. I unlock her cell door and push it open. Callie pauses for a moment on the threshold, looks at Bishop. "I'm surprised you went along with this."

Bishop's eyes are calm, but his face is stiff when he answers. "Thank your sister. If it were up to me, we wouldn't be here."

That's the first time Bishop has said flat out that he doesn't agree with what we're doing. Or at least that he would never have done it had the decision been solely his. Instead of making me angry, his words make me grateful that despite not agreeing with me, he was willing to do this, put aside his anger at my sister in order to help me.

Bishop turns and I follow him, Callie bringing up the rear. "We're going out the back door," I tell her over my shoulder. "Follow me."

"Okay," she says. "Just go."

I have a million questions I want to ask her, about our father and what's happening to Westfall, but they'll have to wait. Bishop is almost at the door leading back into the hallway when I sense sudden movement behind me. Before I can react, I'm flying forward, crashing into Bishop. It takes me only a second to register that Callie shoved me, but it's all she needs, her hand closing around the gun at my waist and pulling it free.

18

Bishop and I turn, his hand on my upper arm, where he's clutched me to keep us both from falling over. "Callie," I breathe, the air in my lungs icy with fear. And understanding. "What are you doing?"

She's pointing the gun at Bishop. Her hands don't shake. Her eyes don't move. "Put your hands behind your head," she says, voice hard.

"Callie." I take a step toward her, and her gaze doesn't leave Bishop as she says, "Don't move, Ivy. Or I'll kill him right now." I freeze. It feels like even my heart stops beating.

Bishop raises his hands slowly, laces them behind his head.

"Get on your knees," Callie says.

"No," I say and the word sounds more like a moan. "*No*." My hand falls to the knife at my waist and I yank it free, grip the hilt with sweaty fingers. Callie registers the movement but doesn't comment. She isn't close enough for me to lunge at her, so she doesn't see me as a threat. Even if I were right next to her, she still probably wouldn't fear me. Fear is a learned response, and I've never given Callie a reason to feel it.

Bishop sinks to his knees, his eyes on Callie. His face is unreadable, but I can see the tension in his shoulders, know he's waiting for a chance to act.

"What are you doing?" I ask her again. "We came here to *help* you."

For the first time since she took the gun, Callie looks at me. "I'm doing what you couldn't. What you *wouldn't*. Did you think you could just make it all stop, Ivy? Did you really think you could change the outcome? This is the way it was always going to end. He's going to die, one way or another."

"You don't have to do this," I tell her. "We don't have to do everything Dad wants us to. Not anymore. You can make a different choice, Callie. You can be someone different." I repeat the words Bishop said to me once. "No one controls who we turn into but us."

She shakes her head, eyes back on Bishop. "This has nothing to do with Dad. This is what *I* want to do."

I don't know if what she's saying is true or if a lifetime of my father's lessons has shifted something inside her that can never be shifted back. But I do know I won't stand here and watch Bishop die. "I'm not going to let you murder him, Callie." The knife in my hand feels like it weighs three hundred pounds, like it's already carrying the weight of what using it will mean.

"Yes, you are," she says. "Because you don't have any way to stop me." She looks me over, head to toe, something close to hate in her eyes. "I still don't understand why you care. Did he tell you he loves you? That the two of you are meant to be? Is that all it took? God, Ivy, you're so predictable." She barks out a laugh. "Did you honestly think we'd all walk out of here and go live happily ever after somewhere?"

"No," I say. "I never thought that."

Callie's hand tightens on the gun and my arm tenses, fingers coiled around the knife hilt. "Please, Callie," I say. "Please, *please*, don't do this."

"I can't believe you're actually begging for his life," she says, mouth a sneer.

"I'm not begging for his life," I tell her. "I'm begging for yours."

For a single moment I see uncertainty flash through Callie's eyes, the tiniest shred of doubt, and I hope it's enough for her to reconsider, to make her lower the gun. But her gaze flickers back to Bishop and her eyes ice over again. "Isn't this where you jump in and make the noble sacrifice? Tell her not to kill me to save you? Isn't that the way it works in fairy tales? The prince falling on his sword?"

Bishop doesn't answer her, just shifts his eyes to mine. We stare at each other and I know Callie is wrong. He won't say those words to me. We are beyond that point with each other. He knows, in a way no one else will ever understand, how far we are willing to go for each other. And he knows that no matter what words are, or aren't, spoken, if I have to kill my sister to keep him alive, then that's what I will do.

Instead, he looks back at Callie. "You always underestimate her," he says. "It's a mistake you've made Ivy's whole life. It's a mistake you're making now."

"Shut up!" Callie says. "You don't know anything about me. You and your family, you took everything from us. Now I'm taking everything from you." She glances at me. "Maybe once he's gone, you'll be able to remember what really matters." Her finger moves on the trigger.

I don't even think about it. The room goes silent, like a bomb's gone off and knocked out my hearing. My vision pinpoints to the single spot on Callie's chest, the vulnerable target right in the hollow of her rib cage that Ash told me about. I raise my arm and send the knife flying, hard and straight and true. I don't wish for it to be a direct hit; I already know it is one. Sound returns in a rush, flooding in as the knife sinks into Callie's body with a wet thwacking sound. She gasps in a choking breath, stumbles backward, the gun still clutched in her hand. Bishop is up on his feet before I can move, snatching the gun from Callie's limp fingers. She doesn't try to take it back, just looks down at the knife handle protruding from her chest and then up at me. She drops to her knees, falls over to her side with a guttural moan.

"Callie," I say, skidding across the floor to her. I land hard on my knees, barely feel the sting of contact with the cold tile. "*Callie.*"

She rolls over onto her back, stares up at me. Her hand is wrapped around the knife handle and before I can stop her, she bares her teeth, her lips white and shaking as she yanks it from her chest, lets it clatter to the floor. That's what makes it real to me: the smell of her blood bubbling up from the gaping wound, the sound of it rushing out of her body, the color of it, more black than red. Not the kind of blood you see when you skin your knee or make a shallow cut. This is dying blood.

"Oh, Callie," I whisper. "I'm so sorry."

It takes her a moment to find the breath to speak, and even then her words are weak and thin. I can hear air whistling from her chest. "I should have known," she says on a thready whisper. "I should have known you'd choose a Lattimer over us."

I take her bloody hand in mine, but she yanks it away, surprising me with her strength, even now.

"You're just like Mom," she says. A tear slips down her cheek. "We were so close to having it all." She sucks in air, her chest heaving with the effort. "It should have been ours."

"Callie." I grab her hand again, and again she pulls it away. The third time, though, she leaves her hand in mine.

I don't kid myself that this means she's forgiven me, or even that she loves me. It only means she no longer has the energy to resist. Her eyes flutter closed and her chest rises and falls so slowly I can count to ten between each movement. Every time I think it will be the last. My breath is sobbing out of me, but there are no tears. I'm a husk now, dried to bone.

Bishop shifts, slides down to sit sideways behind me. "Ivy," he whispers, voice heavy with sorrow. He presses his forehead against the top of my spine, wraps his arms around my waist.

"Remember," I say to Callie, "remember when we were little and we'd build a fort in your bedroom? We'd hide under there and you'd tell me ghost stories? And sometimes"—my exhale shudders out of me—"you'd braid my hair. I always liked that." I take her hand and press it against my heart. "I wish we could have loved each other more, Callie. I wish we'd learned how."

Callie doesn't respond, doesn't open her eyes or squeeze my fingers. Her face is waxy now. Her lashes dark against her snow-pale skin. Her chest rises. Falls. Rises. Falls. Does not rise again.

I hold Callie's hand and Bishop holds me, and in the bruised and terrible silence I am not alone.

19

I stumble out of the courthouse behind Bishop, my hand in his the only thing keeping me upright. He pushes through the back door and I follow. The cold air smacking into my face reminds me that this is real, this is *happening*. I just killed my sister. I still have her blood etched into the lines of my palms. I can still hear the whistle of her failing lungs.

Something wet hits my cheek, and I flinch. Snow. Fat, fluffy flakes drift down from the slate-gray sky. I tip my head up and let them land on my face, melt against my feverish skin. Maybe if it snows hard enough, I can fool myself into believing I'm crying, pretend I'm actually able to shed a tear for my dead sister.

"Ivy," Bishop says softly.

It takes a long time for me to look at him. When I do, he is standing right in front of me, his eyes drinking me in. "Do you think I did it on purpose?" I ask. My voice sounds like my throat is lined with sandpaper. "Do you think I wanted to kill her? Is that why I came back here?" I remember how much I hated Callie that day in the courtroom, how I longed to rip her apart. How much I wished her dead.

Bishop brushes a snowflake off my lip with his thumb. "I don't know," he says finally. "Only you can answer that question. But I know you're not a cold-blooded killer. If she'd given you an out, if there had been another option, you would have taken it."

Wherever Callie is now, I can picture her laughing, calling me the worst kind of hypocrite. And she's right. Because it turns out I do have it in me to kill. I can live with blood on my hands. I just can't live with it being Bishop's. I don't know what to do with my body, don't know whether it wants to fold in on itself or fling itself outward, smash and destroy. I open my mouth, but all that emerges is a faint wail. My eyes burn, but from dryness, not tears. Bishop steps forward and gathers me against his chest, and I push my face into the hollow of his neck. My hands fist into his coat until my knuckles scream, and I think maybe if we can stay like this forever, static and safe, maybe I will find a way to be okay.

But the world doesn't work like that, I'm discovering; it hardly ever gives you a chance to catch your breath. As if to prove my point, Bishop stiffens, pushes back from me just a little.

"Where are Caleb and Ash?" he asks.

I whirl around, eyes scanning the tree line where they were supposed to wait, but there's no sign of them. "I don't know," I say.

Behind me, the courthouse door bangs open and as I turn, Bishop shoves in front of me, hand already reaching back for his rifle.

"It's just me, it's just me," Victoria says, hands raised partway in surrender. She glances between Bishop and me. "Where's Callie?"

"She didn't . . ." Bishop pauses. "She didn't make it."

"I'm sorry," I say. "She . . ."

"She tried to kill me," Bishop says. Not lying, exactly, but subtly shifting the blame for what happened in that hallway from me to him. "You're going to have some explaining to do, Victoria. I'm sorry about that."

Victoria waves her hand. "I'm not worried about that right now, and you shouldn't be either. Your father—"

"What about my father?" Bishop says, taking a step forward.

Victoria catches my eyes over Bishop's shoulder. "*Both* your fathers."

"What about them?" I ask.

"You need to go," Victoria says. "Right now. To your house," she says to Bishop. "See if you can stop it. I'll deal with this." She cocks her head back toward the courthouse.

"I thought President Lattimer's house burned down," I say. Nothing is making any sense to me. I just want to lie down in the snow-sprinkled grass and wake up to a world where today never happened.

"Just partially," Victoria says, voice impatient. "Bishop's parents went back to see if anything could be salvaged." She makes a shooing motion with both hands. "You need to go!"

Bishop is already moving, and even as I follow him a voice inside my head is screaming at me to turn and run the other direction. Find the fence and clamber over it. The voice is telling me that hands torn to shreds on razor wire will be less painful that whatever Bishop and I are going to find waiting for us. But Bishop holds his hand out to me and instead of pulling him back my direction, I run alongside him.

There are more people out on the streets than earlier, and they are all headed the same direction we are. Although a few people shout our names as we streak past, no one tries to stop us. Apparently whatever is happening with our fathers is more urgent than discovering I am back inside Westfall, which does nothing to ease my anxiety.

"Do you think this is where Caleb and Ash went?" I ask. "Maybe they heard something and went to see what was going on?"

"Maybe," Bishop says, face grim.

Bishop's parents' house is still standing, although one half of it is only a charred ruin, uneven remains of brick catching the snow against their bloodred surface. People are lined up outside the wrought iron fence surrounding the lawn. I see a few policemen, but they seem confused, milling around and looking at each other with no one making a move, everyone waiting for someone else to tell them what to do.

Bishop and I shove our way through a small gap in the crowd, and I hear Bishop's quick inhale before my eyes register what they're seeing. My father is standing on the still-intact front porch, the gun in his hand pressed against President Lattimer's temple, his other hand clutching the back of President Lattimer's neck. Erin Lattimer is kneeling on the steps. I can hear the pleading sound of her voice, but not her exact words.

"Daddy!" I scream, before I think about it, the word torn from my throat.

My father's head whips up, scans the fence line until it lands on me. "Ivy?" he calls.

"It's me," I call back. "Please stop, Dad. Whatever you're thinking. Please stop."

"They have Callie," my father yells. "They're going to kill her."

"No," Bishop says, loud, and my father's eyes swing to him. "We got her out." His hand squeezes my forearm. "We're going to come up there. Just Ivy and me. Is that all right?"

My father hesitates, and President Lattimer flinches.

"I'll leave my gun on the driveway," Bishops yells. "We're coming up. Go, Ivy," he urges me. "Go!"

Just as we reach the gate, two policemen rush forward. But Bishop swings his rifle off his back and aims it at them. "No," he says, voice firm. "Back off. *Now!*"

If they were better trained or had more experience with firearms, Bishop alone might not be enough to stop them, but the ease with which he holds the rifle, the strength of his voice, causes both of them to obey his command, and they skid to a halt.

I slip inside the gate and race up the driveway toward my father. I can hear Bishop's footsteps behind me. A quick glance over my shoulder shows Bishop setting his rifle down on the driveway just as he promised. We reach the base of the steps at almost the same time and Erin stumbles down into Bishop's arms. "Bishop," she cries. Her face is ragged from weeping, her hair tangled. One of her feet is bare, and that's the thing my mind snags on, wondering where she lost her shoe and thinking how cold her foot must be.

"Don't come any closer!" my father barks, and his voice snaps the world back into focus.

I stop on the bottom step, the cold iron railing biting into my skin. "Dad," I say. "Let him go."

"Ivy." My father's face softens. "You're alive. You're here." He has dark circles under his eyes and a growth of beard that makes him look like a stranger.

"I'm here, Dad. I came back. But you need to let him go."

"I can't," my father says. His face twists up, but not in rage, in a kind of exhausted sorrow that cuts right through me, rips my heart in two. In a flash, all the anger I've harbored toward him is gone. There is no room for it here, no way it can help me.

"Dad, please . . ."

"He's been having people killed. People who spoke out after Callie was arrested, did you know that?" my father asks.

"No," I say. "I didn't know. But that's still not a good enough reason to shoot him." Once upon a time it might have been, but not anymore. Now he is more than President Lattimer. He is Bishop's father.

"Yes, it is," my father says. "It's more than enough reason."

"That's not why you're doing this," President Lattimer says quietly, startling me. I'd almost forgotten he was capable of speech, all my attention centered on my father and the gun in his hand. "At least be honest, Justin."

"For God's sake, Matthew," Erin cries. "Don't make it worse. Don't goad him."

President Lattimer glances at Erin, something like an apology skating across his face. "This has never been about Westfall. Or the way I run it. Not for you, Justin. It's always been about Grace." The sound of my mother's name seems to suck all the air out of the sky like a held breath, the gasping seconds before a bomb explodes.

"Don't you *dare* say her name to me," my father says. "You have no right."

"I have every right," President Lattimer says. "I loved her, same as you did."

"You let her go! *You killed her!*" my father roars. His eyes are suddenly wild, the gun pressed so hard against President Lattimer's temple that I can see the surrounding flesh turn white. Behind me, Erin moans.

It won't do any good to disagree with my father about who caused my mother's death. I already tried that once and it got me nowhere. "It doesn't matter anymore," I say instead, trying to keep my voice calm, willing the shaking in my hands to stay there and not travel up into my vocal cords. "It was over a long time ago. She's gone, Dad. And she wouldn't have wanted this." I take a deep breath, my eyes meeting President Lattimer's. "She loved him. More than anything." *More than any of us*, I think, but manage not to say.

"Yes," my father says. "She loved him, and he betrayed her. He broke her heart like it was nothing. Married someone else like it was nothing."

"It was never nothing," President Lattimer says. "Do you think it was easy for me? Watching her marry you, have your children? Do you think you're telling me anything I haven't told myself a thousand times? You think whatever you do to me will be any worse than the day I found her dead?" President Lattimer's voice is so raw, so naked, that it makes me want to look away, like I'm witnessing some intimate moment between my mother and him.

Tears are running down my father's face. The moisture makes his dark eyes glow. Snow is catching on his hair now, giving him a crown of white. He looks like a madman. He looks broken in a way I have no idea how to fix. He's not pressing the gun as hard against President Lattimer's temple now, but I'm not fooled. I know my father. I know how strong his hate burns.

"Doing this won't change anything," I say. "The West-falls aren't going to take over. That dream is gone, Dad. But we can leave here. Make a life outside Westfall. Start fresh." This has been my secret hope since the moment I decided to return to Westfall. But now, saying the words out loud, they sound ridiculous, futile in the face of so much painful history.

My father shakes his head. "No. I'm never leaving."

My heart sinks. "If you ever cared about me, Dad, even a little," I say, "please let him go."

"Of course I care about you, Ivy. Of course I do." My father's face crumples. "I love you. You're my daughter. I wanted so much more for you, for all of us."

They are the words I've needed to hear, to believe, for so long. But they are too late. They aren't going to be enough, for either one of us. In my bones I already know there is no way to stop this, but I have to try anyway. "Then put the gun down, Dad. Killing him would only be vengeance, not justice."

My father stares at me, and I fight to hold his eyes, but his gaze slides back to President Lattimer and our brief connection is lost. "Then vengeance is what he deserves," my father says. He shoves President Lattimer forward, aims the gun at the back of his head.

President Lattimer looks at me, a faint smile on his lips. He doesn't seem resigned to his fate, so much as at peace with it. "Your mother would be very proud of you, Ivy." His eyes shift to Bishop, glow with love. "The same way I'm proud of you."

"Dad," Bishop's voice breaks.

"I'm so grateful you and Ivy found each other," President Lattimer says. "I know Grace would be, too." He looks at Erin. "And I'm sorry you always had to live in her shadow. That wasn't fair to you. I wasn't the husband I should have been."

"It's all right, Matthew," Erin says, her words clotted with tears. "I know you loved me the best you could."

"Turn around," my father says.

"Don't," I say, but my voice is swallowed up by the wind, by the force of my father's grief and rage.

"I always loved her," President Lattimer says, turning to face my father. He keeps his head up, his voice strong.

"Not enough. Not as much as I did," my father says and pulls the trigger. President Lattimer's forehead explodes in a flash of blood and bone. One second he is a living, breathing man, a husband, a father, the keeper of my mother's heart, and the next he is a lifeless body, already gone.

"No!" Bishop yells. I stagger up the steps, then stop when I see my father still has the gun in his hand. He's swinging it in Bishop's direction, and I try to move into his path but I'm too slow, my feet clumsy with shock, my hands slipping on the icy railing.

There's a whistle through the air, a sound I know, but can't place, my brain working at half its normal speed. A bolt hits my father in the throat, knocks him backward, blood already spouting from the wound. He slides down the front of the house, leaving a trail of dark gore against the brick.

It feels like I'm observing from outside my body, detached and numb, as I turn my head and see Caleb standing on the lawn, just lowering his crossbow. Ash is next to him, her face contorted with tears. I pivot away from them, watch as Erin slips through blood and snow to President Lattimer's prone body. She presses her face into his chest, and her wails reverberate in the air, stabbing against my brain like knives. I would cover my ears but can't find the strength to raise my arms. I look at Bishop, his shock-wide eyes and pale skin probably a mirror of my own. He collapses on the top step, his face buried in his hands.

I thought I didn't believe in fate, but maybe fate doesn't care what you believe. Because this final, awful result seems inevitable. For all my fleet-footed games of bob and weave, all the ways I tried to avoid the carnage in front of me, it came to pass anyway. Perhaps it was set in motion long ago: when one man wrested power from another; when two children fell in love and weren't allowed to be together; when my mother looped a length of rope over the branch of an oak tree and tightened a noose around her neck.

My father's blood mingles with President Lattimer's, runs in rivulets through the pristine white snow that is still falling, until it forms a single river. Impossible to tell which is Westfall and which is Lattimer. I'm as frozen as the air, unable to move toward my father, unwilling to risk reaching for Bishop only to see him pull away. So I simply stand, hands curled around the iron railing and watch the snow drift down, watch the flakes turn to bloody ice on the bodies of our fathers.

20

I hear a crow calling overhead, the whistle of wind through the snow-laden branches. But other sounds are distant. A knot of policemen is moving up the driveway and while their mouths are open, I can't make sense of what they're saying, don't want to bother trying. When the first policeman reaches me, he grabs my arms, pulls my hands behind my back with a little too much force. I don't resist, can't bring myself to care about what they might do to me.

"Let her go," Bishop says, the first words that have actually reached my ears since our fathers fell. Bishop is still sitting on the steps. He looks boneless; even his voice lacks any sort of force.

One of the policemen has stepped up onto the porch and is trying to gently pull Mrs. Lattimer away from the president's body. "Mrs. Lattimer," he says, "what do you want us to do with her?" He jerks his head in my direction. "Ivy Westfall?"

Erin doesn't get up, only turns her head to look at me. There is a smear of blood across her cheek. She looks very young in her grief, lost and alone.

"What should we do with her?" the policeman repeats.

A whole kaleidoscope of emotions passes across Erin's face: pain, sorrow, anger, disgust, exhaustion. I'm not sure which one is going to win. Bishop must see it, too, because before Erin can reply, he stands, hauling himself upright with both hands wrapped around the railing. "I swear to God, Mom," he says, voice tight. "After all this"—his arm sweeps the carnage on the porch—"if you don't do the right thing here . . ." He is fighting for me, but he is still not looking at me, and my heart drums an insistent, mournful beat.

Erin pushes herself up a little at the sound of Bishop's voice, swivels her head in his direction. She must want vengeance of her own now. How can she not? And I'm the only person available from whom she can extract it. Bishop stares at his mother, his jaw clenched and his chest heaving with tears I know he is trying not to spill. Not here in front of strangers.

"Don't do anything with her," Erin says finally. "Let her go, like Bishop said. Just . . . let her go."

The policeman releases my arms, but I don't move. In some ways, the inside of a cell would have been a relief. I glance back at the fence and see that the people gathered there have not moved. Some are weeping, others are grouped in tiny circles, talking. All the earlier tension is muted, as if the deaths of President Lattimer and my father shocked the anger away, left both sides empty of anything but uncertainty.

Bishop walks down the steps. "I don't want anyone else hurt," he says. "Try to get people to go home, keep things calm, but don't use those guns. We need to diffuse the situation, not make it worse."

"Are you in charge now?" one of the policemen asks. "Or your mother?" No one seems to question the idea of another Lattimer taking over, same as it's always been.

Bishop looks over his shoulder at his mother, still curled over President Lattimer's body. "Me. For now. But I'm going to want input from all sides. Tell people to gather in city hall tomorrow at noon. Everyone is welcome. We have to start figuring out how to put Westfall back together."

The policemen nod, then head down the driveway to begin dispersing the crowd. Bishop follows them for a few steps before veering off across the lawn toward Caleb and Ash. When he reaches them, Ash throws her arms around his neck, and Bishop hugs her back. They stay that way for a moment before Bishop turns to Caleb, pulls him into the same warm embrace. I pivot away, back toward the porch. My father's eyes are open, flat and dark. I wish someone would close them.

"Ivy," a voice says from behind me, something heavy landing across my upper back. An arm, I think, maybe. It's too much work to concentrate. "Come on." There's pressure on my shoulder and I give in to it, allow myself to be turned. "Come on," Ash repeats gently.

"Where are we going?" I ask her. "My father . . ."

Ash keeps guiding me, and I keep following her. "Somewhere warm. And they'll take care of your father." A tear slips down her face. I wish one would slip down mine. "And Bishop's father, too. Don't worry."

Bishop and Caleb are walking ahead of us, the crossbow swinging on Caleb's back. Bishop has picked up his rifle again, slung it in its familiar position over his shoulder. "I don't . . . I don't blame Caleb," I say. Even my mouth feels numb, my lips working hard to form the most simple words.

"I know," Ash says. "He knows, too."

I don't pay attention to where we're going, not noticing the path we're taking until we're on the walkway to the house Bishop and I shared after our marriage. I stumble on the sidewalk. "Why here?" I ask, loud enough for Bishop to hear.

He stops, his eyes meeting mine for the first time since my father pulled the trigger. I can't tell if he's looking at me or through me. "Because there's nowhere else to go."

Bishop finds the spare key where we left it hidden on

the front porch and unlocks the door. I climb the steps and go inside. The house smells musty and abandoned. I stand in the middle of the living room like a statue, while everyone else moves around me. A pair of Bishop's shoes lies in the corner, a remnant of our earlier life.

"I'm going to go take a shower," I say.

No one answers me. I wander down the short hallway and lock myself in the bathroom. The water is cold, but I undress and climb into the shower anyway, hoping that the sting of icy water can bring feeling back to more than my body. I wash my hair, shampoo running into my eyes, making them burn. I scrub and scrub at my hands until all of Callie's blood is washed away. Then I just stand there, let the water stream down my face.

I am shivering violently by the time I emerge from the shower. I leave my filthy clothes in a pile on the bathroom floor and wrap myself in a towel. I can hear Caleb's and Ash's voices from the living room, the sound of them starting a fire in the fireplace. I open the bathroom door as quietly as I can, cross to the bedroom, and slip naked underneath the blankets.

I'm still shaking, my wet hair soaking into the pillow, when Ash comes in a few minutes later. "Hey," she says softly. "Victoria brought over some food."

"I'm not hungry."

Ash pulls the blankets up higher on my body, makes sure my bare shoulders are covered. "Okay," she says. "We'll be in the living room if you need anything."

"Where's Bishop?" I ask, teeth chattering. I don't know if it's from cold or shock.

Ash pauses. "I'm not sure." She lays a hand on my forehead like she's checking for a fever. "But he'll be back."

I close my eyes, roll away from her.

I haven't been asleep. I've been drifting, my mind skipping from memories of my father, thoughts of Callie, longing for Bishop. The soft sounds of Caleb's and Ash's voices from the living room trailed off earlier, replaced by Caleb's muted snores. Bishop is back; I can hear him in the bathroom. It reminds me so much of the time we spent here as husband and wife, all the nights I listened to him get ready for bed. Of all the possible scenarios I pictured for our future back then, this was never one of them.

The bathroom door opens, and his footsteps pause outside the bedroom. I hold my breath, releasing it slowly when he walks into the room, closing the door behind him. I hear the rustle of clothes, then the bed dips as he lies down beside me. I'm on my back, staring up at the ceiling, my arms at my sides. He doesn't speak to me, doesn't touch me. The silence between us gathers and takes on weight, heavy and crushing against my chest. I am thankful that the numbness that descended earlier hasn't fully lifted, or the pain of this moment might be the thing that finally breaks me, the limit to my endurance breached. I want to reach for him, but what my father did to his sits between us like a mountain I have no idea how to climb. How can he still love me now? How can I expect him to?

"Bishop," I whisper. It is the only word I can manage, low and choked from my throat. The blankets shift, and Bishop's hand brushes against mine, slides over it, weaving our fingers together and holding on tight. I suck in a sobbing breath, clench his hand as hard as I can. Tears spill out of my eyes like they've been gathering there all day, waiting for this moment to erupt.

He rolls onto his side and so do I, wrapping my arms around his neck as he pulls me against him. He is crying, too, warm tears slick on his face where it touches my cheek. When we kiss, our sorrow mingles, the same way our fathers' blood did earlier. Bishop shifts over me, yanks off his T-shirt with one hand hooked behind his head. The tears don't stop, for either one of us, as we move together. The pleasure in my body and the pain in my heart merge into one bright streak behind my eyelids. My fingers dig into his back, desperate and too hard, but I can't make my hands loosen. I need to reassure myself that he's here, warm and alive and *with* me.

After everything, still with me.

Once our tears stop and our breathing settles, we lie on our sides facing each other. The night is dark, but the moon reflecting off the newly fallen snow gives the room a hushed, ethereal glow. My eyelids are puffy from crying, my lips raw from his kisses.

"I feel like it's my fault," I tell him. "That I caused it all by coming back here."

"No," Bishop says. He has one arm curled under the pillow his head is resting on, the other slung across my waist. "Our fathers were never going to have a happy ending, Ivy. Whether you were here or a thousand miles away. They had a horrible history, and nothing you did, or didn't do, was ever going to change it."

"But it was my father who killed yours," I whisper.

"You're not responsible for your father. Just like I'm not responsible for mine. They were grown men. They made their own decisions."

"But your father didn't do anything," I protest. "He wasn't the one who pulled the trigger."

"He did other things, though," Bishop says. "When I left here earlier, I went to check on my mother. I talked to her about what went on while we were gone. And what your father said was true. My father was having people killed. Not a lot of them. Some he just had arrested or beaten. Some he had put out. And that's bad enough. But a few he had killed, to send a message about supporting your father. He wasn't all bad, I know that. But he did bad things." Bishop reaches up and brushes my tangled hair off my cheek. "So it wasn't only your father, Ivy. It was both of them."

"I just wish . . ."

"You wish what?"

"My father had good ideas for Westfall," I say. "I really do believe that. I wish he'd been able to see past his hate for your father, so that maybe he could have done something worthwhile."

"Well, if we're trading wishes, I wish my father had learned from losing your mother. Even after everything that happened with her, he still clung to the same ideas." Bishop pauses. "He knew, better than anyone, how wrong it was to take away people's choices. But it didn't stop him. He could never admit there might have been another way to do things."

"They both had chances," I say. "Chances they didn't take."

"It's not too late, you know," Bishop says. "To make Westfall into something better."

"Is that what you want? To stay here and change things?"

"I don't know. I can't think that far ahead." Bishop sighs. "Right now I'm just so tired."

His soft words make me realize the depth of my own exhaustion, bone deep and heavy across my limbs. I scoot closer to him, rest my hand on his cheek. "I'm sorry about your father."

He turns his head to brush his lips against my palm. "I'm sorry about yours." He pauses. "I'd be lying if I said I was sorry about Callie, though. But I am sorry you were the one who had to kill her. I know how much that hurt you." His words don't make me angry. This is who Bishop is, especially with me. Honest. After a lifetime of lies, I'm grateful for the pain of truth.

"I wouldn't go back and change it," I tell him. "Even if I could. I wasn't going to let you die, Bishop. Not ever."

He leans forward and kisses me, lets his mouth linger. "What you said to Callie about you two loving each other more?"

"What about it?" I whisper against his lips.

"You're good at loving people, Ivy. You love *hard*. You're so much better at it than you give yourself credit for."

"It was you," I say, my tears close to the surface again. "You taught me how."

He lifts my hand off his face and pulls it down to rest against his chest. "We taught each other."

21

We bury our dead at first light. Funerals are different than before the war. No big ceremonies, no coffins, no words of comfort. Maybe all those ways to mark a person's passing disappeared when the number of dead reached millions. There was no point in having funerals when there were more people dead than alive. Now, we shroud our dead in homespun cotton, place them in unmarked holes in the ground, and save our words for the living.

Bishop and Caleb got up before the sun to dig the single grave. There's an awful kind of irony in having our fathers buried together, along with Callie. But the ground is too frozen, the space too limited to allow for three separate graves. Sometimes in bad winters mass graves hold more than twenty people at a time. I tell myself they are dead, so what does it matter? I tell myself that maybe this is the resting place they've all earned, forced to merge in death as punishment for the hatred and resentment they couldn't let go of in life.

Bishop stands between Erin and me, clasping both our hands as Ash and Caleb lower the bodies into the ground. Victoria is here, too, but no one else. Callie's body goes in last, and a curl of dark hair escapes her shroud, floats in the cold morning breeze.

"May they rest in peace," Bishop says as Caleb and Ash step back from the grave, from the pile of bones and flesh that used to be people we loved.

Erin weeps quietly beside Bishop, but I am empty again of tears. At least for now. The sun is taking its position in the sky, sending streaks of pale orange through the trees. A few birds chatter in the bare branches. The world keeps on spinning, no concern at all for our losses, the depth of our heartbreak. Strangely, it's a thought that gives me hope. We will survive this moment, this pain. We will outlast it.

"I'll help Caleb fill in the grave," Bishop says.

I nod, and he lets go of my hand and his mother's. As he walks away, I glance at Erin. Her hair is drawn back in a messy ponytail, and she's wearing a sweater I would swear is President Lattimer's, too big for her, the arms hanging past her wrists. I don't know what to say to her, or even if she'd welcome the sound of my voice.

I look into her bloodshot eyes. Neither of us apologizes. We don't offer or ask for forgiveness. We will never like each other; too much has happened for that. When she looks at me, she will always see the destruction of her family. When I look at her, I will always remember her condemning me to a life beyond the fence. But we've reached a kind of understanding, an acknowledgment that somehow we are on the same side now. Because of Bishop. Our love for him will forever be the tie that binds us together.

We arrive at city hall early, file into the rotunda to wait and see who joins us. "We'll stay back here," Caleb says. He and Ash stand near the doorway, as close to being outside as they can get.

"You don't want to come in, join the discussion?" Bishop asks. The light, mocking note in his voice is almost enough to make me smile.

"Don't have a dog in this fight," Caleb says. "But we're here if you need us."

"Yeah," Ash says, "like if all this power starts going to your head. We're available to knock some sense into you."

Now both Bishop and I smile, grateful for Caleb and Ash, their constant presence, their allegiance to nothing and no one but us. Bishop hops up to sit on the edge of the stage and offers me his hand so I can sit next to him.

"A lot's changed since the last time we were on this stage," he says.

"Yes." I can still see my father and Callie walking beside me the day I married Bishop, President Lattimer welcoming me to his family. All of them gone now. The day I stood on this stage and pledged my vows to Bishop, I could never have imagined the words I spoke would someday be true. We are no longer married, but I'm more connected to him now than I ever was when we were husband and wife.

A little before noon people begin filling the rotunda until it's completely packed, the overflow crowd spilling out onto the courthouse steps. Victoria and Erin arrive, and while Erin comes to stand near Bishop and me, Victoria stops to talk to the gathering crowd, offering reassurances and calming the anxious. The crowd shifts restlessly, everyone looking at Bishop for a cue.

"Here goes nothing," he says under his breath, and I squeeze his hand as he steps forward. "Thank you all for coming," he calls out in a loud, clear voice. A shiver runs down my spine: pride mixing with apprehension. He sounds very much like his father. He sounds like a leader. "As I'm sure you all know by now," he continues, "my father died yesterday." A rumble passes over the crowd like a wave. "And Justin Westfall died as well." Bishop turns to look at me and motions me forward with a slight frown. "Come up here," he urges.

I move up next to him, let my eyes scan the crowd. Most people look nervous, scared. They're waiting for someone to tell them what to do, how to behave. After so many years of having their choices made for them, they no longer remember how to make decisions for themselves.

"Both our fathers made mistakes," Bishop is saying. "But while they had very different visions for Westfall, I believe they wanted only the best for all of us."

"What's going to happen now?" someone calls out. "Who's in charge?"

And that's what it comes down to for most of these people. They just want someone to guide them. Bishop glances at me. "I think that's up to you," he says. "I think everyone should get a say, a vote."

A buzz goes through the room, shock and fear, maybe a little excitement. "We want you!" a man yells. "We want a Lattimer!"

"No!" another man cries. "We should all get to vote, like he said."

"But what about for right now?" a woman chimes in. "We need someone in charge right now. Winter is here!"

We're rapidly losing control of the room, people shouting over one another, voices rising so that no one can be heard. "Stop!" I yell, surprising myself. And apparently everyone else, too, because the room falls silent. "You're right. We need someone guiding us until a new government is in place. That should be our first step, figuring out who will run Westfall in the short term."

"Bishop!" a man yells.

"I second that!" a woman cries.

"Only if he has a Westfall working with him," someone in the back of the crowd says. "Ivy needs to be a part of it. That way things will be fair."

I open my mouth to protest; I have no intention of running Westfall, even temporarily, but the man's suggestion catches on and his words ripple around the room. Victoria looks at Bishop. "It's a good idea," she says. "You and Ivy can work together to stabilize things."

Bishop turns to me. We both know what will happen if we agree. Bishop will become the new leader of Westfall. Or I will. I can see it so clearly: the two of us implementing the best ideas of our fathers, keeping people safe while allowing them their freedom. We could make Westfall the place it always should have been. A legacy we can be proud of. The promise of it snaps through my blood like lightning. But underneath that, the little voice I'm getting better at hearing is already asking if fulfilling my father's dream is the same as fulfilling my own.

"What do you say?" Bishop asks me. He's got a faint smile on his lips, and I know he's seeing the possibilities, too. But I pause, really looking at him. Something in his face is weary, his eyes stoic instead of sparkling. Like he's already bracing himself for bad news. My heart turns over in my chest.

I want to see the ocean. I'd rather explore than govern. I don't care enough about the power. I stare at Bishop, hear his words, remember the dream I had for him when I thought I'd never see him again—that he would someday reach the ocean, taste its salty sting.

Bishop has always followed where I led—beyond the fence, back here to Westfall, and now, in this room, he's willing to do it again. Not because he's weak or because he doesn't have his own ideas, but because he loves me and he wants me to have what I need. But I love him, too, and his happiness matters as much to me as my own.

It would be a lie to say a part of me doesn't want to stay in Westfall indefinitely and carry out my father's vision, turn it back into a democracy, a place where people are free in all ways. But then *I* wouldn't be free. I'd be forever tied to this patch of land, these people, this way of life. Here I will always be Justin Westfall's daughter, for better and worse. Before I was put out beyond the fence, I couldn't imagine a life outside Westfall, but now, it's hard for me to really imagine one inside it. Bishop was right; there's so much of this world we haven't seen. And I want to discover it. Westfall feels like my past. The whole wide world feels like my future.

"So, what do you say?" Bishop repeats, and I'd swear the entire room is holding its breath, waiting for my answer.

"Yes," I say. "My answer is yes." I pause. "But only for a few months. Just until spring."

"What do you mean?" Victoria asks. "Why only through the winter?" Around us people's voices begin to rise, everyone clamoring for more information. Bishop ignores it all, his eyes on me.

"Because I think Westfall will do better in the long term without a Lattimer *or* a Westfall in charge." I glance at Victoria, remembering her innate fairness, her determination to try to do the right thing. She's much better suited to the running of Westfall than either Bishop or I will ever be. "It's time for everyone here to find a new way, a new path to follow." I smile at Bishop, take his hand. "And besides, Bishop and I already have plans."

"We do?" Bishop asks, brow furrowed, but that little dance of amusement flaring to life in his eyes.

"Yes," I say. "We do. I seem to remember, once upon a time, you mentioning us taking a very long hike."

"What are you talking about?" Erin says, but I keep my gaze on Bishop. "I don't understand."

But Bishop understands. He smiles, his eyes lit up like the sun at daybreak. He steps close to me, pulls me into his arms. "It'll be rough, Ivy," he says. "And dangerous."

I shrug. "So is Westfall. So is life. It will be worth it." My cheeks hurt from the force of my smile. I loop my arms around his neck and hold on. All around us, voices rage, people shouting over one another. But I don't hear any of it over the sound of my own joy, the power of my own choice.

EPILOGUE

The waves are the same color as the sky, a stormy blue-gray swirl. When they hit the shore, it's with an impossibly loud crash, thundering up the sand toward our bare feet. After so many months of relative silence, broken only by the sounds of our own voices, birds overhead, wind through trees, skittering rocks under our boots, the enormity of the sound is overwhelming, reverberating through my chest. I can already taste the salt in the air, the smell of seaweed thick in my nose. It's like being in another word, an alternate universe from anything I've ever known before. Westfall, and the life I once lived there, seems very far away.

"We're here," I say. "I can't believe we're finally here."

Bishop doesn't answer, his eyes on the far horizon, scanning the vastness of the water. Over all the endless days and nights it took us to reach this spot, I pictured our arrival with running feet and screaming voices, but now, in this moment, we are both subdued. Awed in the face of so much raw power.

"Do you think Ash and Caleb are all right?" I ask, turning my head to scan the bluff above the beach. I can just make out Caleb's dark head. He gives me a wave, and I raise my arm in return.

"They're fine," Bishop says. "Don't worry."

When we'd gotten within sight of the ocean, Ash and Caleb had hung back, urging us to go on ahead. Caleb said he needed to scout out the surrounding area, but I know they just wanted to give us some privacy, a chance to be alone at the end of this long journey.

"We didn't ruin it after all," I say. That has been my biggest fear, that what Bishop and I talked about the day we looked at his grandfather's photo album would come to pass—we would get here and the ocean would be spoiled, destroyed, or simply gone. Even knowing that other people had seen the ocean since the war didn't alleviate my fear. I needed to see it for myself.

"No," Bishop says, and I can hear the smile in his voice, the sheer relief. "We didn't."

I look at him, the line of his profile, the strength of his jaw outlined in dark stubble. He isn't a boy anymore. The year and a half it's taken us to reach this spot has finished the job of turning him into a man, sharpened and honed him. He was right that day in Westfall—getting here was rough and dangerous. Nature conspired against us time and again, starvation and exposure our constant companions. A rockslide almost cost Ash her foot; we spent three months waiting for her to heal before we could move on and begin crossing the desert toward what was once Southern California. She still walks with a limp, but she walks.

And people threatened, too. All of us have killed along the way, but not with any pleasure and always with the unspoken awareness that if we kill too easily or often we will become something we can no longer live with.

But along with the hardships, we encountered kindness in equal measure. A family that shared food with us, a small group that let us stay in their camp, an old woman in a remote cabin who fashioned Ash a crutch of gnarled wood. For every trial there has been an answering blessing, for every loss, something gained. And I was right, too, that day in Westfall, because looking out over the rolling waves I know that this journey was worth every step. It has given us time to mend our broken places inside, make peace with the losses we've suffered, and forgive ourselves for the impossible choices we made. And now we're here, the foam-tipped waves nibbling at our bare toes. A reminder that no matter what damage we do—to ourselves, to each other, to the world—life can still surprise us with its depth of possibility.

"It's a long way from Westfall," Bishop says, echoing my earlier thought.

"I wonder how they're doing." It's hard for me to picture living a life in Westfall anymore. I've grown accustomed to the stars above my head as I sleep, the ache in my muscles as we walk the land. The freedom that comes with defining your world instead of letting it define you.

"I'm sure Victoria's whipped the place into shape," Bishops says, and I smile.

"If anyone could do it, she could," I agree. In the end, we stayed in Westfall through the winter after our fathers died, gathering supplies for our journey and helping begin the process of establishing the new government. By the time we left, Victoria was voted in as president for a three-year term, running on the platform of abolishing the arranged marriages and the promise of intermingling the two sides of town. She said after all that had happened, keeping people safe couldn't come at the cost of personal freedom. We knew it would be slow going, trust between the two sides still a delicate work in progress, but Victoria was as pragmatic and fair as she'd always been, working hard to build Westfall into something better.

A seagull passes overhead, lands near us with a thump in the sand. It tips its head and studies me with dark eyes. Just the latest in a long string of wildlife I never thought I'd see outside the limits of my imagination.

I grab Bishop's hand, his calloused fingers weaving through mine. Hands I know as well as my own now. Hands that have protected me in daylight and touched me in the dark. Hands that I trust with my life.

"Remember when we were first married?" I ask him. "When you asked me who I wanted to be?"

Bishop tears his gaze away from the ocean, looks at me with steady, loving eyes. "Yes," he says. "I remember."

I think back to the girl I was when he first posed that question—scared, confused, falling in love with a boy I thought I could never have, unsure who I was underneath the facade my family forced upon me. I'm still scared sometimes, but I know who I am now. I've been birthed through pain and sacrifice, through joy and unconditional love. I am stronger than I once was, able to make difficult choices without flinching, but I am not hard. My hands are not clean. But my soul is light. I love deeper than I ever thought possible, know the lengths I will go to in order to protect those I care about. I can survive out here, but I can really live as well. I can kill a deer for our dinner and appreciate the beauty of a lone eagle soaring through a brilliant blue sky. I can hold off a stranger with my knife and share laughter with my friends around the warmth of a fire. I can live with the fear of losing Bishop and love him fiercely anyway.

"This is who I want to be," I say. "The girl I am right now."

Bishop's smile is slow in coming, curling from one side of his mouth to the other. His eyes shine. He's happier in this quiet moment than I've ever seen him. "I like this girl," he says finally. "I always have." He runs the thumb of his free hand across my cheekbone. "She's been here all along."

I smile back at him, his words reminding me that he's the person who has always seen the real me, always believed in who I am even during the times I struggled to believe myself.

"Come on," I say, tugging him forward.

"Where are we going?" he asks, laughing.

"Out there," I say, gesturing to the ocean, scary and limitless and beautiful. Just like this life we've chosen. Just like the love we have for each other.

I hold his hand and we step into the waves together.

ACKNOWLEDGMENTS

The act of writing is a solitary endeavor, but this book would not have been possible without the dedication, hard work, and support of so many people. A huge thank-you to my editor Alycia Tornetta for always seeing what I miss and for putting up with my ridiculous and neurotic emails. Thank you also to Rebecca Mancini, Stacy Abrams, Meredith Johnson, Heather Riccio, Debbie Suzuki, and everyone at Entangled for believing in, and loving, Ivy as much as I do. A special thank you to all the readers, book bloggers, and fans. Your support is priceless and much appreciated. The love and patience of my family—Brian, Graham, and Quinn—allows me the confidence and joy to write. I can't imagine my life without each of you in it. You are my favorites. Holly, thank you for always listening, encouraging, and understanding. Not everyone is blessed with such an amazing best friend. I know how lucky I am. Meshelle, Trish, and Michelle, thank you for being such tireless cheerleaders and wonderful friends. I love our small gang. To all my other family and friends, your love and good wishes sustain me daily. Thank you. And, of course, no acknowledgment would be complete without a mention of Larry the cat, who still keeps my legs warm while I'm writing.

EXPERIENCE IVY'S STORY
FROM THE VERY BEGINNING!

THE
BOOK
OF

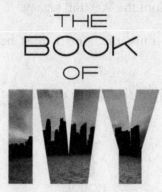

WHAT WOULD YOU KILL FOR?

After a brutal nuclear war, the United States was left decimated. A small group of survivors eventually banded together, but only after more conflict over which family would govern the new nation. The Westfalls lost. Fifty years later, peace and control are maintained by marrying the daughters of the losing side to the sons of the winning group in a yearly ritual.

This year, it is my turn.

My name is Ivy Westfall, and my mission is simple: to kill the president's son—my soon-to-be husband—and return the Westfall family to power.

But Bishop Lattimer is either a very skilled actor or he's not the cruel, heartless boy my family warned me to expect. He might even be the one person in this world who truly understands me. But there is no escape from my fate. I am the only one who can restore the Westfall legacy.

Because Bishop must die. And I must be the one to kill him . . .

Available from Hodder in eBook and paperback

HODDER

Enjoyed this book?
Want more?

Head over to

CHAPteR 5

for extra author content,
exclusives, competitions – and lots
and lots of book talk!

Our motto is
Proud to be bookish,
because, well, we are ☺

See you there . . .

f Chapter5Books 🐦 @Chapter5Books